BEACHC

BEACHCOMBER
A search for the truth

by
Nick Gosman

YOUCAXTON
PUBLICATIONS

ISBN 978-1-914424-90-8
Published by YouCaxton Publications 2023

YouCaxton Publications
www.youcaxton.co.uk

This book is dedicated to the selfless and courageous service of lifeboat men and women the world over. In particular, it is dedicated to the crew of the lifeboat, Solomon Browne, based in Penlee near Mousehole in Cornwall who, on the 19th December 1981, lost their lives attempting to rescue the crew of the MV Union Star who also perished that day.

PROLOGUE:

FRANCISCA TREMAYNE COULD remember the day, the very hour in fact, when her life changed forever.

It was a day like any other, similar, but different, because it was the day at the end of each month when she felt compelled to check the finances; it was a day she always dreaded. Sat in the back shop, she can remember staring at the accounts book. The figures did not look too promising. At the top of the page, September's takings for Tremaynes' Chandlery, in the income column was a line of figures, their takings for that month, it was a short line of not very big numbers. Next to the income was a much longer line of numbers in the expenditure column; they were much bigger numbers. After several more moments willing the expenditure column to somehow swap places with the income column, in the space at the bottom of the page for a signature confirming that month's accounts, she wrote her name; Fran. She hated using her full given name, it sounded like she was a nun in a convent. True, her family was nominally Catholic, but as a thirty-five year-old spinster, she didn't want to be reminded that she was effectively living the life of a nun.

Continuing to stare at the loss they had made that month, Fran exhaled a long sigh and just then it started raining. Looking up from the accounts book, she saw it was 4 p.m. and the rain was beginning to increase in intensity. It was as though even the Cornish elements, fickle though they were at the best of times, were trying to tell her something. It was the end of the summer, the last week of the school holidays and the weather had flipped over into autumn. Fran pondered how she could always remember the last day of summer. It didn't just fizzle out slowly, summer just stopped on a certain day at a certain hour like someone had flipped a switch to the autumn setting.

Shivering in the damp coolness that permeated the storeroom where she had her office, Fran walked through to the front shop with the intention of shutting early. Just then, the tinkling of the doorbell announced the arrival of a customer, or customers. A boisterous family of four entered the shop, clothes and umbrellas dripping. Once inside they immediately fanned out, dad checked through the rack of swimwear and wetsuits, mum the racks of shoes and the children, a girl and a boy of about ten or eleven, rifled through the nick nacks. After a few moments amiably watching them Fran busied herself rearranging some of the things on the counter, while the family oohed and aahed over the things on offer. She was just about to return to the back shop to finish the coffee she was drinking when the man of the family thrust two adult-sized wetsuits onto the counter and said, 'how much?'

Momentarily taken aback by the man's abruptness, Fran checked the price tags on the suits and replied equally succinctly, 'one hundred and eighty-nine pounds ninety-nine.'

The man blew out through pursed lips and said, 'way too much', then, after making a theatrical show of looking around the shop he said, 'seeing as you're not really that busy and it's the end of the season... what about I offer you a hundred and twenty quid for the lot?'

The man's London accent and brash manner rankled. Fran could feel a knot forming in her stomach as she checked the suits price labels again, considering her answer. As she did so, her eyes alighted on the family's expensive 4x4 SUV sitting outside, the fancy Apple watch on the man's wrist and his insouciant smile. They desperately needed the sale, the finances were dire, but fuck it! Finally, she said, 'it's one hundred and eighty-nine pounds ninety nine, take it or leave it.'

It was the man's turn to be taken aback. His brow furrowed, clearly he was unused to being spoken to so abruptly, and by a shopkeeper. He was just about to say something more when Fran heard the ting of a text message. Instinctively looking down at her phone sitting on the counter, she saw it was a GPS distress message. Fran suddenly couldn't breathe. The man was speaking to her, but she was deaf to his words; some nonsense about being spoken to in such a way. Fran sank down onto the wooden stool she kept behind the counter and stared at the text message. It had been generated by her brother's satellite navigation system,*'12-09-2018 Francesca Eloise Tremayne emergency contact for SOS incident detection from Callum Frederick Tremayne currently at location 15o56'57"S 102o16'56"E.'* As she picked up her phone the message repeated again and again, it merged with the tinkling of the doorbell as the family left the shop, leaving her alone in suspended animation. An image formed in Fran's mind of her brother Cal on his yacht, awash in a raging sea somewhere on one of the world's lonely oceans.

After the SOS message there was silence for the rest of the day and for the next week and the next month. There were no updates on Cal's weblog or messages to the family. It was as though he had vanished into thin air. Fran's brother, the only solid rock in her life, had been washed away and the bottom had fallen out of her world.

CHAPTER 1: Housel Bay

SPUME, LATHERED BY the ebbing tide, dragged with it crowds of dark round pebbles, causing them to rattle like the last breaths of a dying man accompanied by a lament voiced on the moaning wind and sighing of breaking waves. A lone figure stood motionless on the tidewrack and pushed their hands deep within the pockets of the oversized black overcoat they were wearing. The figure, a woman, her long, raven-black hair tousled by gusts from a strong north-westerly wind, turned her head resolutely out to sea. In doing so, the sweep of her gaze took in the crescent of white sand, the dark rocky point fading into the first sheets of fine rain and a small, white fisherman's cottage at the far end of Housel Bay. As she took in the mournful scene, the woman's striking features, dark eyes and high cheekbones set within the perfect oval of her face, composed themselves into a haunted look of profound sorrow.

As the keen wind stung her face and tears misted her eyes, the woman, Fran Tremayne, sighed and whispered, 'my square mile,' then staring down at the toecaps of the heavy sea boots she was wearing she sighed again and murmured, 'I've still not managed to move further, dear God, will I ever leave this place?' Looking up at the slate-grey sky, she shouted, 'don't answer that you bastard!' Then quieter, whispering to herself again, 'don't you answer that...' Slowly drawing a hand from her coat pocket, she cupped her forehead and allowed despair to wash over her. Tears came, then guttural sobs, 'damn you, damn you, DAMN YOU!' Instead of echoing around the cliffs fringing the bay as they might have done on a still day, her words were forced backwards into her face by the wind, like a taunt.

Clenching her fists and thrusting them back into the modicum of warmth to be found in her pockets, Fran returned to her task and examined some of the detritus washed up by the receding tide. A forlorn array of tattered objects; several lengths of frayed blue nylon rope, a couple of broken lobster creels and a small army of escaped anchor buoys, that had been washed over the side of various ships and fishing boats as they struggled in the first of the winter storms, resembled oddments laid out on tables in a threadbare bric-à-brac sale. For the umpteenth time Fran wondered whether any of it had come from her brother's yacht, the Nautilus. She imagined the boat's GPS beacon winking out its enigmatic distress message with the latitude and longitude coordinates that had marked Cal's last resting place; or did it? Fran again focused her eyes far out to sea, beyond the waves breaking wildly on the reef where the mournful cries of gulls sounded like sobbing children. She whispered a single word, like a question, 'Cal' and then, like she would receive an answer from him, she asked again, 'will I ever leave this place? Or will I be stuck in this endless feedback loop of memories holding me back... waiting for you?'

Walking past the 'goods' laid out on the tidewrack like a diffident shopper, unbidden, Fran's feet guided her away from breakers, along a windswept track at the head of the beach, towards its rocky point and the white cottage standing at the end of it. Home to the Belts', a dynasty of boatbuilders and to its present incumbent, Jimmy Belts, one of the finest boatwrights in Cornwall and veritable font of all knowledge. Her customary knock on the front door dislodged pieces of flaking old paint, which, like snow, drifted onto the worn flagstones of the porch as she fought her way through crowds of old oilskins. Fran always assumed that, when one of the Belts died, rather than disposing of these essential seafaring garments, they simply left them hanging there as a mark of respect, generations of them. But there would be no more; Jimmy was the last of the line. *Who then would have the task of putting their oilskins away in some final resting place* she wondered? Fran pushed open the grimy door into the front room and was met by a waft of smoke from the small pile of coal burning merrily in the grate at the opposite side of the room. As she entered, Jimmy remained motionless, his back hunched over with his hands stretched out towards the open doors of the old kitchen range as he intently stared into the flickering flames, the only light. At first he seemed reluctant to move from where he was sitting, but his craggy features broke into a smile and he rose to his feet, then made a space for her by the fire and drew up a second chair for Fran to sit on.

Settling back in his chair, Jimmy nodded over towards the range where two large white mugs of tea sat side by side on the hotplate, 'see, I were expect'n you t'call round.' Then, perhaps seeing the surprise on Fran's face, he said, 'don't go think'n I'm a clairvoyant, it's just that I saw ya down there on the beach. Beachcomb'n were ya? Thinking maybe you'd find a message in a bottle.'

Fran scowled and said, 'don't mock me Jimmy Belts, not you as well as all the rest of them!'

Jimmy held his palms up in supplication and said, 'now don't go fly'n off the handle... I'm just concerned. I seen you down there every day this week. You gotta let go. Cal, he's not com'n back.' Jimmy patted his chest with his fingertips, 'you're talk'n to an old sailor. I know the briny as well as anyone who's liv'n I reckon and it don't easily give up what it's taken.'

'You mean old Davy Jones' locker...'

Jimmy snorted with derision, 'fairy tales told by superstitious old sailors. Cal, 'e's come to his rest, of that you can be certain. He ain't in no locker, he's where he belongs, with 'im up there.'

'But... I still feel...' Fran touched her heart, 'here... I can't explain it, but I know he's still alive.'

Jimmy slowly shook his head and said, 'it's just wishful think'n. I don't blame yer for it though. It's like people who's had an arm or a leg taken off, they still feel it's there. Feel pain from it. That's what yer feel'n. You've gotta let 'im go my lovely. Remember the good times. Y'know, that time Cal came into the shop all excited and said he'd bought hisself a boat? Yer da jus' laughed at 'im, but he made summit out'a that old wreck. He had boatwright'n in 'is blood. It weren't a bad boat when all were said 'n done...'

Jimmy would have continued but, noticing that he was talking to himself, he looked over at Fran. Her face glowed in the light of the stove and tears stained her cheeks. After a long moment she said, 'I wish he'd never seen that damn boat.'

Fran's words, spat out with a vehemence that Jimmy had not seen before, made him go quiet. For a while they both sat in silence staring into the flames, then he said, 'I'm look'n for a couple of them big brass gimbals. You got any in that shop 'o yours?'

Fran looked over at the old man and gave a scowl, 'you mean like I wouldn't think to have any, it is a chandlery after all!'

Seeing that his change of subject was not having the desired effect, but unable to stop himself making a point about what he saw as a lamentable decline in the Tremayne's family business and the only chandlery for miles around, Jimmy said, 'it's just that there's more tourist trinkets in there than proper stuff us seafare'n folks need.' Then he chuckled and said, 'yer old da'll be roll'n in 'is grave.'

'Now, tell me Jimmy Belts, how often have you or any of the other fishing folk come into the shop?'

Jimmy cradled his chin for a moment and said, 'well, come to think 'y it, I can't remember the last time I was in.'

Fran nodded emphatically, 'exactly! If it wasn't for all the tourist crap as you call it, the business would've gone under years ago.' Prickled by Jimmy's mocking reference to the grinding work she had put in to keep the chandlery going, yet curious to know what the old man was up to, she momentarily put her indignation on hold and said, 'have you got a project on the go? It's been a while since you had a boat in the yard.'

Jimmy beamed and nodded, 'yep, I have, and it's a beauty. All wood, just like Cal's boat. Why don't you come over and 'ave a look. Bring them gimbals over at the same time.'

Seeing that mention of the decline in her family's business had angered her further, and not wanting one of the few people who ever visited him to leave just yet, Jimmy decided he needed to qualify his comment about Fran's father, so he said, 'about yer da, don't get me wrong. You know 'im an' me were never big mates, we just 'ad an understanding, seafarer to seafarer like. As far as I saw it, yer da's heart were in the right place, but 'is temper were some't terrible to see. He had heart, but he had a devil inside 'im see. It were 'is temper what damaged yer family's business long before you got to runn'n it. But have'n a heart n' passion don't always lead to bad. I'll tell you some't about heart and passion make'n some't good.'

Realising that he had, in his round about way, apologised for what she saw as his tactlessness, Fran's temper subsided and her eyes glowed with anticipation in the light of Jimmy's old range. Here was the start of another one of his stories. His tales were always strange, wonderful... unfathomable.

Jimmy leaned forward into the glow from of the stove and added a couple of shovel-fulls of coal to the blaze raging inside and said, 'see this old range? It were given to me da by an old gypsy man. When I were a nipper, I learned me trade from me old man. He weren't always just a boatwright, me da also built and repaired caravans for the travel'n folks, mostly old Romany families. One day, when I were about sixteen, an old Gypsy man, the head of a big and well-respected family, came to me da and asked 'im to do a job. He said, 'money's no object, I seen yer work.' He said, 'I want yer to fix up me grandfather's caravan, he were a big man, a circus master in 'is day.'

Jimmy paused for a moment and watched Fran's face intently. Seeing that his story had caught her interest he said, 'well, the job were an old showman's caravan. Solid oak, carved inlays, the most beautiful thing I ever saw. Me da looked at it. It were broke in the wheel spokes, the floor were rotted out, the roof were caved in an' all the fitt'ns inside were damaged. Me da said, 'it'll cost yer a year's wages', which were more'n seven thousand pound in them days and were a huge amount of money. The Gypsy man said, 'done!' Just like that, and smacked the palm of Da's hand in the Gypsy way and the deal were done on the spot. Then he said, 'we'll put you up and pay all yer board and lodging.'

Jimmy paused again and said, 'well that old gypsy man were good as 'is word. Me da were put up right regal like, with 'is own caravan. He stayed with the Gypsies Monday to Friday work'n on the caravan; drill'n, carv'n and paint'n for a whole year. In all that time, the old Gypsy man never wanted to check what me da was doin', he said it were bad luck to see it before it were finished. The day came when the job were finally done. The Gypsy man and his four sons came down to see the caravan. Me da had put a canvas tarp over it. When 'e pulled the tarp off with a flourish, he were nervous, cos there were complete silence. Me da were worried that 'is work weren't up to scratch, but when he looked over to where the Gypsy man and 'is sons were stand'n, he were cry'n and 'is sons were cry'n. The old Gypsy said it were the best work he ever saw 'n gave me da two years wages instead of one. He paid it out in cash right then and there.'

Jimmy looked over at Fran and said, 'now that's heart, that's pride!'

Fran stared at Jimmy in wonder and said, 'that old Gypsy totally trusted in your dad, it's like a story from another time, another world...'

'True, but trust needs to be earned, but once it's there, it can't be broke, it lasts a lifetime. Like blood ties, family ties.' Jimmy looked intently into Fran's face expecting an answer.

Fran nodded slowly, 'you mean my brother...'

'Yeah, yer brother. You say you know he's alive, you keep say'n it, but just say'n it ain't gonna bring him back. You gotta believe in yer feelings and follow yer instincts. You'll never lay 'im to rest proper until you know one way or another.'

CHAPTER 2: North Cliff

THE SECOND WEEK of November brought with it a chill wind and, as Jimmy Belts liked to call it, wall to wall blue sky. The unexpected bonus of fair winds and following seas, the sailor's ancient benediction, had Polldon's crescent-shaped harbour bustling with early morning activity. Whilst the larger ring-netting boats lay quiet at their moorings, crabbing boat crews were hustling to bait their pots and set out for their fishing grounds over sandy shoals a few miles out. By mid-morning's slack water, between the tide's ebb and flow when they knew their prey would be foraging, the crabbers would be joined by the ring-netters, their skippers keen to take advantage of the relatively calm autumn weather and the possibility of taking some higher value anchovies on top of their usual catch of sardines. One of her earliest memories as a child, Fran's mood was always lifted by the harbour's vibrant scene. Near the harbour wall, as the narrow main street wound past the Lugger Inn, which incongruously sat out on its own as though it had fallen out with the rest of the village, she instinctively checked on the family's mooring and the boats that lay there. Probably recognising the Tremayne's distinctive burgundy coloured panel van, a 'gift' from the owner of a local building company who had owed her uncle some money, two men waved in her direction from the deck of their boat. Fran chuckled and whispered to herself, 'there's my little fan club.' Checking her watch, it was still only seven, Fran steered the van over to the harbour gates and around to the Tremayne's yard. Cautiously stepping out and down onto the worn old cobbles, so often slicked with fish scales, Fran called out, 'are you two going out today?'

One of the men, either Bran or Breo, since they were identical twins she never knew which, smiled broadly and said, 'and myttin da[1]

---

1 Cornish for good morning

to you my lovely! Then, winking ostentatiously he continued, 'well, somebody's got to go out n' get the money to pay the exorbitant rent y'r charg'n to keep your ladyship in yorn fethus[2]!'

Fran nodded, and thought to herself, *yep, Breo; Breo the comedian to Bran's deadpan act.* Noting the slight difference in that day's clothing preferences, and virtually the only way of telling them apart visually, Fran said, 'ha, ha! Luxury? On a morning like this, I'd swap changing beds up at the guesthouse for a trip out on a boat any day. Oh, and you could come and stand in a freezing cold shop this afternoon as well if you like.'

Both brothers held their sides in a mock show of mirth, and then with less hilarity, Bran said, 'seriously though, you should come out with us again soon... before the sea's get too rough.'

Nodding again, Fran thought to herself, *yeah, and which one's turn will be to chat me up this time? How does it work? And how would it work if I fancied one and not the other? Going out with either of them would be the relationship equivalent of buy one, get one free.* Not for the first time, Fran reflected on the transactional nature of her relationships with men, even as friends. She needed to know more about the boats and fishing; it was likely she would take over the family's fishing business from her uncle one day. But was it going to be worth the discomfort she always experienced when she was around men; the feeling they were assessing her, perhaps undressing her with their eyes. It often felt like her beauty was nothing but a curse inherited from her mother who, like her, lacked the confidence to confront men's unwanted advances.

To Bran, for it must be he, exuding fret and anxiety to Breo's gay abandon, Fran said, 'I might just take you up on your offer this week, so long as we get a reduction on a box of crabs.'

Breo leaned on the boat's rails and gave a jaunty sailor's salute and said, 'yeah, that'd be fine...' then Bran cut in and finished his sentence, 'so long as you cooked 'em n' invited us round for dinner.'

Fran laughed out loud, she loved it when they did that, 'of course, but when?'

---

2 Cornish for lap of luxury

Replying in unison, 'Friday, Friday's best,' then Breo added, 'finish'n off with a pint at the Lugger?'

Walking back to the van, Fran chastised herself for doubting that the twin's motives were anything more than friends wanting to spend time with her. Just then her phone vibrated against her thigh and her heart sank, mother yanking her chain no doubt. To the twins, who had recommenced their frantic preparations, Fran simply gave them the thumbs up.

Back in the van, Fran checked her phone. Texts tend to be short and to the point, but her mother, Ellen Tremayne, could somehow load a few words with an enormous amount of emotional baggage. Fran sometimes wondered how it was possible that, *'what's keeping you'* could exert such pressure on her, but it did. As a child, hugs and reading at bedtime were bestowed on 'girls who've been good,' her mother's words not hers. Far from being a parent's ideal around boisterous children, being seen and not heard was the Tremayne family's guiding principle.

The means used by her parents to achieve this happy nirvana of quiet children were in stark contrast. Where her mother's approach centred around the carrot and stick principle, the carrot being acts of love and kindness associated with normal motherhood and the stick being moral blackmail, for her father, Craig Tremayne, it was all stick. Perhaps adhering to some kind of 1950's era Methodist principle, her father meted out open-handed slaps to her, but he used to beat Cal with his fists. Up until the day that a stroke confined him to his deathbed, Fran lived in constant fear.

After school, she sat at a little desk behind the settee in the front room, out of sight and out of mind, praying that Cal would come home before her father. Her ears would prick up at the slightest sound at the back door, was it her father's heavy tread or the thump sound of Cal's school bag being hefted into the kitchen before he took his shoes off at the door? Five years older, Cal was her protector, her hero and her childhood 'knight in shining armour', taking the sting out of the harsh tongue of her mother and the blows from her father was his way of protecting her. Then he was sent away to boarding school, as her father put it, 'it'll improve his chances,' whereas she must stay to, 'help your mother at the guesthouse, you need to earn your keep if you're going to stay under this roof.'

Now with only two targets, Fran recalled the hell she went through with her mother, as her father vented his anger and frustration on them as the business foundered in the wake of the economic downturn caused by a crash in the mackerel fishery. The sting of childhood resentment that Cal had left her alone was quickly forgotten, as she spent nights and then weeks staying with her mother in a women's refuge in Falmouth.

Like the recurring tripping of a reformed drug addict, repressed memories, which she would rather leave locked away, could break unexpectedly into her consciousness at any time, especially when she had agreed to help her mother at the Tremayne family's guesthouse, North Cliff. In an age where the names of tourist accommodations could be wildly inaccurate or misleading, North Cliff was just what the name suggested, a building sitting on a north-facing cliff. This trite, but accurate description might be reassuring for a would-be tourist, but, for Fran, a trip to North Cliff was to journey back in time; a time she would rather forget.

Ellen Tremayne's pretensions to rebadge North Cliff as a fully-fledged hotel remained on hold for as long as it remained her home. Her fervent wish was to leave North Cliff and find a place of her own, but she remained a prisoner, or more accurately a hostage, to the debts left by her late husband. When a person of substance dies, families believe, often naively, their financial woes will be at an end. Accounts will be settled, fortunes will be released from property sales as the life of a merry widow stretches ahead. This was not to be so for Fran's mother. Her inheritance was a huge mortgage, an army of creditors and burning resentment; resentment of her abusive husband, of her daughter for moving out the first chance she got and of her son for sailing away without a backward glance never to return.

Dark thoughts swirled around in Fran's mind as she turned onto the narrow lane to Pencarrow that wound steeply out of Polldon between high drystone walls, some precariously re-built, the result of an argument with impatient delivery lorry driver or inebriated locals returning from the pub. Finally cresting the hill and turning off sharply to the right, a gravel track crossed open heathland on its way to the rocky prominence where North Cliff stood in splendid isolation. However, today the converted stable block of a long-since ruined Edwardian Manor House, was not alone in its isolation. The courtyard was full. A crowd of half-term holidaymakers, mostly Londoners, had invaded North Cliff's faded grandeur, all of them intent on a frantic holiday away from their breakneck lives. Car doors slammed, babies cried and small children raced around outside the reception area. Fran dodged through the double doors just as a mother stumbled out carrying two huge cases and an infant tucked under her arm. As she did so, Fran caught the frown thrown in her direction by her mother, sitting behind the reception desk, before she pushed through a door marked 'private', sandwiched between the ladies and gents' toilets, and headed down a corridor which led directly to a back door and a small private courtyard where two painfully slim, dark haired women huddled together, sharing the ashtray, sitting on a small wooden table outside. Claudia and Anita, smiled and said in unison, 'good morning, Franciszka.'

Claudia continued and said, 'you are helping with the rooms today? We will be busy! Paula has flu and stays home all week of the holidays.'

Anita waved the phone she was holding in Fran's direction and said, 'but we have happy news from home. Our cousin has new baby, a girl, the christening will be in two weeks.'

Fran stood behind the two older women as Anita skipped through endless photographs of their smiling cousin, smiling relatives and closeups of a tiny scrap of a baby that looked pale and emaciated.

Noticing concern on Fran's face, Claudia said, 'the baby is very small, one and a half kilos only. She was, how is it in English...'

Fran said, 'premature?'

Claudia nodded, 'yes premature by ten weeks. Born in a Warszawa hospital.' After crossing herself, she continued and said, 'we are lucky to have her. The christening will be a big one, a big family celebration!'

Fran left the two women to finish their cigarettes, while they continued to scroll through all the photographs that had been uploaded to their family Facebook Messenger group. She envied them their strong family ties, unlike the dysfunctional Tremaynes.

In an attempt to avoid her mother, Fran used the cast iron fire escape steps to climb to the upstairs landing where she almost immediately walked into her mother coming out of a bedroom with a pile of fresh bed linen. Like a ghost, or some ghastly revenant, her face was as white as the sheets she was carrying. Fran then noticed the heavy odour of stale whisky hanging on her breath, it seemed to literally ooze from the pores of her skin. Her mother's heartbreakingly sad appearance tugged at her conscience for a few moments, before it evaporated when she finally spoke.

'Francesca, so you've finally got here. Surely, you must know we're busy, especially without Paula this week of all weeks.' Prodding the air in front of her, she said, 'you never offer to help any more, I always have to ask. I'm all on my own here, with nobody to help.'

Rolling her eyes in exasperation, Fran said, 'you didn't ask me, I sent you a text and asked if you needed help this week. I had no idea Paula was sick. It's not just you who's busy, I have to open the shop up at nine thirty. I'll do as much as I can for a couple of hours and then I've got to go back into Polldon.'

'Don't give me that, and don't give me any more of your damned excuses!' her mother's last words were spat out, like venom from a snake.

Fran threw her arms up, 'aargh, I give up!' Then turned on her heel and left her mother to her misery. But, in her haste to break away, she entered the one room at North Cliff she always tried to avoid. She found herself in room 105.

When she was eleven or twelve, she couldn't remember which, room 105 was, like now, one of the larger guest rooms. In the 1980's, the room, the only one with its own en-suite bathroom, was home to a resident guest, one of her father's small retinue of men he referred to as 'brothers of the sea'. Men, he said, who had fallen on hard times. Just why these men warranted her father's benevolence she had never discovered, but she suspected they were, or had been, involved in one of her father and uncle's so-called joint business enterprises.

Uncle Blake, her father's younger brother, was what some people might refer to as a hard man, a petty criminal who had been in jail at least twice to Fran's knowledge. It was rumoured that Uncle Blake was involved in smuggling drugs, mostly cannabis, but also cocaine and even people, into the UK via contacts in Belgium and the Netherlands. After his brother's death, Blake took over running the family's fleet of five inshore fishing boats, two crabbers and three ring netters. One night after her father's death, armed with a shotgun, Blake, amidst much swearing and oaths, literally threw his brother's so-called associates out onto the street. Much later, Fran discovered that her uncle had found out about what they, or one of them in particular, a man in his fifties known as Moggs on account of his shifty cat-like eyes, had been up to with his niece. But the damage, as they say, had already been done.

Moggs was the man who had lived in room 105. Fran hastily busied herself changing the sheets on the antiquated old four poster bed that had always occupied the room. As she did so, Fran recalled how Moggs' eyes, full of feline cunning like those of Lewis Carroll's Cheshire Cat, followed her around as he sat in an old leather wingback chair by the window. Mercifully, the chair had been burned, along with Moggs' flea-bitten belongings, in a ceremony reminiscent of a pagan cleansing ritual. Even though the wingback had been replaced by an office desk and chair, Fran shuddered as she passed the spot where it once stood. It was in the wingback chair that Moggs first persuaded Fran to perform fellatio.

Fran could now see that Moggs' grooming had been subtle and cunning. After Cal left for boarding school, she had started coming into the old man's room when her father was in one of his foul moods. It became a refuge where Moggs used to read sea stories, or tell her about his days in the Merchant Navy. Insisting that Fran sat on his knee, the touching first started when he began stroking her hair. This progressed to kissing the top of her head, 'as a reward for being so beautiful.' Moggs also made sure he had a supply of sweets and fifty pence pieces, which he used to hand out for doing 'little favours.'

As she cleaned the sink that she had been sick into that first time, she could hear Moggs' singsong voice in her head, 'now,' he had said, 'you've enjoyed one of my little tales from the sea and you've listened like a well-behaved little girl should, your uncle Moggs would like you to do something for him.'

Bashful, Fran remembered that her face reddened with pride. She wanted to do something for the friend she felt she had, the only person who seemed to take any time to talk to her. So she had said, 'what is it you would like me to do Uncle?' Moggs loved it when she called him Uncle.

'Well, it's something quite easy.' Moggs had then pointed to his trouser zip fastener and said, 'could yer pull that down for me.'

Fran remembered giggling at the thought of doing this for an adult when she had seen Cal undo his own zip himself all the time. But she had done it just the same. As she did so, Moggs moved forward so her hand brushed against his erect penis.

Over twenty years later, the mental image of looking up into Moggs' insouciant smiling face as she crouched in front of him caused Fran to slump forward against the rim of the sink and retch into it, as she did all those years ago, as she tried to wash the mawkish taste of his semen out of her mouth. Even though it had made her sick, she remembered that, at the time, she felt happy, exhilarated even, that she had managed to help make him so happy; the thought still had the power to make her sick to the pit of her stomach. Involuntarily cursing under her breath, Fran whispered to her reflection in the bathroom mirror, 'I hope you're rotting in hell!'

CHAPTER 3: Crabbing

FRAN WOKE WITH a start. It was a blacker than black night of the sort you only get in mid-winter. Rain pattered heavily on her bedroom windowpane and a strong gusting wind buffeted the house, one of a dozen that made up the Victorian terrace that overlooked Polldon harbour. Broken tiles scuttled hither and thither and a few that were loose tapped against each other as though they were waiting impatiently to follow their compatriots and hurl themselves to the ground. As if a leaking roof were not enough, the storm nudged against the house like a monstrous beast, testing the structure's resolve to stay upright, causing the joists to creak ominously as though the wind might soon have its way and tear the roof off entirely. Fran imagined she could hear shingle and large boulders moving up the beach, a primeval grating sound of the ocean's relentless quest to take back the land and return it to his icy depths where it belonged.

Fumbling for her mobile phone, Fran's bleary eyes struggled to focus on the sudden brightness of the screen. Three thirty a.m., the darkest hour, a time when morbid thoughts often came to her. Slumping back onto her pillow, Fran's eyes remained open, the darkness oppressive, almost suffocating, seemed to rest on the surface of her eyeballs like a blindfold. Try as she might to push them away, the contents of the dream she had been having floated in front of her. In it, she had been sitting having tea with Moggs, who, like the Mad Hatter, was sitting at a long wooden banqueting table gorging himself on a variety of cakes that had been served on ridiculously dainty cake stands, the sort her grandmother might bring out on special occasions. In between mouthfuls, Moggs had been holding forth with gusto, his squeaky fat-man's voice seeming to resonate all around her. In her dream, as she had struggled to zone him out, he suddenly broke off from what he was saying and began to howl at the top of his voice, a sound reminiscent of a child frantically calling for its mother. Like a human-sized cat, Mogg's caterwauling, for that was what it sounded like, rang in Fran's ears and, for some unaccountable reason, she found herself joining in and was then unable to stop. From somewhere deep within her being, with each exhaled breath, a guttural sound she couldn't recognise as her own had come in waves, like it was being ripped out of her chest against her will; perhaps it was a lament for what she had lost?

Using the palm of her hand, Fran wiped her sweat-slicked brow. *Why*, she thought, *had Moggs returned to haunt her dreams? What did it mean?* Like a sly, beguiling thief, or confidence trickster, Moggs had robbed her of so much, her childhood and her innocence, but she wondered, *had he also stolen away her ability to have a normal loving relationship with a man, or anyone else for that matter?* Tears formed in Fran's eyes and sobs replaced the animal-like bellowing of her dream. Grief over Cal's disappearance and his likely death was bringing back unwanted childhood memories. Packed away, as she liked to think, in hermetically sealed boxes never to be opened again, images from the past were floating back to her, like unwanted flotsam and jetsam washed up on a beach. Moggs and the men he called associates, who had preyed on her as a thirteen-year-old girl, were like reeking corpses that had sprung back into life.

Fran sat up in bed, smacked her forehead with a clenched fist, and scolded herself in the way she used to as a child, 'c'mon Francesca, get a grip! This won't beat me, it can't. There must be something I can do, or I'll go mad!'

Hand trembling slightly, Fran reached out and picked up her mobile phone from where it was sitting on the bedside table and scrolled through its message log. Since she received few texts, she quickly found the enigmatic SOS message automatically generated by Cal's satellite navigation system, *'12-09-2018 Francesca Eloise Tremayne emergency contact for SOS incident detection from Callum Frederick Tremayne currently at location 15°56'57"S 102°16'56"E.'*

She had received the message twelve times before it finally stopped. She now knew that the coordinates were those of a random spot about two thousand kilometres to the north and east of Perth in

Western Australia, or twelve hundred kilometres due west from East Java or six hundred kilometres from Christmas Island. Since it was the closest land to where the message was sent, Fran liked to imagine that Cal had somehow managed to put ashore on the tiny speck in the Indian Ocean named by Captain Mynors of the British East India Company after he sighted it on Christmas Day. She had even looked out the Christmas Island stamps her grandmother had given her when she had been in the grip of a stamp collecting craze when she was twelve, before Moggs, when her life had irrevocably changed forever. The stamps depicted colourful tropical fish and the sort of sublimely beautiful beach scenes you saw in travel magazines. It seemed absurd to think Cal might have been able to row that distance in an inflatable lifeboat or swim it using wreckage as buoyancy like a storybook castaway, but stranger things had happened and she clung to her dream. The alternative was too awful to contemplate.

Then, like she always did, she came back to the kicker, the one thing that shook her faith in the candy-coated fantasy she had created around his disappearance. If Cal had survived, how then could she explain why he had stopped posting on his blog or his Instagram profile? Why hadn't he just called her to say he was okay? Answering her own question, Fran whispered, 'because he's dead you stupid idiot!'

As though even whispering the possibility that Cal was gone forever might somehow make it true, Fran lay awake, transfixed by her dark thoughts and heavy bed covers as she waited for her alarm clock to sound. She had promised the twins, Breo and Bran, that she would crew for them the next morning, which meant an early start. As the clock's hands crept inexorably towards five thirty a.m., Fran stole herself to search for the courage she would need, but all she found was the familiar growing anxiety in the pit of her stomach as she fought the temptation to text them with some lame excuse.

Registered in Fowey, as were all the Tremayne boats, FY-524 Jasper bobbed cheerfully on its mooring at the Tremayne yard as Breo, Bran and their crew, Lucas, Sergey and Alex, worked to arrange their fleets of crab pots on the deck. In stark contrast, with the kind of dragging exhaustion you can only get after a long, dark sleepless night, Fran took a last pull on her coffee before she got out of the van and walked slowly towards the boat and carefully negotiated the slippery green slime on the quay steps down onto the Jasper's rain-slicked deck.

Breo looked up from baiting the crab pots and said, 'Morn'n me lovely! What's the matter, y' look like you've been on the jynevra[3] all night.'

Fran tried smiling, but knew it probably looked like she was wincing from a bad attack of indigestion, 'no, just bone tired that's all, I'll be fine.'

Always practical and to the point, Bran said, 'did ya mind to put on yer warm skantys[4], there's some sea and maybe a bit of an awel[5] brew'n once we get clear o' the Lizard.'

Sergey, who was coiling the weighted rope they were going to use for the trap lines, shook his head and said, 'thank God,' here he crossed himself, 'you are with us today Fran, at least there will be someone to translate for us!'

Breo laughed, 'you've bin 'ere, what three month, you should be a native Kawr-nish b' now.'

Appealing to his crewmates for support, Sergey laughed and said, 'then you should also be speaking Ukrainian and Polski by now!'

Ignoring the banter, Bran took Fran over to the lines of pots that were being carefully stacked on the foredeck and said, 'y' wanted some experience so once we're out we'll leave you to shoot this string of kowels[6]. Remember, there's always four kowels in a string and three strings in a fleet, that's twelve in all. Mind y' watch them coils, 'an' don't go throw'n y' self after them. It's bin done plenty o' times by folks with more experience.'

Passing by on his way to the wheelhouse, Breo winked and nodded over towards the bow, 'y' can use the sleyneth[7] you showed us last time

_____

3 Gin

4 Underwear

5 Storm

6 Crab pots

7 Skills

18

t' beat[8] them kowels o'er there into summet useful if y' like. There'll be time, we're go'n out as far as West Carne[9]. The weather's foxy[10] n' likely as not t' change before the afternoon's out, so we'll need to be in quick, shoot all the strings we can, then it's back yonder t' haul in our kowels near-in o'er by them cleefs[11] by the Bumble so's we're back for tea-time.'

Fran looked askance at Breo and said, 'you're getting your money's worth out of me today.'

Smirking, Breo said, 'well, we can't miss a chance now can we! Y' did a fine job o' them kowels last time.'

Once the twins were happy that the stacks of crab pots and lines had been stowed properly, Lukas and Alex cast off the bow and stern lines and Breo steered the boat out towards the harbour mouth. At the end of the pier, a group of old men stood huddled by some wooden benches dangling their fishing lines into the water, it seemed like a forlorn hope they would catch anything. A few of the men nodded and waved as the Jasper passed them, her bow now turned towards the open sea. Bran said, 'it's sad. All them men finished up as bummers[12], skippers of their own boats they were, but they lost everything when the bre al[13] run out.'

Moving up to the bow, but before she crouched down on the heavy wooden bench by the forward hatch to begin her work mending the crab pots, Fran took a few moments to lean on the bow rail. It was like a dare. She stole herself to look down at the sea, churning below her. Instantly, her shoulders tightened, her stomach lurched and she had the disturbing sensation she was about to throw herself overboard. After a few moments and before the knot in her stomach became unbearable, Fran tore her attention away from the bow wave and strained to see ahead, it was then she noticed her head and shoulders

8 Mend, specifically used for fishing nets and crab pots

9 Old Cornish for crab fishing grounds lives on in place names

10 Changeable, usually referring to bad weather

11 Cliffs

12 A term used for old fishermen employed to ferry crew out to large fishing boats

13 Mackerel

were silhouetted against the sea mist. As she watched, a bright crescent of light formed around her head and shoulders like a giant halo. So entranced by the strange light phenomenon that had boosted the size of her silhouette to gargantuan proportions, Fran failed to notice that Bran had joined her at the bow rail, until he added his own shadow to the dazzling light show. Nodding at the bright corona that now silhouetted both their heads he said, 'it's a good luck sign. Make a wish, n' ask the Bucca t'call the kankres[14] into our kowels.'

Fran chuckled, 'you mean the bucca-boo? The bogyman mum used to tell me about. She used to frighten me half to death saying I needed to stop crying and go off to sleep, or the bucca-boo would come and sort me out.'

Since he made no reply, Fran glanced over and saw that Bran's jaw was set and his eyes were fixed far out to sea. After a few moments he said, 'if you'd spent as much time out here as we have, you'd know what I were talking about. We all have the tech now, the fish sonar, radar, sat nav, but the sea's like a liv'n beast, it has its moods. There's some days we set out 'n Breo says to me, 'it's jus' no good today broder', so we turn back and head home. I think he feels the moods better than me, he's got the fisherman's sixth sense thick on 'im.'

Fran said, 'doesn't the sea ever scare you? I mean the depth, the dark. Like you said, it's like a restless animal.'

Bran considered her words and said, 'it's our home, our livelihood. The sea's like an unpredictable friend. But me and me broder, we understand it, respect it, and we know what to expect of it. We don't ask it no favours and we don't get them back in return, like yer da, God rest 'im. He wus a Kawr-nish man through n, through. You might've bin born here, but yer mams family aren't local like yer da's.'

Fran's brow creased, 'yeah, and I'm never gonna be allowed to forget it!' She said it light-heartedly, but she'd had her fill of the taunts at school about her 'posh' accent. Then she said, 'so how long before I'll be Cornish then?'

Bran turned his head and fixed her with his piercing eyes, 'a few hun'red years... maybe never. Maybe there's only one chance to be a

---

14 Cornish for crabs

local. Or maybe when enough of your kin 'ave been put in the soil at Polldon churchyard, you'll be a Kawr-nish then.'

Like someone who looked like they had found a flaw in an argument, Fran said, 'who gets to say when?'

'It's a state of mind Fran, you ask'n me's a sign that you're not there yet, see?' Bran gave a wry smile and said, 'anyhow, you'd be long dead before you'll be one of us.' Then he shook his head and said, 'I were mean'n to say to you how sorry we all was, me 'n Breo, all of us, to hear about yor broder going miss'n.'

Fran swallowed hard and said, 'do you think he's alive?'

Bran nodded slowly, 'yes... yes I do, I think he's alive, but don't ask me how. He were a sailor, a good 'n, an' he were a Tremayne. If anyone could survive, it would be him.'

Fran turned her face away from Bran and watched the swell break against the bow for a moment, then said, 'you know, I've spent all this time around sailors and fishermen, but I'm afraid of it, the sea I mean, and drowning. It's depth, the shimmer and the swell of it; just the thought of it scares me. I sometimes think I'm crazy.'

'It's okay to be scared. Our cousin drowned in the sea off a boat when he were nine. Just fell in and never came back up, like it sucked him down and took his life for the hell of it...'

Bran's voice drifted off into silence and they stood together for a while, each of them lost in their own thoughts before Fran said, 'so why do you stick with the sea? It's a hard life and I know my uncle's a hard taskmaster, a hard man actually, I wouldn't want to work his boats.'

Bran, keeping his eyes on the grey, rolling swell of the sea and darkening skies, said, 'when us Nancarrows lost everyth'n, our da sat the older lads 'o the family down n' said we wus done fish'n. He said we had t'sell up 'n find us another life. Breo 'an me was just sixteen an' we said, and I remember it, we said together, 'we here not done with the fish'n.' We left school a few months later an' started look'n for a boat. That's when yer uncle offered us the Jasper, we was just seventeen an' we was on a boat of our own. The sea's in our blood for good 'n ever I reckon.'

As they neared West Carn, the sand banks where there they would shoot their lines of pots, Breo stuck his head out of the wheelhouse door and shouted for the crew, 'ready yer kowels lads, we're go'n fish'n!'

Fran hefted the first pot over the side and, using the side of the boat to slow the weighted rope attached to it, she watched it sink like a tiny elevator car down to the bottom. As Breo kept the boat on a slow, steady course along the sandbanks, Fran lowered another pot as the line came taught, then another then another until the final pot when over the side with the marker buoy. As she watched them descend one by one, she wondered what unsuspecting occupants they would find in the pots they would be checking near the cliffs at Lizard Point.

As they turned for the point, rising swell sent breakers crashing over the bow as they met the first sheets of rain from a westerly squall. Grey-black clouds tinged with orange from the setting sun hung low in a sullen sky. Breo stuck his head out of the wheelhouse porthole, cast a scowl at the weather and shouted to the crew, 'look lively lads and mind you tie yerselfs on!' To Bran he said, 'Broder, we'll take a chance, yeah?'

Bran waved to his brother and nodded, 'yea broder. If it were anyplace else but Gut Carn, I'd say no, but we'll be in the lee 'o the Lizard when the awel gets going by the banks.'

Standing next to Fran, Lukas jerked his chin in the twin's direction and said, 'what is he talking about! Are we going to the other pots?'

Fran's jaw was set hard, the pitch of the boat and crash of the waves made it difficult to hear anything, but she shouted over the rising wind and nodded, 'yes... we... are... going... on!'

As they approached a large white buoy marking the start of the lines of pots, the crew braced themselves on the mid-ship's rails and clipped on to the safety line. As Bran used a long gaff to hook the buoy, he was almost swept off his feet by the wash, but Sergey grabbed the hood of his oilskin before he lost his footing. Working together, the crew hauled in six lines of pots, secured them in the fish-room[15] and Breo powered the boat into the heavy swell and back towards

---

15 On a small crabbing boat, this is a term for the mid-ships area where the fish are stowed.

Polldon, but it was no use, the rising storm pushed the boat back like an invisible hand.

Bran grabbed Fran's arm, 'get yersel down below, we're gett'n pushed off toward Falmouth, that'll be where we're land'n. Tell the others. I'm head'n up to the wheelhouse to give the boy a hand.'

Despite the conditions, Fran couldn't help smiling, Bran often called his brother 'the boy', a half-serious reference to the fact that he had been born ten minutes before Breo, then she shouted back, 'was it worth it d'you think?'

Bran nodded, 'there were a day when the fish were so thick y'could walk on em all the way out to the Cley Deeps, twenty mile out. Now, we're pick'n up the scraps 'o what's left. We gotta risk it to keep the boat!'

Fran's stomach tugged. It was the rent charged by her uncle, her family. The responsibility for the crews that fished from Tremayne's boats suddenly seemed to weigh heavy. But there were never any looks or recrimination, it was the way of their world, how it worked. It had been the same for generations.

CHAPTER 4: Buddy

SIX A.M. ON a crisp, bright Sunday morning in late February saw Fran seated on the bench outside her porch, pulling on her sea boots. Traditionally, Sundays were held sacrosanct, the preserve of the not-to-be-disturbed lie-in until eight a.m. at the earliest, but that was before Jimmy had tugged her arm and pulled her to one side towards the end of a raucous New Year's Eve get together in the Lugger Inn. At that moment Fran's life had changed, or had been, at the very least, modified. Jimmy had made his move shortly after the chimes of Big Ben when she had made her New Years wish, a silent prayer addressed to nobody in particular consisting of just three words, *bring me hope*.

Initially she had been wary, after all, Jimmy was a man of mystery at the best of times, but *what*, Fran thought, *could be so important at ten after midnight that couldn't wait until morning?*

In the relative hush of a small anteroom behind the bar, the preserve of only the most regular of regulars where they could find privacy for business that needed a dark corner to be discussed, Jimmy had said to her, 'I've got something for you.' In response, Fran remembered that her shoulders had tightened and she had braced herself for something, but what? Maybe it was something Jimmy had kept for her from her father, or a last note from Cal who, like herself, often confided in the old man. Whatever it was, this was not the time, she wasn't ready.

Noticing that Fran had become tense, Jimmy had smiled and said, 'it ain't nothing bad me lovely. I got somethin' that'll maybe bring a bit of a spark into them long walks you like to take on the beach. Like I said, I seen you there quite a few times all alone, and I said to m'self, she needs a friend... well, I got you one!'

At the time, Fran had visions of Jimmy acting as matchmaker for a crusty old sailor friend who had come to him and asked if he could find a woman to accompany him on the journey into his declining years. She had thought, *who could be better? Craig Tremayne's spinster daughter, a virtual old maid in a culture where most of the local women were married off with kids by the age of twenty.*

In reply, Fran had blanched and said, 'this isn't one of your badly timed jokes is it Jimmy Belts, because if it is, I'm going back to the bar. I've been chasing a hangover all night and I'm not going to be denied by one of your schemes!'

'Now hold on Fran, it ain't nothin' like that. Look, it's a dog – I got you a dog, if you want 'im that is. He were a stowaway on a Spanish fishing boat. I saw 'im get'n badly treated by the crew and I thought I'd find 'im a home. He's a little-un, a terrier, a rat dog. He'd be handy around your old house I reckon.'

Fran had been taken aback and said, 'but why don't you take him? You're in as much need of company as I am.'

Jimmy shook his head, 'me cat, Davy, they wouldn't get on and you know what they says about black cats and sailors, I wouldn't want no bad luck!'

A few days after New Year, Jimmy made good on his promise and brought the little stowaway to her house, complete with basket and dog blanket. From that moment, Fran's schedule had been disrupted, in a good way. It had only been a few weeks since he had taken up residence, but Buddy, the name that had sprung immediately to Fran's mind when she first saw him, had already got into the landlubber's habit of long walks. So, on this particular Sunday morning, the little dog, already waiting by the front door, gave a friendly bark when Fran came downstairs. Kneeling down, she gently stroked Buddy's head and said, 'just wait a sec, I know you're keen, but us humans need some strong coffee before heading out this early on a Sunday!' Buddy cocked his head to one side as if to say, early? It's already eight thirty!

As she crossed the narrow strip of grass that ran along Marine Terrace and down towards the path leading to Polldon Cove and the beach, Buddy ran a little way ahead and stopped just before he got to the fringing dunes. Sand, or, in this case, the brilliant white of crushed mollusc shells that made up the beach above the tide-wrack, seemed to totally phase the little dog. Jimmy reckoned it was because Buddy had spent most of his life at sea and needed to find his 'land legs'.

Panting and looking over towards Fran, Buddy waited until she approached. When she bent down to reassure him, he immediately leapt into her arms and she carried him over the dunes and down onto the squeaky dampness of the beach. Once there, Fran bent down and gently placed him on the sand, 'there, you see, it's not too bad?' Buddy cocked his head to one side and watched his mistress walking for a moment before he followed, bouncing in and out of her footprints as though he still refused to trust the unsteady surface.

As was her habit, Fran turned southeast and headed towards North Cliff with the intention of walking around the point and into Housel Bay, the place where all the best beachcombing was to be found. As always on her walks, flocks of herring gulls and black-backs wheeled overhead, the wind gusted as she walked towards the cliffs and the bracing salt air crystallised her thoughts ready for the day ahead, but now things were different, something was missing, the weight of solitude that used to sit on her shoulders had gone. Fran watched as Buddy, forgetting his earlier hesitancy, shot ahead again and careered towards a large group of waders searching for their early morning lugworm in the shallow breakers. When the birds rose in a fluster sending Buddy running back to Fran for further reassurance, she gently rubbed his ears and immediately felt a glow of companionship she hadn't experienced for a long time warm her soul.

As they rounded the cliffs into the strong wind that always blew across the bay, a flutter of an unfamiliar excitement ran through her body, a feeling she had not encountered for a while. *What* she thought, *was the reason for this?* Surely not her impending visit to Jimmy to present him with the binnacle she had found amongst the junk in the backyard storage shed of the chandlery? Nevertheless, it had been quite a find. It was likely that her father had reclaimed it from an old 1900's Falmouth steam fishing boat. The compass was in working order and the magnets that corrected for off-course wanderings that would otherwise be caused by the steel hull of the boat were all still where they should be. She knew Jimmy would be pleased, it was just what he was looking for to complete restoration work on the wheelhouse of the fishing boat he was converting into a houseboat for the out of towners, as he called them, a retired married couple who had commissioned him to do the work. Despite his initial complaints that he was getting too old to do big refurbishments, he hadn't needed much persuasion, Jimmy loved a challenge. It would be a fitting gift in return for his bringing Buddy to her.

Once over the boulder strewn reef at the base of the cliff, the beach stretched away in a graceful curve and Fran's eyes scoured the inevitable debris that was always left there by the receding tide. It seemed to be a day for plastic bottles. Thrown overboard by careless cruise ship passengers or crews on container vessels, plastic was now the scourge of the sea and its inhabitants. Fran had read an article in a Sunday magazine that claimed you could find plastic bottles washed up on even the most remote and uninhabited islands in the world. She could believe it, on this particular morning, Housel Bay had captured quite a little haul of the miscreants.

As was her habit, part of Fran's beachcombing included collection and disposal of as much plastic she found or could carry; she always brought a large basket for the job. As she bobbed down to pick up a large food container, Fran's eyes were drawn to a pool that always formed in the lee of several large rocks that rose out of the tidal part of the beach. From where she was standing, she could see there was an object sticking out of the pool, which looked like it was attached to something below the surface. Her stomach involuntarily tightened; it looked like the head of a corpse.

Something Fran always dreaded was finding a dead body on the beach. Some poor fisherman who had been washed overboard out at sea during a storm and drowned. Thoughts of Cal's forlorn corpse washed up somewhere flooded her imagination with gruesome images. She was just about to shout after Buddy to try and distract him from the pool, but she was too late and he ran off towards the rocks as fast as his legs could carry him. 'Buddy no! No, come here... please...' her plea was a forlorn hope. Buddy danced around barking. He couldn't contain his excitement as Fran approached to where, in the clear water, there was what looked like a corpse's head resting on the sand at the edge of the pool.

As Fran got closer, she could see that the head, which had seemed at a distance to have a tangled mat of hair attached to it, was in fact, sitting in a large clump of seaweed. Buddy was sniffing the air, but was not tempted to enter the pool, which was quite deep. Fran wondered whether, like many sailors, he was unable to swim.

Confident now, that the object in the water was not a corpse, Fran wondered what it was. It was indeed the size of a man's head. Oval in shape like a rugby ball, the surface of the object was pitted and, rather than being covered with sand, was actually sand coloured. As she tugged at the seaweed to bring it closer, Buddy barked his encouragement. Once she had hauled the surprisingly heavy object onto the sand, Buddy was all over it, sniffing and whining excitedly.

Fran grabbed Buddy's collar just as it looked like he might take a bite, 'no you don't fella! Let me take a look before you start eating this thing for breakfast.'

Lifting it up and out of Buddy's reach, Fran turned the object over in her hands. It was surprisingly solid and dense, yet it had been floating in the water. Finally, concluding that it shouldn't be left on the beach, or it was perhaps the remains some kind of unusual sea creature, Fran resolved to take it to show Jimmy when she brought the binnacle over to his boatyard later that day. 'Jimmy will know what it is; he's a proper know-all. It'll be a little mystery for him to solve!'

Despite its quaint, but rather rundown appearance, Belt's Boatyard enjoyed an imperious view of goings-on along the Helford River at a point overlooking the village on the opposite bank. At that tidal point in its meanderings, the Helford River was all rush and business, no doubt anxious to have done with it, after all its miles of sedate meandering, and finally pour itself into the sea at last.

Although he was, like Fran, an outsider, a son of a boatwright from Wroxham on the Norfolk Broads, unlike Fran, Jimmy's highly revered skills in wooden boatwrighting had somehow given him a fast track to local resident status. After over thirty years living by the Helford, Jimmy still had a strong Norfolk accent, which Cornish folk needed some experience to navigate. A native of Bath and Bristol, not a million miles away from Cornwall and being the daughter of a

Cornish father, Fran always felt a little aggrieved about this. Somehow, Jimmy's expertise as a boatwright had allowed him to skip over the many generations needed to become, as Bran quaintly put it, proper Kawr-nish. Having said that, being a fellow outsider might have been the reason why they were drawn together, that and her father's strong personal regard for him. Fran had, therefore, known Jimmy all her life and he, in turn, had become something of a surrogate grandfather to her, after the death of her own.

As Fran drove up to the pitch-coated clapperboard shed where Jimmy had his office, she felt a wave of excitement at the prospect of presenting him with the binnacle. The old man must have seen her van arrive, because the door of the office opened and Jimmy stepped out, waved and started walking over to her. Recognising his rescuer, Buddy jumped down off his spot on the passenger seat and ran towards him.

Jimmy crouched down and ruffled the little dog's ears as he barked his greeting. When Fran approached, he stood up and said, 'now I 'ope yer not spoil'n 'im. He's little and you can't be give'n 'im too many doggie treats and the like.'

'Don't worry Jimmy, I'm sticking to the rules, just a few dog chocolates when he's good, but the rest of the time it's strictly the food you recommended.'

'Good girl!' Then, craning his neck to see past Fran into the van, he said, 'you said you 'ad summat for me.'

Fran smiled and drew back the van's sliding door, 'tadah! What do you think?'

Jimmy's eyes lit up, 'well, well! It looks like an original 1930's Mark II, Hezzanith Standard binnacle, intact with all its magnates no less. Well, you've struck the jackpot there, me lovely, I seen 'em sell at auction for up to a thousand pound or more.'

'It's all yours, free, gratis, complements of Tremayne's Chandlery.' Then, seeing that Jimmy looked rather dumbfounded, she said, 'it is the right instrument for the boat you're restoring?'

'Well, yes, of course, but I need to pay for it, so it's all business-like.'

'Take it as a gift, or a gift for a gift, for bringing me Buddy.' Fran bent down and stroked the dog's head for a moment and then said, 'he's made such a difference to my life, not just the walks, but he's been great company. I can't thank you enough, really.'

'It were noth'n, really it weren't, 'e had your name written all over 'im the moment I saw 'im that day on Polldon Quay. Y'know he's a sailor's dog, he's more at home on a boat, that's plain to see. Maybe he can teach you a thing or two, help find yer sea legs.'

As they walked around the yard and inspected the old fishing vessel Jimmy was renovating, the conversation finally got around to reminiscing about Cal. 'Y'know', Jimmy said, 'for me sins, I were the one who helped Cal with 'is boat. I never would've done it if I'd have known what he were go'n to do with it. When he came into the yard with one of 'is wild looks on 'im, I knew there were trouble brew'n. He said he'd bought an old seafare'n yacht with the money yer da left 'im. He asked me to help 'im sail it over from Falmouth. It were called the Leviathan, but he told me he were go'n to rename it Nautilus, 'cos he said it were Greek for sailor and the original name had negative associations for 'im, 'is words, not mine. Anyhow, that were a mistake right then... rename'n a boat's bad luck. I'll tell yer straight, I thought 'e were mad. It were an all-wood hull, rotten to the beam when I first saw it. When 'e said he'd spend every last penny yer da left 'im on 'er, I said 'e were mad to 'is face. It were like 'e'd lost 'is senses.'

While Jimmy was talking, Fran thought his words sounded like a confessional. She had never heard the story about Cal buying the Nautilus, she had only found out what he was doing when he had almost finished it. By then, it had looked amazing. She thought at the time it must have cost a fortune to refit, but she didn't think to ask where he got the money. To her, Cal was the all-knowing big brother, never to be questioned.

After he had finished his story, Jimmy said, 'look, it's get'n dark, but why don't we 'ave a walk along the river, it'll stretch Buddy's legs and ours.'

Returning to the yard, Fran remembered about the strange object she had found on the beach and said, 'hang on, before we go, I've something else to show you in the van.'

Opening the basket, Fran beamed at Jimmy for a moment and then, with a flourish, lifted out the object she found on the beach.

'More gifts?'

'No, it's a bit of a puzzle for you to solve. I found it in a tidal pool on Housel Beach the other day. I've no idea what it is, but Buddy can't get enough of sniffing at it.'

Jimmy hefted the object, sniffed it, then nodded to himself and said, 'I'm pretty sure this is ambergris, or, not to put too fine a point on it, sperm whale shit.'

'Of course! I've read about this stuff in a magazine article. Some bloke found a huge piece of it on a beach in Australia, it turned out to be worth a fortune. Perfume companies use it in their expensive colognes.'

'Go steady there me lovely. I said it *could* be ambergris. There's a few things we could do to check whether it is or not, but I've got what we need in the workshop.'

Once back inside his workshop Jimmy brought over a blowtorch and some mounted needles. Laying these on a bench he said, 'if it's ambergris, this here hot needle will melt it and it'll go sticky and black.'

'How do you know all this?'

Jimmy tapped the side of his nose with his forefinger, 'I haven't been at sea an' around mariners all these years and not seen a bit of the ol' sea gold now and then. A sailor man I once knew said he'd sold a small bit to a dealer in London for a tidy sum. I'm not want'n to get yer hopes up, but look, it's melt'n under the heat of the needle... y'know it could well be sea gold Fran. A bit this size could fetch quite a sum.'

Fran stared at the unprepossessing chunk of flotsam and said, 'who would believe it could be worth something.'

Jimmy said, 'it's a sign, that's what I think. You're say'n you can't rest until you know for sure about Cal, whether he's alive or... gone forever. Why not take to the sail and find 'im yersel' girl. You got the knowledge an' the know-how, all y' need is the learn'n, 'an now you 'ave the means.'

'What means?'

'The ambergris of course! If it is sea gold, then you'll maybe have enough to do the skipper's train'n 'an get yer ticket. I know some people I can ask. They travel the high seas regular like, 'an they'll maybe take you where y'need to go.' Then, changing the subject he said, 'c'mon, let's go for that walk. It's dark, but I knows me way about well enough after all these years!'

Even with the company of Jimmy and Buddy's enthusiasm for anything and everything along the way, in Fran's imagination, the river, sly and menacing, appeared to slide mischievously along its banks and, as moon shadows started to dance along the moorings in the gathering darkness, she noticed some darker pools, not of light and shadow, but almost like they were a shifting hole, so dark it showed against the lesser dark on the far bank.

Fran stopped still and stared for a while as a dark shape split into two. Jimmy noticed her staring and said quietly, as though someone might overhear, 'take no heed, it's just the shapes I call 'em. Pay 'em no mind, they mean no harm. They're just go'n about their who knows what to who knows where or where from.'

'You think they're real? Who are they, what do they want?'

'So you think they're a who? I'm think'n they're a what rather than a who.'

'Isn't that rather frightening, them being a what? It means they're inexplicable.'

'I know what they are I jus' haven't found a proper name for 'em yet.'

'I saw them, tell me what they are... what it is.'

'It's your imagin'ins is all. They haven't taken form yet, like things that'll happen, but not taken shape yet. Yep, just shapes f'now like, until they form up into what'll be, if you understand me.'

'You mean you can tell what they might become? Tell the future... that's crazy!'

'Maybe for you my lovely, but I seen them in the very act of change'n into somethin'. I seen your da's dy'n before it happened. And I know why it had to happen then. He had it come'n sooner by the rule, I calls it. He weren't an evil man, but he weren't no angel either. He made it happen to his sel'. The shapes took form and his end were wrote by them.'

'Have the shapes been telling you about what happened to Cal? What will happen to me?'

'That's for you to know, but only if you let them.'

'I don't want to know…'

'That's fine then, that's fine. Know'n's not like help'n. Know'n's jus' know'n. There's now't y' can do about it anyhow.'

Fran shrugged her shoulders and shivered, pushed her fingers through her unruly hair and frowned, thinking, deciding, then she said, 'I feel it, y'know, fate. That friend you have who found the sea gold, do you know where he sold it.'

It was Jimmy's turn to frown, concentrating, 'I'm pretty certain it were a French dealer, 'e were from somewhere near Paris I think. I don't hold with your internet, but y'should be able to find 'im there right enough.'

Fran smiled, 'who needs the internet when I've got you… look, I've got another favour to ask, please could you put in a good word for me with your contacts, ones going down under.'

Jimmy nodded, 'I know just the man. He's quite mad, but 'e knows 'is stuff. Jack McGivern, Givvy we call 'im. He were a banker in Dublin no less 'afore 'e got the mariner's bug, now 'e's a Yacht Master runn'n down to the Antipodes a coupl'a times a year with a pay'n crew. Only an Irishman would be crafty enough to 'ave the crew pay for the privilege of sweat'n their behinds off, day 'n night.' Jimmy chuckled to himself for a bit, then said, 'I'll go 'an see 'im, 'e's based over Falmu'th way. I need t' go there anyhow to do a bit 'o business.'

In a rare gesture, which was as far as intimacy could go for her, Fran touched the old man's arm and said, 'thank you Jimmy, I really appreciate it.'

'Oh, don't go thank'n me jus' yet me lovely. You'll probably be curs'n me for gett'n you into trouble soon enough!'

CHAPTER 5: Jimmy' asks a favour

JIMMY'S OLD FORD van was somewhat out of place amongst the luxury cars standing in the customer's car park outside the offices of the Falmouth Sea-breeze Yacht Charter and boatyard. Ignoring the stares, he drove his van around the back and parked it pride of place next to a huge shiny new four-wheel drive truck sitting in a space reserved for 'J. R. McGivern Managing Director'. As he arrived, a tall, lean, curly-haired man in his 50's stopped talking to a gaggle of well-dressed businessmen and waved.

Disengaging from the group, obviously clients he was buttering up ready for the 'kill' as he called it, Jack McGivern strode over, grasped the proffered hand with both of his and beamed at the old man for a moment, 'Bless ya Jimmy, you're look'n better than ever. That there new boat refit's do'n you good. I can see you've got back yer old zip me man!'

Without giving Jimmy a chance to reply, or refuse, McGivern towed him over to where his group of would-be clients were standing and announced, 'this here's me mate Jimmy Belts, one of finest Boatwrights in the country, outside of Ireland of course!'

Having been momentarily silenced by the approach of what they might have thought as a vagrant who had shuffled into the yard to ask for some money to buy a cup of tea, the little group of men suddenly burst into smiles and murmured greetings. McGivern, nodding approvingly, winked at Jimmy, drew him aside and whispered, 'just give me a few minutes Jimmy lad whilst I finish talking with these 'ere posers an' we can break out the Jameson's.'

Good as his word, Jimmy watched whilst McGivern worked his group of clients. There were exclamations, no doubt in response to one of the Irishman's drôle comments, then the mood became serious, then hushed as he went in for kill. After a few minutes of discussion, there were nods all round and McGovern clapped his hands like an Appleby horse-trader closing a deal. Then, in what looked like a carefully choreographed move, a beautiful young woman with flowing red hair and the fair, almost porcelain-white complexion of the Irish, walked purposely out of the marina offices with a sheaf of paper tucked under her arm. Seeing that the deal had been agreed, the woman's rouged lips parted into a dazzling smile as she approached and the group laughed at something she must have said as she joined them. Still smiling, the woman led the businessmen back to the offices and McGivern peeled off and came over to where Jimmy was standing.

Jimmy said, 'success then?'

McGivern nodded, 'aye, Mora'll take care of it from now on. As she's always say'n, I can't be trusted with money when there's Messrs Jameson, Bush and Mills about.'

'Yer still wrestl'n with the drink there Jack?'

Coming from anyone else, a comment about his drunk ranting and all-day boozing sessions would have got short shrift, but instead McGivern looked contrite and said, 'Jimmy, I swears to ya, I'm gett'n the better 'o the drink. Mora's got me sorted out.'

'An' Riley, are you two settled up an' all?'

Wincing at the mention of his wife's name, McGivern said, 'na, we aren't divorced if that's what y' mean. To be sure, if we did, she'd take me for every penny I got and more besides. We're separated. An' since we never had kids, it's gonna stay that way as far as I'm concerned me old mate. Y'know, there's some women who put years on ya, then there's others that take 'em off, Mora's taken years off me, that's for sure. I feel like a young man again.'

'She's young right enough.'

'Aye but she's not just a pretty face, she's got a smart business head on 'er shoulders an' the clients love the honeydew she pours in their ears.'

Seated in his private office, McGivern opened one of the bottom of the drawers of his desk and produced a bottle of Jamesons whiskey and two glasses. Noticing it was the twenty-five-year-old reserve, Jimmy said, 'Jesus Jack, yer treat'n me today aren't yer?'

'Not at all, I save the good stuff for me mates. Anyhow, we haven't seen each other for a while. Here get that down ya.'

Jimmy sipped the golden-coloured liquid, smiled his appreciation and smacked his lips, 'now that's smooth. I could suck this stuff down me pipe all day long.'

'Aye, that's the problem, and why I only drink the good stuff with me mates, otherwise... well, it can get a wee bit messy as you know.'

Jimmy settled back and the plush leather chair he was sitting in creaked expensively, 'look, I've got a favour t' ask yer. It's about a friend o' mine, Fran Tremayne. She's look'n to sail down to the Antipodes. She don't 'ave much experience mind, but the sea's in 'er blood, 'er da were Craig Tremayne.'

Jack nodded, 'knew the fella, bit of a temper on him by what I remember; she take after him then?'

Jimmy shook his head, 'she's the result of all Tremayne's rage'n and beat'ns, she deserves a chance Jack; as a favour to an old friend.'

McGivern cradled his chin in the fork of his palm for a moment and said, 'Y'know, normally I never takes on a crewmate without know'n the cut of their jib in a tight spot, but see'n it's you... Look, I've got a three week shakedown for a new crew in a couple'a month's time. All five I've got signed up so far are green through and through like, so I wus look'n for more experience for the rest.

'Fran, she's gett'n the train'n for 'er ticket. She's a smart 'n and she's bin around boats all 'er life.' Jimmy paused and, gilding the lily slightly, said, 'she 'elps 'er uncle, Blake Tremayne, runn'n the fish'n boats and the Polldon chandlery.'

Jack laughed, 'You've sold her to me Jimmy me man.' Then, leaning forward, he said, 'yer not... y'know, got somethi'n go'n with 'er have ya?'

'Like I said, she's a friend. I promised 'er da on 'is deathbed I'd see she were alright. I got 'er interests at heart is all.'

Jack blew some air our through pursed lips and said, 'I know Jimmy, but I can tell yer close to 'er like. I wouldn't be surprised if you and 'er were going together.'

36

'Jacky lad, I'm a seventy-year-old man, almost twice 'er age, I swears to ya, we're just friendly.'

'Just mess'n with ya mate! Consider her signed on. The crew shake down'll be around the west of Scotland up to Cape Wrath and round the north coast. It'll likely be a bit wild with the spring tides n' all, but it'll be a good test of the crew's metal.'

Jimmy looked serious, 'aye, that it will. Them's huge seas up there sometimes and there's the whirlpools and rip tides. Aye a real test!'

CHAPTER 6: Yacht school

WOMEN HAVE A sixth sense about these things. Out of a fairly large pool of trainers, Neil Meadows had somehow managed to be Fran's instructor at the Falmouth Yacht School all the way through six weeks' worth of back-to-back courses.

From the very start of the Coastal Skipper's course, Meadows had been there. She was the only woman out of a class of six and the only one who didn't actually own a yacht. 'But my brother Cal had a yacht' she had felt compelled to say, when Meadows did the usual painful round robin check-in at the beginning of the surprisingly hard first day of theory, kind of an all you need to know about sailing that condensed a lifetime of nautical knowhow into a single day.

At the end of the first morning, during which the class had covered basic navigation and how to create a safe passage taking account of coastal terrain, tides, currents and wind speed, Fran was comparing notes with her fellow students when she noticed Meadows had taken a seat opposite and was regarding her thoughtfully whilst dunking a chocolate digestive biscuit into his mug of tea. The group was talking about how tricky interpretation of the chart information could be when Meadows paused mid dunk and said, 'come on Fran, you make out like you're a novice, but I can see that you know your way around a nautical chart like a pro.'

Up until that point, Fran had been enjoying the company of her classmates and felt a wave of irritation break over her otherwise sunny mood. But Meadows was, after all, the instructor, therefore it was natural for him to be showing an interest in his students, so she buried her annoyance and said, 'well, I have to come clean and admit that I've spent quite a few hours on fishing boats with my Dad; since I was a thirteen actually.'

Meadows' expressive features registered something like a light bulb being switched on and said, 'of course, Francesca Tremayne, Craig Tremayne's daughter and there's Tremayne's Chandlery in Polldon. You're fishing boat owners, I should have known.'

'So, our family's fame has travelled as far as Falmouth?'

'Well, I've heard the name recently from...' here Meadows pulled himself up short and proceeded more cautiously, 'I, er, heard about your brother, in the paper, his tragic... death.'

Fran's throat tightened and it suddenly felt difficult for her to breath. She had hoped to get through the several weeks of skipper and Yachtmaster training without the albatross of her brother's disappearance settling on the masts, but it was, she supposed, inevitable that somebody would have heard the name and the story and would put two and two together. In response to Meadow's hesitant and deferential enquiry, for some reason unknown to even herself, Fran had blurted out in a voice that sounded strangely different, like someone else had taken control of her emotions and was speaking for her, 'he's not dead Neil; I'm going to find him! And I'll thank you to say nothing more about it. Have you any idea how difficult it is not knowing, not being able to be sure? How would you like it if the only place you could mourn your brother was somewhere in a chunk of water the size of Wales?'

Fran's raised voice had hushed conversation around the rest of the table and all eyes were on her. Before the impulse controlling her could say anything more, Fran had rushed to the ladies' toilets and barricaded herself into a cubicle. With the door firmly locked on her stall, Fran's knees gave way and she sank down until she was sitting on the loo seat. It felt like her feelings were held back and hair-trigger sensitive, so they ambushed her without warning. Head in her hands as she tried to shut the world out, Fran's senses fell to listening to the metronome sound of a dripping tap; it was then that her inner voice spoke to her, *accept it, you're consumed by Cal's... disappearance? Death? I must know, must know for sure... I can't bear this not knowing...* Tears had come then, they escaped from under her palms and moistened her knees.

Sometime later, it may have been ten minutes but seemed longer, someone tapped tentatively on the door of the ladies, obviously a man, because he didn't come in, then she heard Meadows' voice, 'Fran, we're going out to the marina to do some familiarisation before our first cruise tomorrow. I am so sorry, I should have been more... it was thoughtless of me.'

Fran opened the door to find her instructor standing listening at the other side, she said, 'it's okay, my fault, I'm sorry. I don't know where that came from, it's just so... hard, you know?' Fran's voice had broken then, and for some reason, she had laid her head on Meadows' shoulder and spent a few moments soaking his jacket. That was the start; some kind of green light had been switched on and Meadows had pursued her ever since.

Six weeks later, on the final day of the Yachtmaster's course, Fran walked purposely to the Yacht School from where her van was parked overlooking Falmouth Haven on a breezy early spring morning. Fran looked up at the skies and made a mental note of the raggedy clouds scudding high above and the white wave crests scampering across the water out in the Carrick Roads. A smile played across her lips and she thought to herself, *well at least Neil will be kept on his toes today, no time for long meaningful conversations when there's an eight foot swell and three nervous students to worry about.* Fran sighed with contentment as the heels of her rubber boots boomed on the pavement as she walked; it was like nothing could stop her. The heavy weight on her chest had been lifted and aching sadness had been replaced with a pure joy she had not felt in a very long time.

After more than six weeks of training, this was it, judgement day, when students would be tested on their yachting and navigational skills during a cruise that would include some night sailing. Fran had surprised herself how much she enjoyed the courses on navigation, something about the precision required to use a sextant to calculate the angle of stars above the horizon and triangulate her position, it seemed like a perfect marriage between the celestial with the mathematical. She thought of her old maths teacher, he had always kept the faith and finally taught her the basics of trigonometry against all the odds, *well Mr Crippen, you'd have been proud!* Despite sharing his name with a notorious 1900's murderer, her maths teacher was young looking, almost boyish in appearance, even though he was balding, very mild mannered, and, of course, patient. Sometimes it just clicks with a teacher, and the impossible becomes possible. It had been like that with Neil Meadows, despite frequently giving the impression he was going to invite her out or declare undying love when he persisted in lavishly praising her. Perhaps the only thing that held him back was the fact he was married already.

Now, as she approached the marina, the timpani of halyards slapping on aluminium yacht masts sent a thrill through her body. Somehow, all the classroom hours and training on the boats had cured her of her fear of the sea, or had perhaps tempered it with a certain feeling of mastery, however delusional that might be in reality.

When Fran stepped onto the walkway out to the yachting school berth, Meadows met her at the gate and saved her the trouble of punching in the key code by opening it. 'Good morning Fran, it looks like we might get a bit thrown about today, but you'll be glad to know that the swell will die down this evening.' They walked together over to where two men with greying hair were standing, then he said, 'you know Tom and Eustis; I think they were with you on the coastal skipper?'

After both men made their greetings in unison and Fran, hiding her shyness as she always did on these occasions, had responded with an overly effusive greeting of her own, Meadows settled into his instructor's patter and said, 'now, I think you've all been on the Apollo, she deserves her grandiose name, she might be just a twenty-four-footer, but she's a J24 Keelboat. Just remember, she's pretty nippy in the water and less forgiving than our other twenty-four footers, so you'll need to make sure you're nimble at your stations when we come about. For the navigational theory part of the assessment, we're going to use the sextant to calculate our position using three situations; coastal landmarks, lights at Lizard and St Anthony's and celestial bodies. The weather's going to clear later today, so we should be okay to get good sightings on everything.'

Good as his word, the evening saw Meadows and his students riding a low swell with the lights of Lizard, St Anthony's and Dodman Point winking reassuringly in front of them and, above their heads, Draco, Ursa Major and his fainter little cousin, Ursa Minor twinkled in a clear sky and were clearly visible despite Falmouth's light pollution. Confident that everyone had triangulated their position correctly, Meadows shouted, 'well team, that was how we do that! Now come about and we'll head for home.'

As Tom and Eustis leaned against the port rail, Meadows positioned himself beside Fran, who had taken a spell at the tiller, 'enjoying yourself Fran? If your smile was any wider it'd break your face.'

'Yeah, I think my mood almost scored a ten all day. Y'know, before I started the yacht training, I was afraid of the sea. Even though I've been out helping on fishing boats with the crews quite a bit over the years, I'd always be uneasy. I feel like I've kind of mastered it in a small way, my fear I mean.'

'Well, you certainly aced the navigation, your dad would be proud of you.'

Fran shook her head, 'my dad didn't give a damn about me. We weren't close; I think I was a disappointment to him from start to finish. Anyway, I feel like I achieved something in the last few weeks. Did I tell, you the story about my scholarship?'

Meadows shook his head and smiled indulgently, 'no, but I think you're going tell me.'

'It's all down to whale shit, sperm whale shit to be precise.'

'I don't follow.'

'I found a big chunk of ambergris on Housel Beach. I sold it to a dealer for fifty thousand Euros! I could hardly believe it. Some old whale somewhere out on the ocean dumped out its guts and left me more money than my old man ever did!'

'That's the most unusual story I've ever heard. It's definitely worth putting it on the school's blogspot.'

'Ha ha! Just don't mention my name, or where I found it, otherwise I'll have everyone knocking on my door asking for a loan.'

Meadows looked thoughtful for a moment and said, 'look, why don't you stay with us tonight, it'll save you driving back over to

Polldon and it'll be just a short walk over to the School the next morning, what do you think?'

Meadow's house was, as he had said, very close to the Falmouth Yacht School, but what he hadn't said was that his wife and children were not at home. Fran inwardly cursed her naivety, or was it something else? Did she feel flattered by the older man's interest in her? He was charming and amusing, but now it was late, she had drunk way too many dry white wines to be safe on the road and she was going to be sharing an empty house with a married man who looked like he was in the habit of straying. 'Never trust a man in his fifties', a girlfriend had once warned her after a fling with a workmate had gone horribly wrong. *Good advice*, she thought, *so why don't I take it?* Even though her brain was befuddled, the instant she realised Meadows had lied to her when he previously intimated his wife was home, at the very point when she had prepared a plausible excuse to leave, her words betrayed her like they always did. Maybe it was Mogg's conditioning; an implanted reflex that, despite what she knew would happen; the unwanted kiss on the lips and caress of her buttocks that inevitably led on to something more, she was somehow unable to say no.

Snapping on the main light in the living room, Meadows bent and heaved out the base of a large settee and said, 'here's the put-up bed we use when the girls have friends stay for sleepovers; it's pretty comfortable by all accounts.'

Somewhat relieved, Fran flopped down on the bed and said, 'this'll be fine for me. I'm pretty tired so I guess I'll go out like a light.'

Fancy a nightcap to get you off?'

Before she had considered her reply more carefully, Fran said 'yeah, why not, it can't do any more harm after all the beer and wine we've consumed this evening.'

Meadows brought over a couple of large glasses and an already opened magnum of chilled Prosecco and said, 'it's going to be a bit flat, but it's pretty good and there's another in the fridge if we finish this one.'

The wine went straight to her head. Vaguely aware she was slurring her words, Fran found herself in Meadows' arms in a heated embrace that kept on going. Her head swam and, as they began to kiss deeply, she found herself unable to muster the will to break away from him and instead responded when he started removing her blouse and pushing down her jeans. The last thing she remembered was standing up and taking the rest of her clothing off herself, like she would if she was going to sleep in her own bed.

Waking next morning in a haze, Fran couldn't work out where she was at first, then it hit her, she had stayed with Meadows, the man she could now hear whistling a tune in the kitchen preparing coffee. She then realised she was naked. In answer to the next question that popped into her head, she reached down and felt tell-tale soreness and discharge between her legs and also in her behind.

Fran threw herself back down onto the couch and covered herself with the duvet as Meadows came into the room wearing just a towel and carrying a tray with coffee. Sitting down next to her he said, 'we were pretty drunk last night, and you were pretty wild...'

Perhaps the look of revulsion on Fran's face cut him off short, because he did not say anything more. Not only had she allowed her yachting instructor to make out with her, but it was obvious he had taken further advantage by having sex and all without any protection or asking if she was on the pill. Recovering her composure slightly, she said, 'I'm going to find some breakfast down by the Marina. I need to clear my head a bit before we start today.'

Meadows didn't push the issue and let her go. It was then she was sure he had taken advantage of the situation and perhaps felt some level of guilt. Deciding not to risk having a shower, Fran put her clothes on in silence and left.

Later, feeling completely defeated and humiliated, Fran sipped her coffee in the Marina Café and washed down the morning after pill she had picked up at the pharmacy on the way. *Why*, she thought, *do I allow men to keep taking advantage of me this way?* It had ruined everything; she had stolen defeat from what would have been a rare victory. Answering her own question, she hissed under her breath, 'I'm a bloody fool that's why!' The young woman serving behind the counter must have heard because she gave Fran a wry smile, then came over and said, 'fancy a top-up me darl'n, it looks like you need it.'

CHAPTER 7: Fate comes knocking

'HELLO, IS THAT Francesca Tremayne?'

The Irish lilt was unmistakable, so Fran said, 'Mr McGivern?'

'Now don't you be call'n me Mr, it's just plain Jack. Look, Yer mate Jimmy said I should talk to you 'cos I'm look'n at take'n on crew for a trip down to Australia and he said you were look'n for a place.'

Taken aback by Jack's forthright manner, Fran said, 'I am Mr... Jack. I wasn't sure whether Jimmy had spoken to any of his contacts about me...'

'Oh, aye it's the way of the man to never say what he's up to, he loves to spring a surprise all mysterious like.'

Fran laughed, 'that he does!'

'Look Fran, Jimmy told me all about you, I knew yer daddy a wee bit, not so much, but I've had occasion to do a bit of business with him back when I was get'n started. As far as I'm concerned, anyone out of one of the old Cornish fishing families has got t'have saltwater in their veins. I mean, I was a banker sit'n in an office in Dublin 'till a few years ago when I finally got my head straight and my priorities sorted out. Now, Jimmy told me about what happened to yer brother, all I want from you is to know the story about why yer want'n to go there the hard way. Why not just get on a plane and fly there? I mean, it's gonna be more than three months of hard sail'n down to Freo[16], hav'n said that, it's likely we'll be stop'n along the way in the Canaries, Caribbean, Fiji, places like that to stock up and have some R n' R, but it all depends on the winds t'be honest with ya.'

'I know it'll be tough, but like Jimmy said, it's the circumstances around his disappearance, we're really not sure where he is. I know he took the usual westerly route following the trade winds, but messages to his trip log and social media stopped long before we

---

16 Fremantle docks near Perth, Western Australia

got the distress signal. The UK authorities haven't been very helpful and the Australians have no idea where he is and there haven't been sightings of him there, so it's a total mystery. The only way I can think of finding him, or something about what happened is to sail there and make enquiries along the way; I do know his stopping points because he messaged about them.'

'I wanna to do something to help. Yer old mate Jimmy's given me a pretty solid recommendation and says you're a good'n, so what I'm gonna do is offer you a place on the crew at a reduced rate. Don't, for goodness sake, tell anybody about the arrangement, including me colleen[17] Mora, or she'll have me guts for garters! Now, we're go'n to have a shakedown trip around the north of Scotland in July. It'll be a chance to meet the crew and to familiarise yerself with the boat. The one we'll be use'n is a hundred and thirty foot traditionally rigged gaff schooner called Nostromo. We'll need a crew of six, plus m'self and Mora, that's eight in all to handle the watches, a boat like the Nostromo doesn't sail herself, if you know what I'm say'n. It'll be bloody hard work even with eight of us.'

'Jack, I don't know what to say... thank you!' Fran paused for a moment and then said, 'I've got a little dog, he's a terrier that Jimmy found on a fishing boat. I love him to bits and don't want to leave him behind...'

'Don't fret yerself, Jimmy's told me all about him too, he's literally a seadog, right, so I guess he's more at home on a boat than on land. We need a dog anyhow, they're good luck and good for reducing stress levels, so if y' don't mind share'n him with yer crewmates, then I'm happy to have him aboard.'

All the time whilst McGivern was on the phone, it seemed like Fran had been holding her breath, so when he rang off, she immediately collapsed into a chair. That was when the reality hit her and she thought, *now I've got to tell my mother I'm disappearing off on a yacht like Cal; she'll go mad.*

After hanging up her call with Jack, Fran noticed that she had another unknown caller whilst she was talking, 'mmm, it's certainly a day for

---

17 Irish for woman or girl

phone calls!' After quickly checking the store and the chandlery entrance for customers, Fran returned to the back office and hit the redial button on her phone.

A well-spoken man replied after a couple of rings, 'Hiya, how can I help?'

Fran thought she recognised the cultured Home Counties accent of one of Cal's old school friends and said, 'Ben... Ben Gates, is that you?'

'Yes, it is the one and only Ben Gates. I'm guessing it's Francesca Tremayne I'm talking to 'cos I just called you.'

'Ben, it's been ages, I think the last time we met was when I came along as Cal's plus one at a school reunion dinner, that must be five years ago.'

Ben laughed, 'yeah, and I remember that everybody thought Cal had finally snagged himself a woman. It was a great disappointment! A couple of the guys thought he'd married in secret when they realised you both had the same name. Quite a laugh if I remember rightly!'

Fran laughed along, but the way she remembered it was that Cal, for some reason best known to himself, had actually played along with the misunderstanding and made out that she was his girlfriend. Not knowing how to react, Fran had initially gone along with it thinking it was one of her brother's jokes, but in the end she remembered pulling him aside and saying, 'look Cal, what the hell are you doing? Are you crazy?'

'Sis, where's your sense of humour?'

'Cal, everyone thinks I'm your girlfriend and a couple of your friends have actually started referring to me as such. This isn't funny anymore. Now come clean with them or I'm walking. What's got into you?'

'Sorry sis, it's just that... I actually feel rather embarrassed I don't have a girlfriend, so when people started assuming that you were, I just thought, what the hell, why not. We'd make a pretty good couple you and me, don't you think!'

'You won't get round me that way, now please will you set the story straight before I tell them myself...'

To Ben, Fran said, 'yeah, that wasn't one of Cal's best jokes I'm afraid, it was rather embarrassing.'

'But you guys were pretty close before he went off on his round the world thing.' Ben paused for a moment, sighed, then said, 'I don't suppose you've tracked him down yet?'

'No Ben... we've not heard anything, I, I...'

'It's okay Fran, I'm sorry. Look, the reason I phoned is I was doing a spot of spring cleaning and stumbled across some of Cal's belongings, things he left behind in the flat. You remember he stayed with me the week before he left?'

'Yeah, he was escaping Mum's wrath at him leaving if I remember rightly.'

'Look, about Cal's belongings, there's too much to send by post and I'm away on business overseas for a while next week so I've got to prepare. I'm not sure how you're fixed this weekend, but why don't you come up to London to collect them? You're welcome to stay overnight at mine and we can nip out to the pub for a few drinks and do some catching up.'

After her recent experience with mealy-mouthed Meadows, as she'd started to think of him, Fran was on her guard and wondered why Ben couldn't just send Cal's belongings in the mail. From one of his social media posts, she knew that Ben was himself single after breaking up with his live-in girlfriend, so it looked like a ploy. And yet, she wanted to look though what Cal had left behind, maybe there would be clues to why he disappeared, so she stole herself and said, 'yeah, that'll be fine. I haven't been in London for a while, and it'd be good to catch-up.'

After hanging up her call with Gates, Fran absently tapped the screen of phone with the nail of her forefinger like she hoped it would offer up an explanation for Ben's call. She thought, *why now? And why bring up Cal's stupid pretence at his school reunion?* Fran made a silent pledge to be on her guard and keep in check the impulse, which had so recently been exploited by her sailing instructor.

CHAPTER 8: A trip to London

STILL BASKING IN the unaccustomed glow associated with being relatively financially flush, Fran decided to forego a long and uncomfortable drive up to London in the van and instead booked herself on the Cornish Riviera, the plush overnight sleeper train that runs between Penzance and London Paddington. As an added luxury, to avoid what she always thought to be the rather awkward situation of having to share a bunk with a complete stranger, Fran chose a single occupancy cabin but saved some money by driving part of the way and boarding the train at Truro.

On Friday evening, before she boarded the train, Fran bought some nibbles and a bottle of chilled white wine for her journey. As she paid for her goodies, she inwardly thanked the sperm whale whose vomit or poo, she couldn't remember which, was paying for all this unaccustomed extravagance. Recently, she had begun to refer to her benefactor as Humphrey, who she could picture swimming about somewhere in the vastness of the world's oceans calmly going about his business completely unaware of the transformation his bodily waste had made to the life of one very grateful human being.

At 10 o'clock on a Friday evening, Truro station was completely deserted and the little coffee places were boarded up. A chill wind blew along the platform, but rather than hitting the sack when she boarded, Fran was looking forward to a spell in the lounge before retiring. As the train entered the station, the impressive sweep of carriages and gleaming paintwork wouldn't have been out of place in Victorian England.

Stepping up into the carriage, Fran could hear the sound of female chatter coming from the lounge car, so after dropping her bag in her cabin, she headed back to join them. Near the bar, she found a group of four women sitting around a table, which was loaded with wine bottles. Seeing her come in, one of them said, 'come and join us gal, the bar's closed, but it looks like you've come prepared!' there were inebriated giggles all around. Two of the women made room for her at the table and she sat down. It was then she noticed there were two men sitting at the table opposite. The woman next to Fran whispered, 'see those two blokes over there? Ignore 'em, they've been trying to chat us up since we left, they're a right pain.'

Fran said, 'I could call the guard if you like.'

The woman said, 'I'm Barbara by the way; yeah, we tried to find the guard but he's hiding somewhere. They're never around when you need them and always ready to pounce if you've lost your ticket.'

Fran said, 'yeah, tell me about it.'

Just then, one of the women who Barbara said was called Sal, stood up and went over to the men who were laughing loudly and said, 'you shut your dirty mouth. We've had it up here with your effing nonsense, now just piss off both of you. We've called the guard, so you better watch you don't get yourselves kicked off!'

In reply, both men got up and faced off with Sal, who refused to back down. Unperturbed, Sal pushed them both back in their seats and said, 'push off, you don't scare me, waddya gonna do anyway, now piss off!'

To Fran's amazement, the men backed down and after more heated words they decided to leave. The other women, Fran included, gave Sal a round of applause and she bowed and said, 'thank you, thank you, all in a night's work.'

Barbara whispered to Fran, Sal's a policewoman. Even though she's off duty, she could've nicked them for threatening behaviour, but she knows how to handle herself. If you stand up to them, most men are just like naughty kids really and just do as they're told.'

Fran smiled while she poured herself a drink and said, 'still, I'm bloody glad she was here, I wouldn't have fancied taking care of them on my own.' She envied Sal her confidence, *that* she thought, *is what I need to do more of, stick up for myself instead of just backing down all the time.*

Later the next day, sharing a taxi with Gates on the way back to his swish terraced house in Highgate, Fran reflected on an evening that had gone according to expectations. There had been dinner at one of his favourite Italian restaurants then there was reminiscing about old times followed by more drinks at a local pub. Their conversation during the evening had confirmed her previous assessment that her brother's old school friend was a self-opinionated boor who liked the sound of his own voice. She had never understood what Cal had ever seen in him and he had clearly not changed.

During the evening, Fran had been careful to watch what she was drinking and how much, but she was still feeling unsteady when they got out of the taxi and Gates helped her up the steps to the front door.

After Fran had settled into one of Gates' large over-stuffed settees, he asked if she would like a nightcap, but, since she had recently been in the same situation and was not going to make the same mistake, she said, 'thanks, but I'd better not.'

Settling himself on the settee next to her holding a glass of scotch, Gates said, 'are we being all abstemious now? I always remember you were a pretty hard drinker in your youth.'

'That was a while ago, I've learnt my lesson; copious quantities of drink and good judgement don't go together.'

'Oh, I see, I'm getting the not-so-subtle brush off, eh?'

Gates' tone put Fran on her guard and she said, 'Sorry Ben I'm just tired. Is there any chance I could take a look at Cal's things. I'm anxious to find out if there are any clues as to why he went to Australia in the first place. Maybe some idea of what he was thinking of doing.'

Without answering, her now petulant host got up from the settee, retrieved a cardboard box from the dining table and unceremoniously dropped it onto Fran's lap, 'there you go, your brother's earthly remains. You're welcome to make of them what you will.'

Seeing that Gates' jaw was set and he now wore a mask of the utmost irritation, Fran said nothing and instead, began sifting through the contents of the box. After a few moments she said, 'is this it? Just a few old letters, some cards and a few clothes he left behind.'

'Yep, 'fraid so, but there is a diary in there that you might find interesting.'

Delving deeper into the box, Fran pulled out a folio-sized bound notebook and said, 'you mean this?'

'Yeah, I've read a bit of it. There's stuff in there about planning the trip, but it's the journal that you might find interesting. It confirms a few things about old Cal's preferences if you know what I mean.'

Fran felt her stomach tighten and she became wary, 'and what do you mean?'

'It turns out that your Cal was wrestling with his sexuality and couldn't decide whether he preferred young women or young men, but in both cases, it seems he liked them young.'

'You mean he was gay?'

'Not gay, but something in between. Anyway, I'll leave you to read between the lines so to speak, but there were a few instances at school that make sense when you read that diary. '

'It was Fran's turn to lose her temper, 'how dare you insinuate about Cal when he's not here to defend himself, or tell his side of the story?'

Gates snorted, 'for God's sake, he can't defend himself because he's dead! You need to be organising his funeral, not fretting over what he's written in his diary. Mind you, I'm not sure what you'll put in his coffin.'

Taken aback by the hostility of his words all Fran could think of to say was, 'I don't believe he is dead and I'm going to find out what happened to him!'

Seeing Fran's anger, Gates softened his tone and said, 'look, at school your brother was a loner, a quiet lad that just wanted a quiet time, but he was good looking and he was preyed on by the older boys. I wouldn't be surprised if he was... forced to have sex; boarding school's full of that stuff and Bramerton was no different.'

'Didn't you do anything to help him?'

'I was his mate at school, no matter what you think now, but he made rather a fool of himself in a way that didn't help him. One day, we were standing in the lunch queue and Cal and I were horsing about as usual. I had something he wanted, a candy stick decorated to look like a cigarette, so I stuck it in my mouth so he couldn't get it. Suddenly Cal grabbed the back of my head and bit off the end of the stick. It was a stupid impulse. Everyone thought we were kissing.

I tried to quell the rumours, but it got out of hand. Cal was bullied remorselessly after that. They would wait for him after school, forced him to fight, toilet flushed him. In the end he paid some older boys to beat on the bullies, but his life was a misery after that.'

'Cal never told me about what happened at school... he must've been so frightened. We had a close relationship at home, he was my big brother and he looked after me, stood up to my dad and took some of the beatings that were meant for me. I was devastated when he was sent to boarding school. My parents said it was so he could get a better education.'

Gates paused for a few moments while he considered his words, then he said, 'from what Cal confided in me, he blamed you; he reckoned it was because of you he was sent to Bramerton. He said his parents thought you and he were getting too close.'

Fran was shocked and hurt by what she was hearing, but old memories had already started to surface, ones she had pushed to the back of her consciousness so she could deny their existence. Once again gripped by an emotional force she seemed unable to control, Fran said, 'but I never egged him on, or came on to him, I was confused, the guests at our boarding house abused me Ben, I was sexualised at an early age.'

Gates saw he had touched a raw nerve, so he shook his head and said, 'y' see, Cal saw it differently, he recounted to me a charming little story about a day you spent in the woods together, do you remember that? He said you were messing about and it ended up with Cal swinging from a tree branch. It was playful, but you tugged down his shorts and, well, grabbed his privates. He said you were like a thing possessed; you got him off, a thirteen-year-old girl, so where did you learn to do that? He was seriously pissed off when he was sent to boarding school, he was a square peg in a round hole, he never said it, but I think he resented you for it.'

'That's not true! Cal was sent away to punish me; he was the only friend I ever had. I never did anything to cause my parents to send him away, it was just spite by my dad.'

Seeing that Fran was about to start crying, Gates grabbed her shoulders. After watching her for a moment he suddenly leant forward and attempted to kiss her on the mouth, but she pushed him away.

'Get away from me, what the hell are you doing Ben?'

Gates' anger flared again, 'what do you think; I'm getting some from you like everyone else. Cal said you were a right little slut with the guests at your family's guesthouse!' Then he lunged towards her, but Fran managed to break free and run upstairs, only to find she had trapped herself in what looked like Gates' bedroom.

Running into the room, Gates shouted, 'perfect! Just were you need to be, on your back!' Pushing her down onto the bed, he tried to pull down her skirt and panties. Using his considerable weight, Gates was able to pin her down; it was then that Fran felt him struggling with the zip of his trousers. While he tried to free himself, Fran used the distraction and pushed him off her onto the floor where she kicked him hard in the groin before fleeing downstairs. She knew she had hit the spot, because she could hear his agonised howling, so, before leaving, she had the presence of mind to retrieve her bag from the kitchen table and the cardboard box with Cal's belongings.

Fran was shaking as she half walked, half ran down the street away from Gates' flat. Part of her was elated despite the grotesque end to the evening, at least she had stood up for herself for once and not allowed Cal's so-called friend to push her into something she didn't want to do. Then there was trauma of hearing Gates' stories about Cal's time at Bramerton and the implications of what he said were contained in Cal's diary. Fran could not bear to think that Cal resented her, blamed her for what happened to him at school. How had her brother found out about what Moggs and his cronies had forced her to do? Perhaps he had stumbled onto what was happening? If he had, he must have been as traumatised as she was; but he had never said anything about it. *God!* She thought, *what a mess!* She resolved there and then to have it out with her mother once and for all.

CHAPTER 9: Home truths

FRAN FELT SHE was already piloting her life's ship across storm-tossed seas, at once exhilarating and frightening with the ever-present possibility she could founder on some hidden reef and sink without trace. But before her ship could leave the harbour and embrace the transformation that surely lay beyond its walls, she needed to confront her mother.

Fran's mother, Ellen Tremayne oozed resentment for a life that now lay largely behind her, which had been full of disappointment. When she was just nineteen, her beauty had caught the attention of one of the wealthiest men in a place, where such men were rare, but he had turned out to be a tyrant who eventually drank himself into a stroke and an early grave leaving her with nothing but misery and bad debts. Despite the house in Polldon, the boatyard, a fleet of fishing boats and the ship's chandlers, after a brief honeymoon period, the early part of Ellen's tempestuous marriage had been spent in fear living in women's refuges, first alone and then with her children. Five times she fled the family home to cower in a damp tenement house in Falmouth with other frightened women. Five times she vowed to leave her husband and every time, Craig Tremayne had talked her round, begged her to forgive him, to give him another chance and she had believed him every time. She had been in thrall to him throughout her young life, believed his lies and turned a blind eye to his womanising. Perhaps, deep down she felt she could eventually tame him, change him into the man she thought she had married; but it was like parlaying with the sea and just as futile. As if by holding up her hand she could hold back the tide and stop the breakers smashing into her as they washed away all hope.

North Cliff had been Ellen's idea, a venture that she would operate so she could have a stake in the family business. At first it had been successful, but her husband had snatched away even that small triumph. Tremayne's resident guests, as he had called them, turned out to be nothing but trouble. Mateus Ogden, known only as Moggs in his latter years, had been the first of these guests. The son of a highly respected Romani-English family, it was known he had plenty of ready cash, so in desperation, Tremayne begged Ogden for a loan when the fishery crashed. Ellen well remembered the night when he stood in their kitchen, Moggs' eyes, full of feline cunning, had slid around the room and her and Fran taking it all in as he counted out fifties from a huge role of cash he took out of his coat pocket. But, like all loans, it had come with strings. So, when Moggs decided he would take his ease, as he had put it, a serviced room at North Cliff had been part of his retirement plan. Knowing that Moggs had more than loan repayments hanging over her husband, Ellen knew she could not refuse. Moggs was the only man she ever knew her husband to be afraid of. And, of course, Moggs had "associates" who came and went from time to time; they never paid and always ate and drank their fill.

Fran chose her day carefully, Wednesday afternoons were always best, before her mother made up the staff payroll and after she had finished with the weekend guests. It was a day in the week when mother had some time to herself during the day; Fran had no wish to be at North Cliff during the evening, after dark there were too many bad memories lurking there.

After pulling the doorbell, Fran walked through the front entrance and followed the sound of music playing on a radio in the back kitchen where she found her mother sitting at the wooden table where housekeepers, Claudia and Anita usually took their meals.

Without turning around, her mother said, 'it's not like you to come here willingly; you must be wanting something.'

'Is that where we are now, I'm just the help...'

Turning now to face her daughter, she said, 'and reluctant help at that.' Pausing for moment she said, 'well, how did your trip to London go? You said you were picking up some of your brother's things from Ben.'

'Yeah, right, Ben, and what a nasty piece of work he turned out to be; you could have warned me.'

Ellen shrugged, 'last time I saw him he was in short trousers. He's a banker, they're all supposed to be up themselves, but he'll have some money, you could do worse.'

'It wasn't a social call, well, I guess it started out as a social call, but ended up with him trying it on. I won't be going back, but I got what I went there for.'

'Which was, what?'

'Cal's things, the stuff he left in London before he left. Don't you remember?'

'Oh, I remember all right. I remember a son that we did everything for disappearing off and traipsing around the world to find what? Himself? He was never a sticker and now he's...'

Ellen left the last word hanging, fell silent and might have resumed her brooding, but Fran saw where the conversation was going, so she decided to drop her own bombshell before it went any further and said, 'I'm going after him. I'm going to find him and find out what happened.'

Ellen fixed her daughter with an icy stare, 'what's that supposed to mean?'

'I'm leaving here. I'm going on a boat, a yacht; same as Cal. It's the only way I'll be able to find him. I need to travel in the same way, stop in at some of the same ports he messaged from and see if anyone knows anything.'

'And what am I supposed to do? God help me that I should ever have to rely on you, but that's what it's come to. Where's money going to come from for this trip? It's not coming out the business! Look, your brother made a choice, now he's made his bed, he's going to have lay in it and rot for all I care, just like his father!'

'I have the money', here Fran smirked to herself; she had omitted telling her mother about Humphrey the whale.

'It's all very well for you to smile you useless good for nothing!'

'At least I wasn't stupid enough to get married to a wife beater. Oh, a great life we all had together at the Callows, waiting to see if Dad found us or not. Scared to go out to the shops. Yeah, I had a great time growing up with you two as parents. Now it turns out that Cal was sent away because of me.'

'Where did you get that from?'

'Here', Fran pulled Cal's diary out of her bag and waved it in front of her mother, 'it's all in here, Cal's diary. And there's more besides. There's stuff about the sort of company you and dad were keeping. While we're on the subject of the filthy scumbags that we used to have staying here, it's all here in black and white. I've tried to block it out, but...'

'Block what out! What the hell are you talking about?'

'Abuse! The sexual abuse I put up with for years, the abuse I now have to live with all because you turned a blind eye to it. I'm never going to forgive you for what you've done to me.'

'Oh, here we go. Look, Miss High and Mighty, times were hard, we couldn't turn away steady business.'

'But what sort of business was it? You must have known what was happening to me.'

'Same as happened to me when I was your age, but I didn't squeal about it, some things in life you just have to get on with.'

'But I was thirteen!'

Since it was clear that nothing more would be gained by staying and much to be lost, Fran turned on her heel and left her mother shouting after her. Just before she slammed the front door, Fran heard the sound of breaking glass and a stream of abuse she had never heard before, even from her mother.

Later, much later, when Fran had time to gather her thoughts, she called her Uncle Blake. After experiencing the momentary chill she always felt at hearing her uncle's voice, which sounded exactly like her of her father's, she basked a little in the warmth that radiated from him when he spoke to her. He was, in truth, her father's antithesis, at least as far as she was concerned. It was her uncle who had run Moggs and the others off. She remembered the fear they had in their eyes; five grown men cowering like boys with Uncle Blake standing over them with a loaded shotgun. Half expecting something similar to what she had got from her mother, she need not have worried.

When Fran got to the bit where she explained what she was going to do to try and find Cal, he was immediately conciliatory and said, 'don't worry lass, I'll take care of the shop and find some help for your mother. A spell at sea will help get your head straight. Things'll be right with your mother in time. She's bitter cos me old brother never left her right after all them years o'hell he brought 'er.'

CHAPTER 10: Shakedown

FOR ONCE THE grey clouds and heavy rain forecast for Dublin turned out to be wrong and instead of the mad dash from the plane to the airport terminal she had been expecting, Fran savoured a leisurely walk, carrying a crew bag on her back with her jacket thrown over one shoulder. Following the passenger safe route to arrivals, Fran watched the baggage handling cart approach the plane she just had just disembarked and jostled around slow-moving fellow passengers; she was travelling light so she could get over to the animal reception centre to pick up Buddy as soon as possible. In fact, she wanted to avoid baggage altogether. Briefly searching her memory, Fran couldn't remember a time when she felt less encumbered by baggage; metaphorically that is, life's baggage. It felt like a heavy weight had been lifted from her shoulders and she was floating on air.

When Fran arrived in animal reception, Buddy had already been released from his travel-crate and was drinking some water from a large bowl. As she entered, one of the veterinary nurses said, 'I guess this little chap's yours; he's quite a charmer.'

Fran laughed, 'yep, he can be when he wants to! He's a ship's dog; we're off on a sea voyage around the north coast of Scotland. I think he's going to be the unofficial mascot on the longer voyage down to Australia we've got planned for later in the year.'

The nurse playfully ruffled Buddy's ears and said, 'you'll need to make sure Buddy's documentation is up to scratch for that trip, the Aussie quarantine authorities are very strict.'

Australia, the thought of a long voyage and the places she would see along the way was seductive, thrilling even, but anxiety around Cal's fate and what she might discover hung like dark clouds on the distant horizon, so Fran shifted her thoughts back to the journey ahead of her. Weeks ago, in her phone call with McGivern, he had mentioned that the Nostromo was large, more than one hundred and thirty feet, and clearly quite old, since she was a traditionally rigged gaff schooner, a type of yacht that was popular around the beginning of last century, which would explain the relatively large crew required to sail her. She had, however, been able to glean more information from a conversation with Jimmy one evening at the Lugger Inn when she had plied him with drinks as a thank you for putting in a good word for her with McGivern.

'Oh, aye, Nostromo is what you'd call a super yacht these days, but she's quite old, 1930s' if I remember right. She were built for some bigwig American financier by Hilditch's of Carrickfergus at their now defunct Lough Boatyard in Belfast. She were a fast boat then, advanced and way ahead of 'er time. I did the some boatwright'n on 'er in the mid 80's and again when Jack bought her. It were originally called, summit German, but after the War she were renamed Nostromo. She were a beautiful piece 'o craftsmanship when I were work'n on 'er.'

Jimmy had become sentimental at that point and veered off into a long rambling list of technical details, but she had got the impression that Nostromo was big and old and needed a lot of looking after. Nothing had prepared her for the reality.

Nostromo had been undergoing some repairs at Whites-Robson's Shipwrights in Howth outside Dublin and, when Fran arrived there, the broken cloud that had allowed some fleeting glimpses of sunshine at Dublin Airport burst through in a kind of glorious welcoming fanfare. Even as she waited to be admitted at the yard gates, Fran could make out the outline of a large three-masted yacht berthed nearby.

After a few minutes, a smiling young man in his twenties with sand-coloured hair jogged towards her and unlocked the gates. As he fiddled with the combination lock, he said, 'you must be Fran right? I'm Flip, one of the crew actually. We've been arriving in dribs and drabs all afternoon. It must've been quite a journey up from Cornwall!'

Fran held out her hand in greeting, 'Yeah, it was', then nodding towards a three-master berthed at the quay, she said, 'is that her over there?'

'Yep, it sure is, all one hundred and eighty feet of her, she's quite a beast.'

'She keeps growing! Jack said she was a hundred and thirty feet and now you're saying she's a hundred and eighty!'

Scenting the sea air and that something was going to happen, Buddy barked and danced around Fran's feet. Flip bent down, 'so this is your dog? He seems to be right in his element.'

'You could say that. He was a rescue dog from a Spanish trawler. A friend of mine found him and thought we'd get on since I come from a family of Cornish fishermen. On the practical side, he's a Terrier, a rat dog, great for keeping the vermin down on-board ship.'

'That's so cool, a proper seadog. I've never been in one place long enough to own a dog; I've always wanted one.'

'Now's your chance, Buddy's pretty easy-going with strangers, I guess he's used to crews on long fishing voyages. My friend Jimmy reckons he's been on boats since he was a pup.'

As they got closer to the berth Flip said, 'I hope you've got a head for heights' the main mast's really high. Jack's been telling us greenhorns that we've all got to take a turn in the crow's nest, whatever the weather, to make sure we don't bottle it when it really matters.'

As they exited the sheds and walked onto the quay, Fran looked up at the stern of the first of three yachts and read the single word "Nostromo" picked out in gold lettering against a large expanse of white with three masts towering above. The boat emanated a kind of presence that demanded respect. The sleek shape of her dark-coloured hull sweeping the eye inexorably forward towards the bow told of a vessel that could eat sea miles and, in the right hands, could be a formidable tool, a veritable time-machine transporting it's crew in both time and space; the ocean was her playground and she the ultimate rich man's plaything. The sight made Fran stop for a moment. Trotting beside her, Buddy cocked his head questioningly to one side and looked up at her. Flip, who was already at the gangway, called out, 'yeah, she does that to you when you first see her, she's pretty awesome!'

When Fran stepped onto the deck, Buddy's excited barking caused Jack McGivern to leave off from chatting with his crew, 'ah ha! That'll be the last of our crewmates.' Motioning for her to join them, he said, 'c'mon, Fran isn't it, we're doin' the introductions.' As she got closer, Jack shook her hand, and winked at her, it was a friendly gesture like she had known him for years, then he said, 'how's that old rascal Jimmy Belts, keep'n in fine fettle I hope. Just the other day I was admiring some of the ash beams he installed; fine work it is, fine work.'

Turning back to his crew, Jack said, 'that's our crew complete folks, now we are eight, that's just about enough to keep this here lady in check. You've got to remember that it's easy for a boat like this is to be master of its crew and not the other way around. At time's it'll be like she's get'n away from ya, but we've got to work together and show her who's boss. Under a full complement of thirty thousand square feet of sail and more than thirty winches, she'll take us up to twenty knots if we sail her right. While the flash youngsters are kitted out with the latest automatic winches and computerised furling systems, Nostromo is old school. The sails will need to be hoisted and lowered by us, the crew. If you were look'n to know how to crew a real boat, this is it, a sailor's sailboat if ever there was one!'

'When you come onto the boat, you leave your old selves and lives behind, you become different people, a team with a single purpose, to push the boat through the water to get the best from her that she'll give ya! If you're all wondering about her name, Nostromo means shipmate in Italian and right enough, she'll be our shipmate if you treat her right, but God help ya if y'don't!'

After Jack had finished, a young red-haired woman who had been leaning on the rails with the air of a person who had heard the skipper's pep talk many times before, came over to Fran and said, 'Mora O'Hare, good to meet you at last.' Rather disconcertingly and without waiting for Fran to respond, O'Hare got straight down to business and said, 'I was think'n with your family be'n fishermen an' all, you'd be good for senior deckhand, but that job's already gone to Marty Childs, he's been with us quite a few times over the years, so we thought he's due to have the job of bosun's mate this time. Jack said you run a guesthouse down in Cornwall is it? What d'you think about be'n the cook? You'd need to work with me as the mate and my second in command the bosun Teddy Styles on provisioning.'

'That's fine with me, I like the idea of having a job of my own on board.'

'Fine, now that's settled, since you were a bit late get'n in, I'll introduce you to the rest of the crew. Now this 'ere's Jen, you already met Flip, they come as a pair, and another deckhand, Tan Morgan, and last but not least, Teddy Styles our bosun, he's answerable to me and Jack, who's the skipper.' There were nods and a murmur of greetings all around, then Mora said, 'right, I'll leave you all to get acquainted. We're have'n our first meal together on board cooked by yours truly, but from then on, it's over to you Fran!'

While Mora was talking, Buddy had taken the chance to make his own tour of inspection around the decks, sniffing around dark corners, pushing against a door here and peering down a hatch there, but seeing she had now disappeared below, he scampered over to join Fran and the others.

Marty said, 'he's a smart'n that's for sure. He knew that when the boss was around he needed to make himself scarce! He's a crack'n little dog, how long've you had him?'

'Just a few months really, but I don't know what I'd have done if I'd had to leave him at home.' Fran sighed and wondered how much she should say about herself, so she decided to keep things simple and said, 'Jack might have mentioned, but I recently lost my brother at sea, Buddy's been part of my therapy.'

Marty and the others nodded, then Marty said, 'dogs are good for that. They keep you grounded, they give ya so much love.' Then, whilst the others drifted off to the crew mess to see what there was for the evening meal, Childs carefully looked around before he continued, 'so you've sailed with Jack and Mora before have ya?'

Fran shook her head, 'no, this is my first time, one of many firsts actually. For instance, it's my first time as crew on a yacht. Mora made a thing of saying I'm from a Cornish family of fishermen, but it was my dad and now my uncle who run the fishing boats. I go out with the crews when they need an extra hand, but this type of sailing is completely new to me.'

Marty nodded, 'well, how should I put this, it's a bit of advice really, just mind yourself around Mora, she's good at what she does, like organising stuff, but she keeps a jealous eye on her man if y'know what I'm saying. When she's got the green-eyed monster control'n her, she can be quite a piece 'o work.'

Fran furrowed her brow; she did not like what she was hearing. It was only a few hours into her time on the crew and she was already feeling uneasy, so she said, 'what *are* you saying exactly?'

'All I'm say'n is you need to keep a distance from Jack. I'm not say'n he's got a wondering eye or anythin', it's just the last time we had a lone female on-board, Mora got it in her head there was someth'n go'n on with Jack and her; it caused a bit of unpleasantness, that's all.'

'Why are you telling me all this now?

'Cos forewarned is forearmed as they say. I used to work the roll on roll off ferries, mostly DFDS between Harwich and Hook of Holland. It's hardly cruise liner stuff, but in my experience work'n with crews on a boat, it's always good to know what the trigger points might be. Jack's a friendly guy, everyone's a mate, it's not him you've got to worry about, it's her.'

'So what about in reverse, does Jack get jealous?'

'No, not'n like that, in fact, she's a terrible flirt, always eye'n up the young bucks when we're on shore leave. Nah, Jack's cool with it, he takes the view that if yer an old chosser and you're with a pretty young woman half yer age, y'need to let her have her head, if you get my meaning.'

Fran wearily shook her head and sighed, 'I guess I should say thanks for the heads up, but it's not inspiring me with confidence.'

Marty smiled, 'don't worry, I'll keep yer right, I'm the bosun's mate remember, it's my job to look after crew relations and help run a happy ship. When all else fails, I get out my accordion and get the crew to sing a sea shanty or dance a hornpipe!'

CHAPTER 11: Night-watch

TWELVE NOON AT Howth Marina and under breaking clouds and the promise of fine weather ahead, like a cricketer taking his first ball, Jack McGivern stepped onto the aft deck. With a keen eye on the mizzen mast anemometer, he nodded to himself and said, 'right everyone, we've got ourselves a fifteen knot wind to the abaft, so we'll raise the staysail then release the forward slip line so we pivot off the quay nice and easy-like before we let go aft. As I said in the briefing, we're gonna be cruis'n up to Bangor tonight to visit our friends in Northern Ireland. It should be an easy twelve, or so hours sail'n, but we're go'n to have the tide com'n at us through the North Channel, so she'll likely make heavy weather of it if the wind's not right. We're also go'n into some busy shipping lanes, so we'll need to keep our eyes peeled during the watches. Now let's get to it and show our little crowd watchers on the quay over there how it's done!'

As Fran followed Teddy up towards the bow to help with the foremast winch and Flip positioned himself at the bowline, she felt tension rise in the pit of her stomach; this was the moment of truth. Up until that moment, except for training cruises, most of her knowledge of sailing was theoretical; visions of mealy-mouthed Meadows and his obsequious smile loomed in her mind. Then there was the rather unwelcome news that Mora might have her steely eye on her in case she showed signs of what, her lusting after her boyfriend? McGivern was an easy man to like, as Marty had said, he was everybody's friend. Apart from learning the ropes as a deckhand, Fran felt she was already in an impossible situation. Whilst she did not want to let Jimmy down by being unfriendly to someone he liked and respected, she had, at the same time, to avoid Mora's jealous rage. *God help me*, she thought, *I don't know what's going to be harder, crewing the boat or navigating the stormy waters of McGivern's tempestuous relationship with his Master's Mate!*

Despite her earlier misgivings, Fran's first few days of sailing had been surprisingly straightforward. The route around the coast from Bangor had swung around the Mull of Kintyre, past Islay and included a provisioning stop in the charming little port of Tobermory near the northern entrance to the Sound of Mull. During the trip, Fran's day-to-day activities had changed along with her sleep patterns and mealtime routines. She felt more present and she was able to observe how she felt and went with the flow. When she was tired, she slept, when hungry she ate and when she was in awe of the beauty surrounding her she felt able to just sit in awe and take it all in. It was like she had found a healing balm for her battered soul.

In the quiet of her first early morning watch, in meditative mood, Fran stood on Nostomo's sleek deck, closed her eyes and allowed her senses to drift. As she did so, the soles of her feet absorbed the vibration, murmur and whispering of hundreds of feet of rope and thousands of hull timbers straining at the fulcrum point of the elements, the wind, the tides and the currents flowing beneath and around. Nostromo had become a living thing in a way that Fran had never experienced on fishing boats. She felt part of it, bonded to it, nurtured by it; although a deep respect for its power remained, she knew then that her fear of the sea had finally been purged from her being. Walking aft to check the helm, she passed the companionway and noticed the ship's bell fixed under the cockpit and the inscription etched upon it, "Unter der Linden." According to superstition, Nostromo's previous name immortalised on the ship's bell to dispel the wrath of the fates. Fran felt the sense of history; of past voyageurs on this magnificent vessel, almost one hundred years of them, her senses tingled with the thrill of it.

Becoming aware that someone was watching her, Fran glanced over at the abaft deck steps and noticed a figure sitting there; it was McGivern, he was smoking a cigarette and smiling at her. When he noticed she had seen him, he said, 'hah, I caught ya! I know what yer do'n 'cos I've done it myself many a time, you're feel'n her aren't ya?

She's like a living thing, noth'n like a steel boat or a motor yacht. Of all the charter boats we're run'n, with Nostromo it was love at first sight.'

Fran smiled and walked slowly over to where McGivern was sitting, sat on the steps next to him and said, 'so what brings you up on deck this fine morning skipper?' Just then, Buddy spotted her and came running over, the chance of petting by his mistress and the boss was too good to miss.

McGivern instinctively reached out and began stroking the dog and said, 'I'm so glad you brought Buddy with ya, he's already turn'n out to be a big hit with the crew.' Then McGivern drew in a deep breath and let it out; he did it a couple more times and said, 'agh! It's the damn sea sickness. I always get it at the start of a long cruise, it'll pass right enough. Ha, ha! A man who owns sailing yachts who gets seasick; ridiculous right?'

'You're not alone, I've seen it with fishing boat crews, even old lags who've been at sea their whole lives. I think sometimes its nerves, the sea and its moods can play on them.'

'Yeah, but it's not the only reason why I'm out here, Mora's thrown me out.'

Feeling a little uncomfortable at such a forthright admission, Fran said, 'Jack, you don't need explain yourself to me, we hardly know each other.'

'I know, but my philosophy's always to let it out rather than bottle it up so to speak. It's about money, it's always the devil that ruins ya in the end. I bought meself a pub back in my home village of Clonakilty in County Kilkenny. I was help'n out family, y'know that blood's thicker than water and no more so in Ireland. Mora's business orientated, she's the brains of the outfit really and she's always say'n we're not a charity. But we McGiverns are a big family, farmers. There's never been much money for us. It's my step grandfather's boy I'm help'n actually. When my nan remarried after the death of her husband, they never had children, so my step grandad kind of adopted me as he'd no kids of his own. I was the youngest of nine in our family, I felt lost, left behind, but he doted on me. We'd go fishing for hours on end. One day, we were fishing off a pier near my grandaddy's house and

I got a fishhook stuck through my thumb. I was going to run inside to my grandmother, but he stopped me. It was then I discovered he was afraid of her; she had the money and the trousers so to speak. So my granddad an' me made a pact not so say anythin'. He cut the barb off with pliers he had, then pushed the hook all the way through my thumb, Christ it was painful! But I said noth'n about it; he winked at me when my grandmother asked what happened, it was our secret. I guess yer wonder'n why I'm tell'n you all this?'

Fran smiled, 'I think I understand.'

'Yeah, well, the Irish and Cornish folks have got a lot in common when it comes to family, its our wealth, 'cos we've not got much else. Look, Jimmy told me a bit about why ya comming on this trip down to Australia. I want to help all I can with yer brother. It's what I'd do if I were in your position. Just give us a list of the stopping points he made and I'll see if we can fit some of them in. I'm not promising anything, but we'll try.'

Fran's eyes filled with tears and she said, 'thank you Jack, you don't know how much that means to me.'

McGivern smiled, 'aye, but just don't go saying anything to Mora!' Then he winked, 'it'll be our secret, like me and my granddaddy.'

Not naturally a morning person, Fran had come to enjoy the night watches and the company of the bosun, Teddy Styles, her watch mate. Hair thinning on top with a bluff outward appearance, Styles was an early-retired postman, father of two sons who were now in their twenties and one of the first of the crew she had really got to know. After three nights on watch together, Styles chose the first watch before midnight, in dense fog and a rising wind as they skirted the small isle of Eigg, to talk about his divorce. At the end of the half hourly check on the weather, heading and sail trim, Fran sounded four bells, halfway through the watch, before they both returned to the cockpit. In the dim light, Fran took the helm and corrected the course, then, to nobody in particular it seemed, Teddy said, 'do you want to know the reason why Catherine left me? Too fat, yeah, I'd swapped my job on the round for admin, a desk job so I'd see more of the boys and have more regular hours. Turned out to be a big mistake;

I put on a lot of weight. After a while she wouldn't touch me, go anywhere near me. There were trips out to see friends and eventually the overnighters started. That's when I found out she'd been seeing a mate of mine. We got over that, but there was another punch in the gut coming, prostate cancer; she left me for good after that. Coming on the boat saved me, I was looking for a way out, like suicide, I don't think I would still be here now if it wasn't for Jack taking me on his crew.'

Fran, who had been listening intently with her eyes watching Teddy's face said, 'I totally get that. I... my father, he was abusive, allowed abuse of me at the guesthouse we ran, still run. I was brought up in women's refuges. I thought I would never get out from under what happened to me, but I might've found a way. You know I said my brother died at sea? He was on a solo round the world trip on his yacht. We're actually not sure what's happened to him, we've heard nothing from him since a distress signal he sent somewhere about six hundred miles off Western Australia; messages from him stopped before that. All this, crewing on the boat, is my way of trying to find him, or find out what happened to him.'

Teddy said, 'it's the not knowing what happened that must be the hardest part; I feel for you, I really do.'

Whilst they had been talking, the wind and swell had increased, so when Flip and Jen arrived for the middle watch, Styles said, 'you guys need to watch your heading, the winds are pushing us back onto the mainland. If y'think there's any danger of us get'n blown off course, we'll need to get all hands-on deck to trim the sails accordingly.'

After leaving Flip and Jen up on deck, the physical exhaustion she always felt at the end of her watch meant that sleep came naturally and quickly and the sound of the ship's bell just punctuated her slumbers; it was Buddy's barking that woke her. From under her cot where he stayed during the night, Buddy jumped up onto her chest in an attempt to get her awake. The ship's bell was ringing continuously, the alarm call for all hands-on deck. Fran returned Buddy to his bed under her cot and said, 'stay here champ, it's too dangerous for you to come up on deck with me.'

71

Grabbing her clothes as quickly as possible, Fran struggled with her one-piece waterproof suit, threw on her life jacket and half ran, half stumbled towards the steel-clad steps, which took her up on deck. At the top of the ladder, the violent bucking of the swell caused her to lose her balance and she struck her head on the rails as she tumbled downwards. Already shaking, and with a gash on her temple, when Fran finally managed to get the hatch cover open, she was met by a maelstrom of the elements, all bent on tearing off anything that was not lashed down and hurling it into the sea. Fran had heard fishing boat crews talk about the huge seas they had faced, but what she was seeing seemed hardly possible. The bow dipping into the maw of a hole in the sea it would seem impossible to rise out of, but she did and the wash over the decks was enough to knock a big man off his feet. Moving towards the port bow, Fran clipped her safety harness onto the jack-line and moved forward toward three figures braced on the rails and shouted, 'what's wrong?'

The middle of the two figures shouted, 'the jib, we can't move 'er, she's stuck fast 'an she's dragg'n us towards the Skerries!'

Then Mora's voice, 'some God dammed idiot left it too late, the winch's jammed solid.'

A huge wave and the resulting wash dragged everyone off their feet and all floundered until they regained their feet at the port rails.

'Someone's gotta go up.' It was Jack's voice.

Flip said, 'I'll go, it's our watch!'

'No lad, it's my responsibility, I'll go up!'

Fran said, 'no Teddy, don't do it, it's not safe!'

The figure next to her, O'Hare, shouted, 'let him go! Someone's got to do it or we'll be pushed onto the reef God dammit!'

Styles clipped his harness onto the halyard whilst Fran and the others grabbed the halyard hoist and took up the slack, whilst he inched his way up the mast. McGivern shouted, 'keep him fast, make sure you keep the tension on the main halyard in case he slips!'

As the almost impossibility of a man climbing a one-hundred-and-fifty-foot mast in a storm unfolded, Childs and the rest of the crew struggled with the helm which almost dragged them off their feet in the raging tempest. Visibility was almost zero and everyone braced themselves for what seemed like the inevitable crash. Then, all of a sudden, the boat shuddered and Childs shouted, 'the helms going slack, I think the rudder's damaged.'

McGivern shouted, 'get them engines started, get us away from the reef or we'll founder!'

A grey line on the horizon gradually reddened and with daybreak, the storm lessened into a heavy swell with hard rain. With help from Tan and Flip, Fran had just got the stove working and served hot sweet tea to the rest of the exhausted crew when McGivern wrenched open the sea door and stepped into the galley. The Skipper's face was drained of all colour and he stood for a moment swaying on his feet before he said, 'I can't believe it, we've been blown into the head 'o Loch Nevis on the mainland, that's more than twenty miles off course!'

Styles said, 'skip, I'm sorry, it's my fault, I shouldn't have left Flip and Jen to it after my watch.'

Fran said, 'and mine too Teddy, we shared the watch, I should've seen the signs. A rising swell and the wind changing like that. We were all just tired.'

McGivern would have said something more, but O'Hare said, 'yeah, that's right Teddy, an' I'll have you know we're holding you responsible.'

McGivern reached out towards his girlfriend and gently squeezed her shoulder like he was holding her back and said, 'Mora me darling, not now, we can't have this discussion here and now like this.'

O'Hare shrugged him off and said, 'you're always so soft on them Jacky, one of these days you'll live to regret it!'

O'Hare snorted in derision and left, the slam of the door reverberated around the crew's mess, but the figures either slumped on chairs or resting their heads on tables stayed silent.

CHAPTER 12: Unexpected shore-leave

THE NEXT MORNING dawned fine. Nostromo's three bare masts raked the cloudless sky as she drifted with the slack tide in the mouth of Loch Nevis. Behind her and hidden from sight lay the busy port of Mallaig, the gateway to isles, whilst ahead and just visible, the tiny village of Inverie, nestled in the mountainous terrain of Knoydart, the most remote and least populated of the peninsulas crowning the northern flank of the west coast of Scotland. As McGivern paced the stern deck above the dive platform, he anxiously scanned the horizon out to sea before he shouted down to his two divers, 'Marty, Jen, the currents around Skye and the head 'o the loch run pretty fast, so you guys need to be careful down there, we're still making eight knots with the sails stowed.'

Pausing from his task of carefully checking his oxygen tanks, and noticing that his Skipper's brow was creased into deep lines of concern, Childs gave a thumbs up and said, 'we'll be right skip, we're not dive'n on the Titanic y'know.'

The remark, a reference to the mate's escapades with salvage dives on World War II ships resting at the bottom of Scapa Flow in Orkney, only irritated the skipper more and he said, 'okay, so it's a walk in the park, but what's the plan?'

Jen said, 'we're just gonna go down, have a look and try and set the rudder so it's straight, right Marty?'

Childs nodded, 'yeah, it's just a temporary fix 'til we get her into shallower water where we can get to work on something more permanent use'n the welding gear.'

Impatient to get over the side and the job done, the pair hefted the heavy tanks onto their backs and checked the facemask seal before they both sat side by side on the large stern platform. Flip did a final check on both their tanks, gave the thumbs up and they both took a graceful backwards dive into the water.

Fran watched as first Jen, and then Marty, took up position under the stern and hung there just below the boat having a conversation using diver's hand signals. In the crystal clear water, it was like they were still near the surface, but they were probably already twenty feet down, the underwater scene had a surreal quality to it, like they were floating in outer space. After they finally disappeared under the stern, Fran switched her attention to the scene of intense beauty in front of her. In the clear morning air, tree-clad mountains reared up on either side of the entrance to Loch Nevis, the tallest summits hidden by fluffy orographic cloud, which had the appearance of the steam you might see issuing from the vent of an active volcano. As they drifted further into the lee of the mountains, standing like sentinels on the left bank of the loch, the sea, now a striking ultramarine blue, was almost flat calm. Over the sigh of the wind that had died to a whisper, it was possible to hear wavelets slapping languidly on the hull; the sound had a deeply calming effect on Fran who, despite having been tasked with keeping an eye on the progress of the dive, began to nod inexorably into sleep.

Just as Fran had given herself up entirely to her slumbers, the tranquillity of the scene was broken by a rushing sound of gas escaping from aqualung breathers closely followed by the reappearance of Jen and Childs from the depths. As she pivoted expertly out of the water and onto the stern platform beside Fran, Jen laughed and said, 'a great dive watch you make!'

Startled, Fran's face was a picture of surprise, 'whoa! Ha-ha, very funny, so what's the damage?'

Jen said, 'yeah, well, the rudder's pretty knackered. It looks like we hit something under the water.'

Childs, who had now joined the women of the platform, said, 'the rudder stock's bent backwards and binding on the coupling with the rudder blade. It's a pretty sturdy copper and steel construction, so we must've given it quite a knock.'

While Marty was speaking, McGivern reappeared on the deck above them and said, 'great work, we're sailing straight now so we can tack over further into the mouth of the lock and do the rest under power.

Jen said, 'I can't believe we're going to be staying in Inverie. I spent three weeks there on a university ecology field trip in my second year. The estate around the village is owned and run by the Knoydart Foundation. It's essentially a community buyout from some old Nazi sympathiser who previously owned most of the western part of the peninsular.'

Fran said, 'so you're going to be able to introduce us to the locals.'

Jen smiled, 'it's no problem 'cos they're all really friendly; the owner of the pub's a bit of an old misery guts though, no one likes him. The downside is he owns the Inverie marina, a bit of grand name for the bit of the pier he runs as a boat mooring for visitors in the summer.'

As they were talking, a large white catamaran outboard motorboat entered the mouth of the loch, heading towards the mainland. Seeing the Nostromo was in some kind of difficulty, the launch changed direction and chugged over to them. As she drew alongside, the skipper, a florid faced young woman wearing a woolly hat and a big smile shouted, 'are you guys okay?'

McGivern said, 'not really, we've got a damaged rudder.'

The skipper of the launch said, 'the best thing is for you to head back to Mallaig there's not much help for you in Inverie.'

McGivern nodded, 'yeah, I know, but I think we'll be able to sort it if we can just get into shallow water. We've got the gear on-board to fix 'er.'

'It's Mr McGivern, isn't it? I think we've met before, I'm Sally Hardcastle, I help run the ferry.'

McGivern smiled, 'now don't be call'n me mister, Jack's the name. Yes, I remember ya from a couple 'a years back wasn't it?'

'Well, you're very welcome. It's Friday, so it's fish and chip night. If you like, I'll let Pip at the café know we've got visitors; for eight is it?'

McGivern shouted, 'yep that's right, make it eight cod n' chips with all the trimm'ns, it'll be on me!

As the ferry headed away towards Inverie, Jen said, 'I told you they were friendly! The pub and restaurant only opens in the summer holidays; it's a bit of a waste of time if you ask me, so the locals have built their own, "The Wee Nook" they call it. There'll be a fire and beers, it's the best day of the week; usually nothing much happens, and I mean nothing!'

Fran said, 'it sounds idyllic, I can't wait!'

Although it was her turn to take a spell below, the hypnotic beauty of their surroundings had cast a spell, so, unable leave the deck, Fran gave Flip and Jen a hand in holding a shallow line towards the opposite headland before they tacked over for the final approach to Inverie harbour. After they had set the sails for the turn, Childs took the helm and Fran went back on deck to help.

Without a fully functioning rudder, the sails needed to be set and re-set to ensure they kept on the right heading, it was hard physical work, but exhilarating. With the harbour rapidly approaching, a few whitewashed houses could be seen nestling in amongst the trees on the shore, which extended up onto the mountain slopes. The wooded mountain scene contrasted with barren treeless landscapes that she associated with the Scottish Highlands. Motoring now, Jen and Flip leant together on the rails and embraced, the uninhibited expression of their love matching the exuberance and thrill of their surroundings. '*Surely it can't get better than this*', Fran thought as she watched the young couple and felt a pang of regret that she was still to find someone to share her life. Despite the hurt and disappointment, and her wariness of men, part of her knew there was somebody out there for her and she hoped that she would recognise him if and when he ever appeared.

Early evening and the rocky summits of the highest Knoydart peaks, bathed in the ochre glow of the setting sun, appeared to gleam like the electrum prepuce on ancient Egyptian pyramids. The crew of the Nostromo, in two of the motor launches they used when the boat needed a deeper water anchorage than a harbour provided, sat silent, each of them lost in their own thoughts on an evening that was the exact opposite of the one they endured the previous day; such is the caprice of the sea. As they motored onwards towards the shore, with Buddy sitting regally in the prow, Nostromo's huge presence seemed to dominate even the vastness of the sea loch and the eyes of the villagers were drawn to it.

As the crew walked around the shore to the village in the gathering dusk, Jen nodded towards the small groups of people passing them carrying bundles wrapped in white paper and said, 'fish and chip night's in full swing at the Brightwater Café. All fresh from the Mallaig fish market, it's the best cod and chips I've ever tasted.' Opposite the village shop, a group of figures were standing around a makeshift tractor wheel fire bowl positioned outside an open-fronted wooden structure, Jen said, 'there's the Nook. It's a just a shelter, not a bar, and the pub's shut remember, so we'll need to get some beers from the shop if were gonna have something to drink with our fish and chips.'

The team split up, half going for food and the rest crammed into the homely confines of the village shop. As they waited in line, Fran put a friendly arm around Jen's shoulder and said, 'just as well you're with us, you can't have fish and chips without a beer!'

Then, from behind them, a man called out, 'Jen, is that you?'

A bearded man in his thirties with a crop of ill-kempt hair appeared from the back of the queue. He was dressed in wellington boots, yellow waterproof dungarees, thick fisherman's sweater and the kind of oilskin jacket worn by fishing boat crews.

Jen smiled and said, 'Fran, this is Danny Tipps. If there's anything you want to know about the natural wonders of this place, its trees and the wildlife, Danny's your man!'

Danny said, 'so you just came in on that huge yacht sitting out there?' Then he chuckled and said, 'it's not yours is it? I always thought you sounded a bit posh.'

Jen blushed, 'good God no, but the skipper's here, Jack McGivern, he's just gone to get us fish and chips.'

Danny said, 'hah, now that's the kind of leader I can get on with, not of the people but for the people, if you know what I mean.'

Jen turned to Fran with a smile, 'before we go any further, there's something you need to know about Danny, he's Inverie's resident Marxist-Leninist revolutionary.'

Danny said, 'very funny, but I'll have you know, we've never properly explored true Marxist doctrine, the Russians and Chinese were simply totalitarianisms masquerading as communists. A true communist state has yet to exist.'

From further back in the queue, a man's voice said wearily, 'oh God, here we go. These poor people have just landed here from God knows where and you're already bash'n their ears. Give it a bloody rest Tippsy!'

Danny said, 'just ignore him ladies, that's just my boss letting me know he's here.'

Jen and Fran giggled and Jen said, 'Danny's the only guy I know who's chat up line sounds more like a party political broadcast.'

Fran smiled, 'it sounds better than some of the awful chat up lines I've heard over the years.'

Danny looked wounded, 'I am not chatting anybody up! Can't anyone around here have a grown-up conversation.' Then, as they got closer to the front of the queue, Danny lowered his voice and whispered conspiratorially, 'now my advice is to just buy the minimum number of cans you need to get you through the next hour or so until the shop is about to close, then, they put the cans that got busted in transit over on the tables in the Nook and you can finish your evening drinking free beer.'

Jen said, 'free, but flat beer though Danny.'

Danny said, 'after the first few, it doesn't really matter if it's flat or not.'

Fran said, 'it sounds like you've got this all figured out Mr Tipps, you've done this before.'

Danny winked, 'crafty, eh?'

After eating their fish and chips, Jen, Flip and the others went their separate ways for walks, leaving Buddy to clear up the escaped chips and fish scraps under the tables while Fran, who was by then firmly ensconced with Danny in the Nook, fell into deep conversation.

Danny said, 'so Buddy's your dog?'

Fran said, 'yep, long story, but since we came on the boat together I've hardly seen him. He loves the attention he gets from the rest of the crew, so who am I to interfere? I do miss him, though it's good to have him with me this evening, even though he's only stayed to eat the discarded chips.' Then, moving away from the fire, Fran took a seat at the table opposite Danny and said, 'what really brought you here? The community thing fits with your political views, but it's got to be more than that.'

'You're right, it's the work we're doing that keeps me here. I graduated in ecology at Durham Uni and drifted for a while. I even got jobs on archaeological digs, anything so I'd stay doing science, but be working outside. Then I applied for a forester's job here; it was supposed to be for a season, but that was almost ten years ago.'

'I get that, the chance to just follow what you're interested in. I feel so imprisoned by my life and all the responsibilities I have for the family business. My dad died and left Mum and me in quite a mess financially. My uncle picked up some of the pieces and keeps the fishing part of the business going, but then there's Mum and the guesthouse and the chandlery that I run...'

'It sounds like quite a business empire you've got.'

'Don't go thinking we're shipping magnates or property developers, there's plenty of those in Cornwall, but we're not them.'

'So what persuaded you to crew on a yacht. You had your own business going on, so why jack it all in and go work for someone else?'

Fran considered this for a moment, then said, 'my brother was lost on a solo round the world yachting trip. Gone, just like that. He's five years older than me. He was the centre of my world when I was a little girl, he stuck up for me. My dad was an alcoholic and when he was drunk he used to become violent. I've spent a fair bit of my childhood in women's refuges.'

Fran paused and thought, *yeah, there I go, the poor me speech I always trot out to all and sundry like a tired old record.* But then she noticed Danny continued to remain silent while he watched her intently from where he was sitting across the table, then he said, 'yeah, what can you say. I think Phillip Larkin had it right when he said, "*they fuck you up, your mum and dad. They may not mean to, but they do. They fill you with the faults they had. And add some extra, just for you.*" There's a few more verses, but those are the ones I always remember.'

Fran shook her head, 'I know the poem you're quoting from, but, for me, Larkin's just making excuses. I think, know for sure actually, that my dad fucked us up on purpose, he was vindictive like that.'

CHAPTER 13: A walk in the woods

THE EARLY MORNINGS on board the Nostromo were always busy for the ship's cook. Over the previous week, Fran had acquired a couple of enthusiastic helpers in Flip and Jen who were both very handy with knives and could cut vegetables like the sous chefs that Fran had seen in upmarket London restaurants.

Noticing Fran's mesmerised stare as he made short work of the remainder of a bag of carrots, Flip said, 'impressed, eh?' Then, winking at Jen, he said, 'well it's down to helping cook at scout camps. Me and Jen didn't meet at uni like most couples do, our relationship was forged under the flapping canvas and smoke-filled air of the camp kitchen. In fact, we've been together since we got together on a scout camp in the Summer Isles on the West Coast of Scotland, so, what with Jen's time in Inverie on her uni field trip, we've spent the best days of our lives under grey clouds and driving rain.'

Slightly puzzled, Fran said, 'I thought Scouts were boys.'

Jen said, 'quite true, most of the troops still are, but the Scouts went mixed in the 90's and ours in Epping was one of the first; us girls blazed the trail with the boys so to speak. Personally, coming from a repressed all-girl school, suddenly being presented with a huge number of boys it was like unexpectedly coming down to an all you can eat breakfast!'

Flip said, 'yeah, we got together when were fourteen and kept together through Venture Scouts and uni; we recently celebrated ten years together, we're like a very young old married couple.'

Jen laughed, 'as always my dear, you need to leave the talking to me, you're not making any sense!' Then, nudging Fran, she said, 'talking of romance, you and Danny were deep in conversation last night, I thought we'd never get you back onto the boat.'

Fran said, 'hardly, well, okay, Danny and me did get into a rather deep conversation about social injustice.'

Jen said, 'that sounds like Danny alright, straight in at the deep end; no light chatter for him!'

Fran shook her head and laughed, 'actually it was quite refreshing to have a conversation that didn't revolve around fish, boats or beds. Actually, he's invited me for a bit of a "tour of the bounds" as he calls the fences they've been putting up to keep the deer from eating the tree seedlings; it's part of the re-wilding project, he says some of the fences are more than two kilometres long, they're fencing whole hillsides.'

Jen said, 'don't I know it. They had us drilling holes with an auger and banging in fence posts almost from day one of the field trip. At the end of my first day everything ached! It'll be interesting though. Once we're finished, you get yourself over there; don't worry, we'll clear up.'

Following Danny's hastily drawn map, Fran walked along the metalled road to the village from the harbour and turned off up a track that led into dense forest fringing the sea loch. As she entered the trees, the sun's rays, having reappeared from behind a bank of cloud, filtering through pine fronds and freshly unfurled silver birch leaves of iridescent green, transformed her surroundings. Groups of tiny birds, fire crests, chattered in the high branches of a large stand of mature pine trees that overhung the track. More familiar birds, wrens, blackbirds and robins, filled the air with sound; nature's orchestra now complete as spring gave way to early summer. Beyond the soundscape of small perching birds, the percussion sound of a distant woodpecker could be heard as it punctuated the distant mournful cry of a red kite, the top predator waiting his chance for the first easy meal of the day.

Through the mist and first warmth of the sun, it seemed like Danny's dream of the rebirth of a new revitalised Caledonian forest, was taking shape all around her. Further along the track, now steeply inclined upwards as it penetrated a dense understory of holly and dogwood, a rich organic scent percolated the damp air, here and there mingled with the more acrid scent of fox, badger and the distinctive pungent odour of the pine martin. Only in this most isolated part of the Scottish Highlands could such a rare animal, the martin, be numerous enough to have become a nuisance, tearing open food bags left out by careless visiting campers.

Danny's pod, the name the villagers gave to the squat wooden cabins built by the Knoydart Foundation for its workers, was set back from the track, perched on a stilted platform that gave the main window a view over a dense thicket of his beloved trees. Fran found the man himself, standing on the veranda brushing his teeth. He waved her over and then promptly disappeared inside, reappearing a few minutes later with two steaming mugs and a pile of buttered toast. Unused to visitors, like the hermit he was, instead of the usual welcome chatter, Danny rather disconcertingly briefly resumed the conversation they had been having the night before and then he said, 'I thought we'd need to feed the inner man, or woman, before we set off.'

Perching on an intricately constructed stick chair with a willowy back and with every outward appearance of a tense woodland animal preparing itself for flight, Fran took the offered coffee and a slice of toast and said, 'enchanting though all this is, I can't stay too long. I'm wanted back on the boat to help with sail repairs this afternoon.'

Danny smiled, 'just like Captain Bligh on the Bounty, keeping the crew under the thumb to prevent malcontents from jumping ship and melting into the native crowds in foreign lands.'

'A rather poetic way of putting it, but yes.' Then, laughing, she said, 'do you always manage to put a leftist spin on everything?'

'The shackles of low-paid work are all around us.'

'Believe it or not, we're crewing the Nostromo willingly and even paying for the privilege!'

'There you are! The elitist classes have found yet another method of exploitation. You think you're on holiday, right? But you're paying to crew on the master's boat. All you're doing is lining his pockets. The only one having a holiday is Mr McGivern and he's doing it at your expense!'

Fran shook her head, 'there's clearly no winning with you Danny. Whatever I say, you'll find a capitalist conspiracy hiding somewhere.

Actually, Jack's been pretty good to us, it's his girlfriend you've got to watch.'

'Ah, the feisty Mora O'Hare, yes, we copped some of her fiery temper the last time they were here. There was a falling out between her and Bruno, the guy who runs the brewery, restaurant and so-called marina. It was something to do with mooring fees. Even though McGivern's yacht was anchored way out in the loch, Bruno was claiming a hefty fee for administration; whatever that is out here in the middle of nowhere. Anyway, he'd met his match with Mora, they had a huge and rather entertaining shouting match on the quay with everyone watching the show. She definitely had the last word though, because he ran back to his bolthole like a frightened rabbit! I'm guessing he's keeping out of her way this time though.'

Giving Danny a wry smile, Fran said, 'Danny Tipps, I bet you're no fun at parties, you always seem to find the negative side to everything and everyone. What will you be saying about me when we've finally sailed away?'

Danny sighed, then, pointedly ignoring her question he said, 'yeah, everyone says that, but I'm not sure what else I would talk to people about besides trees. It's become a kind of defence mechanism, but you managed to survive a whole evening; you'd be one of the first in a while.'

'So, who is the real Danny Tipps?'

'He's a bit of recluse if truth be told. I came here with my girlfriend after finishing uni. We stayed here together for a summer and part of a winter as volunteers; then she went back to the damp house in Manchester we'd been sharing with her mates. We kept in touch for a while, but when I told her I'd got a permanent job here, she said she'd found someone else. The kicker is, that someone else is a guy who's part of the community that lives on Eigg, just a stone's throw from here, and she's now living there with him. Since then, I've been here on my own. There's not many available women and those that come in are usually just volunteers.'

'So, apart from the work, what is it that keeps you here?'

'It started out as an experiment really. I've always hated my own company and living on my own, but the experiment's taught me a way of making peace with myself. I've laid my demons to rest.'

Fran relaxed on the chair she was sitting in, demons were something she understood, then she said, 'for years I've been telling anyone who'd listen that I was abused as a child, I've kind of worn it like a badge, an explanation for the way I come across to people; I never let anyone get close. The truth is, it's only recently that I've started to come to terms with it and allowed myself to start the process of moving on instead of it defining me, like I'm this victim, poor wounded me.'

Fran paused and took a moment to consider why she was telling Danny, a complete stranger, all of this. Ever since she could remember, in her interactions with people, she always felt numb inside, like she was going through the motions of being friendly without really feeling anything. It was like she had, at some point, engaged some kind of emotional autopilot and she couldn't figure out how to reengage her real self again, as though it had become permanently stuck.

Then, she felt it, a prickle of a connection like an unfamiliar thrill in her senses, and, without understanding why, Fran experienced something she had not felt in a long time, a need, a longing even. She wanted to reach out and confide something to this kindly man sitting patiently in front of her, to make an offering to him of a rare and precious gift that might, in so doing, fractionally unburden her troubled soul.

During her pondering, Danny had remained quiet, almost as though he were willing her to continue, to take a first step. Then, at last, Fran said, 'other than my mum, who doesn't really count since she's as emotionally dead as I am, I haven't told this to anyone before. To be honest, I feel embarrassed, ashamed by what happened when I was a girl, so when I feel the need to explain how I am with people, I'll say something about abuse, but that could mean anything, loads of people say they've been abused, but I was systematically raped by several of the resident guests in our family guesthouse. My mum knew and didn't do anything about it; just turned a blind eye and blamed my dad, but she let it happen and my dad didn't care. I resented my brother for leaving home and then disappearing on his yacht, I felt betrayed; he was the only person I ever loved. But...' Fran took a breath and paused for a moment before she said, 'but now I know he was running away from something, his own demons, not from me. I need to find out what happened to him, that's why I'm doing this trip with Jack down to Australia.'

Danny nodded, but stayed silent and allowed Fran's words to hang in the air between them for a moment, as though he were deciding whether he should accept the gift of Fran's confidence. Then, as though what Fran had said had been too emotionally charged to answer directly, he adopted a universal male response focussing on the practical and said, 'it's a bit of a long shot, finding him, the ocean is a pretty big place.' Then Danny paused and Fran thought she saw tears form in his eyes, then he said, 'you've been holding this inside you for a long time haven't you?' Fran nodded, but when she didn't reply he said, 'it must've been hard for you to say what you just did about what happened to you at home, a place where you should've been safe. I couldn't imagine what it must've been like when your mother didn't do anything to protect you. It sounds like some horrible nightmare. I am so sorry Fran that this happened to you.' Danny's voice faltered and a single tear fell leaving a trail of dampness on his cheek that Fran for a moment felt compelled to brush away, but she restrained herself; the autopilot was kicking in again. Keeping her response practical, she said, 'I know where Cal stopped, on his way, before he was lost that is; it's a start. So, what about you? You also seem like someone who's lost too.'

Danny composed himself for a moment before saying, 'yeah, you could say I'm a self-condemned prisoner. I came here when I was young, looking for something, now I've got old.'

'Thirty-five's not old; we're the same age. I don't feel old, but I feel it's time that something happened in my life.'

'You mean, finding a partner, settling down.'

'I've never been unsettled and I've never made anything but a fool of myself with relationships. I don't know how to say this, present company excluded, but I don't trust men.'

'From what you've been saying it's hardly surprising.'

'It's not that I don't want to find somebody and maybe it'd work out, but I doesn't feel like I've done anything yet. Cal's disappearance has given me a purpose for the first time in my life.'

Danny made a move to leave and they both stood up together. Finding themselves facing each other, Fran felt like there was an electrical field sitting between them, like it would hurt if she were to reach through it, yet she felt compelled to make some kind physical contact. Surprising herself with the suddenness of her impulse, she reached out, brushed her hand against Danny's and curled her fingers through his, feeling the warmth of his touch; it was an intimate gesture. Then she said, 'thank you.' It was all she could find to say before she felt compelled to release his hand.

But the message had been received, Danny smiled and their eyes met for a long moment before he said, 'c'mon, let me take you on a tour round what we've been doing. I don't get much of a chance to show somebody from outside.'

As the Landrover bumped along the forest track and finally reached the top of the hill behind Danny's pod, a wide vista of hills and of heathland opened up. Danny said, 'it looks empty yeah, but look more closely and you'll see trees growing on the slopes we've been fencing. This lot's only been enclosed for a couple of years, but further on, there's a corrie where it's been closed to deer for fifteen years, then you'll see what I'm talking about.'

After passing through the sort of commercial pine plantation that covers most of the highlands of Scotland, the track turned up hill and then ran along the banks of a vigorous and noisy mountain stream. Further on, it became clear that the steam issued from a high corrie nestling between the precipitous flanks of a ring of tall mountains, their peaks hidden in cloud, whilst their lower slopes were bathed in bright sunshine. The scene resembled a painting that hung in the family home at the head of the stairs. Since her mother was religious, Fran had always assumed it was a picture of Eden or heavenly paradise. It was of ethereal mountains, glowing skies fringing idyllic, lush green slopes. It was probably Switzerland or the somewhere else in the Alps, but she realised it could have been a painting of what she was now seeing.

Leaving the Landrover parked below a stoutly built wooden footbridge, after walking over it and across the bustling waters of the stream they had been following, the path turned steeply uphill and could be seen disappearing over the lip of a high corrie just below the cloud-line. Danny stopped and swept his hand in the direction of the slopes above them and to their right and said, 'this here's Ladhar Bhein, make sure you pronounce it "Loor Venn", otherwise nobody knows what the hell you're talking about. It's one of the highest mountains in Knoydart. Fifteen years ago the slopes around this corrie were completely bare, now, you can see mixed Caledonian pine, deciduous alder and silver birch growing. There's bird species, plants, moths and insects here that you wouldn't have seen before these slopes were enclosed. In another ten years, some of the trees will be topping out and this place will be covered in forest, a new Caledonian rainforest, 'cos it's always raining.'

While he was talking, Fran could see that Danny was literally and metaphorically in his element and she said, 'so these are your babies then?'

'Yep, the trees are the closest thing to family I've got these days; sad, eh?'

'Not sad, you've found your thing, your calling in life.'

'I guess, but I'm only a small cog in a machine. Re-wilding was seen as an idealist's dream a few years ago, now it's an international movement, and we're part of it. In another few years, we're gonna bring in a top predator, probably European lynx; I don't think we'd get away with grey wolves like the Americans in their national parks.'

While he continued speaking, and was distracted by his enthusiasm, Fran allowed her eyes to trace the lines of Danny's face and to read his expressions. Like a series of camera snapshots, she committed to memory his determined jaw, the raised cheekbones giving an almost feminine appearance to his fine features, which then gave way to his blue-grey eyes and bushy eyebrows. Hiding under his straggling beard and unkempt hair, was a man with a handsome, almost boyish face; perhaps, she thought, it was the reason why he had grown a beard.

Fran had decided that she liked Danny Tipps and his idiosyncrasies and his zeal for communism. His heart was in the right place and she could tell he had a propensity for love, which, whilst currently largely vested in forests and wild landscapes, she felt that he could be coaxed into loving someone; Fran mused on this and enjoyed Danny's outpouring of enthusiasm, and his company.

Whist they were moored at Inverie, Childs, with Jen's help, had managed to patch up the rudder, but it was far from a permanent repair, so McGivern concluded that discretion was the better part of valour and decided to cut short the shakedown cruise and head back to Dublin for dry dock repairs. The crew were disappointed at missing out on a passage over to the Hebridean islands, but it was nothing compared to O'Hare's fury with Styles who she had decided was incompetent and needed to go. With the cruise down to Australia just a few weeks away, McGivern begged her to reconsider, since it would be nearly impossible for them to find such an experienced bosun who could handle a boat the size of Nostromo in time. In the end she backed down, but everyone knew the situation was bound to cause problems later on since Teddy as the bosun and O'Hare as the mate would need to work closely together.

On hearing the news, forsaking his usual good humour, Childs confided to the others that, 'if Mora's constantly questioning the bosun's decisions, it's just not gonna work! She'll never admit it, but when it comes to sett'n the sail and reading the weather, Teddy knows his stuff, yer can't blacken a man's name after just one mistake.'

Although Fran had agreed at the time, she felt uneasy, since she was, by implication, also responsible for what happened. She knew now they should have reefed the sails and left just the storm jib in place to help control the vessel. Styles had been complacent for some reason, distracted perhaps by his ongoing divorce. It was clear that he was running away from the situation, weren't they all, but the Nostromo could have foundered on a reef with potentially fatal consequences.

Setting sail on the slack tide in the late afternoon, Fran suspended food preparation in the galley and came up on deck. Taking up position at the stern she watched groups of people gathering on the jetty for the arrival of the Mallaig ferry. A man appeared on the harbour wall and stood apart from the rest of people standing on the pier. Taking his hands out of his pockets, he shielded his eyes from the glare and looked towards the Nostromo as the crew were making their preparations to leave. Fran knew immediately it was Danny and felt a jolt like electricity go through her at the recognition. Feeling like an excited schoolgirl again, she waved furiously in his direction and couldn't remember the last time she felt that way about a person; maybe she never had.

Thinking he was reciprocating with a wave of his own, Fran then realised that he was holding something up for her to see. Even at the distance they were from the quay, Fran could see it was the letter she had slipped into his coat pocket without him seeing. When she had left him earlier in the day, Danny had seemed miserable and he said to her, 'so we're to be ships passing in the night? I won't hold it against you if you sail away without a backward glance. As a hermit living on a largely uninhabited speck off the coast of Scotland, I've become rather Zen about relationships. Just remember where I am if you ever need me.'

Fran had smiled and said, 'rubbish, I'm coming back, just try and stop me!' Then she had kissed him. She realised, at that moment, it was what she had wanted to do since she they had first met, but had no idea why. After only two days with Danny, she had begun to notice a growing schism between her instincts and her reasoning self, the self that felt empty and unable to feel anything. The same self that had been bludgeoned into a stupor by Moggs and his cronies, her father's brutality and her mother's ambivalence. Seeing Danny on the quay had produced a joy that had consumed her senses, it was then she knew that, in time, her instincts would win out and she could be a whole person again. But before that happened she needed to lay the ghosts of the past finally to rest; finding out what happened to Cal was part of that.

Then, joining Fran at the stern rails Jen, always anxious it seemed to keep tabs on any hint of onboard romance said, 'I see you've taken a bit of a fancy to Danny then? You wouldn't be the first, but he never lets anyone in apparently.'

'That's not how he sees it. He's more complex than you might think.'

Jen grinned, 'I'm seeing the signs Fran, and I've already spotted you checking out his crazy Facebook pages.'

Ha-ha, how did you guess?'

'Oh my God, you're following him aren't you! Well, if you want my opinion, I think he's lovely.'

Digging her hands in the pockets as a chill breeze started to blow along the loch, Fran's fingers curled round something and she drew out a small envelope that she found there. Turning so that Jen was unable to see what she was doing, she opened it and a beautiful little wooden spoon fell into the palm of her hand. Hanging from it was a small square of cardboard attached with string and on it was written, *just make sure you remember to return and set me free.'* Then there were three *xxx's* and a large *'D'.*

'Well, that Danny's enigmatic to the end. I didn't know he was a spoon carver.'

Fran spun round, it was Jen. She said, 'sorry, I just can't resist. I'm a soft soap for romance.'

Only half joking Fran said, 'then why don't you buy yourself a Mills & Boon?'

CHAPTER 14: Westward ho

AFTER SOME SPARE parts delays, the Nostromo launched from its dry-dock berth at Whites-Robson's Howth boatyards in early September with a new rudder mounting and a new shipmate aboard, Ben Cribbs, a thirty year old computer programmer and keen dingy sailor who replaced Tan Morgan who, as Mora put it, hadn't pulled his weight on the shakedown. Ben, anxious to prove his worth from the start, arrived aboard two weeks early to help O'Hare with provisioning, taking on procurement of spares and equipment, a job that everyone loved to hate. He quickly became Buddy's best friend. Seemingly unable, or reluctant to leave the Nostromo after the shakedown cruise, while his mistress was away in Cornwall, Buddy struck up a friendship with Ben who fed him an array of tidbits he kept in his coat pockets. The two spent hours together and seemed inseparable. Buddy was not the only member of the crew to appreciate Ben's quiet charm. His tanned features, designer stubble and lithe surfer's good looks, were, it seemed, irresistible to the master's mate. O'Hare flirted openly and Ben more than once succumbed, spending a few stolen hours together in her cabin when McGivern was working at their charter business's Dublin office. If he noticed at all, the older man chose to turn a blind eye; as he used to say, 'if yer an old chosser and you're with a pretty young woman, y'need to let her have her head now and again.'

Back aboard the Nostromo, during the first days after their departure on the long voyage down under, Cal's existential presence pervaded Fran's waking hours. She could almost feel him tugging at her shirtsleeves, her heart, her very being. She saw his face reflected in every burnished surface, instead of the washed-out and pale version of her own face reflected in night-time windowpanes, it was his, like an ever-present twin. If it was a sign, she was listening loud and clear, 'I hear you my brother, I hear you and I'm coming.'

Reinserted back into the crew's watch rota, Cal's presence in her waking hours had taken the habit of following her into the superficial slumber that comes when you know you'll be woken from it. Tossing and turning as she fruitlessly pursued a physical need for sleep, Fran found herself spooling though memories of her childhood and of Cal like a filmstrip, speeding through, backing up and replaying them at will, it was something she couldn't recall being able to do before, like a new gift had been miraculously bestowed upon her, or was it a curse?

On the second night of blue water sailing across the Bay of Biscay, the filmstrip became stuck on a particular scene that she couldn't get past. It was the moment of Cal's departure and she appeared to be floating above herself at the moorings near Jimmy's boatyard. She could see the Helford River snaking around on its way to Falmouth Bay. Cal was standing on the deck of the Nautilus with his arms folded; Jimmy and herself were on the boatyard's wooden pier. There was a conversation going on. The scene, at first playing in full sunlight, faded to grey and the shapes of the Helford, the Nautilus and the figures fell into shadow.

She realised that the three figures now in shadow had become darker; they were like the shapes they'd seen that night when she walked with Jimmy along the riverbank. The shapes danced around each other and a fourth appeared as though it had coalesced out of Cal's body, it stood next to him on the Nautilus, but held itself slightly apart, watching, waiting, perhaps impatient for Cal to start his journey. It was like she and Jimmy were holding them back and that Cal's shadowy companion was impatient for them to get on their way.

Fran felt herself floating downwards to get a better view of the figure standing next to Cal. Who could it be? Still unable to tell whether the figure was male or female, its head turned towards her, but before she could see the shrouded face, she woke with a start. One bell sounded time for her to start the middle watch. Shifting on her upper bunk, she peered over the side and saw Jen's brightly lit face framed by the supports of her bunk below. She was slowly turning the pages of a book she was reading. Looking up at her, she nodded towards the book and said, 'I've taken your advice.'

Crinkling her brow, Fran said, 'what advice? I don't usually give out advice.'

Jen tittered and closed the book so that Fran could see the front cover and the title, "Prisoners Of The Night."

Jen said, 'Mills and Boon, a real classic. Actually, so far, it's not too bad and a distraction from your snoring.'

'Oh, gosh, I must've been lying on my back.' Fran paused a beat and then said, 'I'm sorry.'

'About what?'

'What I said back when we were leaving Inverie, I meant to say before, but it's just I was raw after leaving Danny. God! I don't know what I'm saying.'

At that moment, the little wooden spoon Danny had given her, now suspended on the pendent cord around her neck along with her crucifix, dropped down. Reaching up, Jen gently held it in her palm for a moment, then said, 'Danny's quite a one; quiet waters run deep, I'll say that for him.'

'I know, but how can I be having these feelings after only two days?'

'It was the same for Flip and me; I knew he was for me when we first met. Our love started as snogging and groping in a damp canvas tent, but it eventually grew into an adult along with us.' Fran would have answered, but before she did, Jen changed the subject and said, 'I'm worried about Ben, he's been acting very strangely. I think he's suffering from some kind of anxiety.'

Dropping down from her bunk, Fran said, 'none of us really know him and since he couldn't make it for the shakedown, he's a bit of an unknown quantity.'

Jen whispered, 'not to Mora he isn't.'

'How do you mean?'

'I've seen him around her, and I've seen them emerging from dark corners together,'

'You think they're playing around, right under Jack's nose?'

'Yeah, definitely. You know me, I can tell a mile off.'

'Your romance radar you mean?'

'Yeah, I guess so.'

'Maybe he's just nervous, worried about getting caught with Mora.'

'No, it's not just that, he's really anxious when he's up on-deck working with us, you've maybe not noticed it 'cos you're down below in the kitchens quite a lot during the day.'

'Okay, I'll have a chat with him whilst we're on watch. I've heard about this happening on the trawlers sometimes. When you're away for a week or two, out of sight of land, the limitless horizons, it can get to some people. The Cornish call it the bluewater fever.'

Up on deck, Fran found Cribbs sitting on one of the wooden benches in the cockpit, to one side of the companionway; it looked like he had been waiting for her, so Fran said, 'did you check the heading already, or should I have a look?'

'T'be honest, I've been sit'n here wondering whether I have any business being on this boat. I mean, just now, when I started walk'n back to check the helm, somethi'n I would've never had a second thought about if I was on my mate's ketch, the deck seemed to shrink like it was too small to carry me. My legs went and I almost pitched over the side.'

As soon as he mentioned going over the side, Fran's eyes flicked down to Ben's harness and checked he was clipped into the jack-line; then, reassured, she said, 'it's the bluewater, it shrinks the boat, I've heard about it from fishermen who've switched from coastal to trawling. It's nothing to be ashamed or worried about, it'll pass in time, if you let it.'

Cribbs dragged his fingers through the quiff of sandy-coloured hair on the top of his head, it was matted with sweat like he was perspiring heavily, then he said, 'I didn't realise what it'd be like, being out of sight of land. It kind'a feels like I'm on this tiny platform above the huge drop of the ocean. I've been too embarrassed to say anything, after all, I've been on boats often enough, but the feel'n of vulnerability out here is gonna take some get'n used to.'

Fran stretched an arm out towards the western horizon she said, 'have you ever tried describing the sunsets you get out here. They all seem to be diffident, for me, they're like flavours, this one's a peachy gold with crimson overtones.'

Ben chuckled, but he kept his gaze inside the confines of the deck rails and said, 'yeah, right, I get ya, a bit like a fine wine, plenty of depth.'

'C'mon Ben, take a look with me now and tell me what's there, describe it using your other senses, what does it make you feel, what might it taste like, feel like.'

Ben drew in a long breath, like a man who was taking his first step onto a shaky foot bridge or moving out onto an exposed ledge and said, 'definitely strawberries, with a hint of cinnamon and orange, like Christmas.'

Fran nodded, 'now you're getting it. Just hold those thoughts and watch the horizon as the sun goes down, it'll be changing, I want you to describe what it tastes like.'

For ten whole minutes, Ben described the light show and the shimmering halo of the horizon until the upper part of the corona slipped into the sea and the light was finally gone. Then he said, 'you're good at this Fran, you missed your calling, you should've been a shrink.'

Fran shook her head, 'believe me, I've done my time as someone who's been afraid. I was afraid of the sea, but not anymore. For me, it feels like the Nostromo's holding us to her, I love feeling the way she moves though the water. I've felt the fear of the sea plenty of times, but I've learned to give myself up to it, like riding a bicycle, you just have to let go and trust yourself to know what to do.'

Towards the end of the night, as the faintest glow of light appeared as a steel-grey line on the eastern horizon, Fran checked the heading, walked for'ed towards the cockpit and rang eight bells, the end of the middle watch. As she did so, she caught a trace of cigarette smoke; less acrid than Marty's Woodbines, she knew it must be the skipper's menthols. Wanting to let him know the winds were still not blowing right for their intended passage to Madeira and a landing there for fresh supplies, Fran followed her nose and found McGivern sitting on the deck with his back against the aft locker doors. It was a favourite spot of his and a pleasant little sun trap when conditions were right.

Joining him there, Fran said, 'skip, have you got a minute?'

'Sure, come into my office. There's no better place on earth to do some think'n with the sea skimming underneath and her sails filled with a steady blow.'

Fran said, 'it's the steady blow I wanted to talk to you about...'

'I know, I know, I checked the compass, we're not go'n to the Madeira's, I'm think'n we shouldn't fight it and head into Morocco, I've already let the port authorities know and I've booked us a mooring at the Rabat Yacht Club.'

Before Fran could reply, there was a scratching sound and Buddy pushed through a gap in the doors at the top of the companionway. On seeing them, he let out a delighted bark and scuttled over to they were sitting. McGivern ruffled his ears and said, 'he's a fine wee dog he is for sure. Y'know, he's not been off the Nostromo since we got back from Scotland, I keep say'n it, but he truly is a seadog right enough!' Having sat down and seeing that Buddy had now placed his head in Fran's lap, he said, 'but he still knows who his mistress is; better than the company of an old bugger like me! He has taste, I'll give him that!' McGivern then cracked a toothy smile, 't'be honest with ya, like Buddy here, I prefer the female company.'

Fran's face reddened slightly as she said, 'I guess I should be flattered.'

'Don't be worry'n yerself colleen, me other half, Mora, keeps me on the straight and narrow!'

It occurred to Fran that McGivern might be flirting with her. After all, his girlfriend was trying it on with one of his crew and, as her grandmother used to say, 'what's good for the goose is good for the gander'. If he was, Fran was not going to respond, she had no desire to be part of a love triangle. Kind and generous though he appeared to be, she had the impression there was a transactional undercurrent to Jack's dealings with people; you scratch my back, and I'll scratch yours – the way of the Irish perhaps. If Jack was looking to get back at Mora for her transgressions with Ben, she was determined to stay out of it. She chastised herself and made a mental note to avoid situations like this where it was likely she would be alone with him.

Although it was the end of her watch, McGivern seemed in no hurry to let her go to her bunk and said, 'once we're out of Morocco, we'll catch the Canary currents that'll take us down to past West Africa; that's where we've got to stay out as far as possible, over towards the Americas to avoid tangl'n with pirates.' McGivern looked thoughtful for a moment and said, 'are you sure Cal got on further and around the Cape? D'ya think there's a chance he got into some trouble?'

'With pirates you mean? If they hijacked his boat, why the distress signal near the Christmas Islands, thousands of miles away?'

McGivern said, 'point taken. Our landing in Rabat could be a good chance to see if the Moroccan authorities heard anything about him; I think y'said he'd landed there.'

Fran said, 'I'm on it. It's a bit of luck that's now where we're headed.'

'Yeah, right, after Morocco there's a lot of bluewater sailing and nothin' much until we get around the Cape of Good Hope, so?'

CHAPTER 15: Now you see me

DRAGGING THE SHIP'S grocery cart behind her, Fran walked slowly towards the Rabat harbour office and immigration buildings. Having decided not to wear a headscarf, despite local customs, her jet black hair flowed back from her head as she shook out the tangles. Inclining her face upwards towards the haze-tinted blue vault of the sky, through her dark glasses, she could make out the contrails of jet planes taking off or landing at the nearby airport. All around her there was business and bustle. The breeze was warm and carried to her senses the musty smell of dried decay with a tang of citrus and sea salt, like a hastily prepared spritzer cocktail. O'Hare had warned her to cover her head with a scarf, but she was feeling mischievous, excited even and she thought, *who was O'Hare to be giving out advice about unwanted advances from men anyway?*

The gleaming white stucco buildings, painted blue and gold, seemed overpowering after the empty vistas of the open sea. Groups of French tourists with their children in tow crowded the charter offices whilst a separate small crowd had gathered to admire the Nostromo; she was always the main attraction wherever she went. Although there were other super yachts, she was old school, wood to her heart and something special. Fran wondered whether her newfound propensity for love now extended to the Nostromo.

Having passed through immigration, Fran re-emerged outside and followed a broad boulevard to the office of the Harbour Master, which itself had the appearance of a ship under steam with gleaming steel rails around its upper and lower decks. She thought of Cal and the certain knowledge that he had also been here, had walked along the same street and had entered the same office to speak to the same officials. Dipping into her purse, she brought out her passport, a head and shoulders photograph of Cal and another of him standing proudly in front of the Nautilus. Like the Nostromo, it was distinctive, a wooden-hulled, Ketch-rigged fifty-five-footer, there was a chance that someone would remember it.

Adjusting to the cool, echoey, almost church-like entrance hall, she crossed to a reception desk and the single man on duty. Nerves almost getting the better of her, Fran decided not to even attempt speaking French, so she said, 'Good morning, I have a question about a missing person.'

The man drew his fine, tanned features into a look of concern and said, 'I am afraid madam, that you must speak to the gendarme about such matters. I can ask one of our staff to assist you.'

'He is my brother; he sailed here on his own boat from England. He was lost at sea, but we know he was here in November last year. His name is Callum Tremayne. His yacht was registered in Falmouth, England number 14/1923.'

Showing customary deference to another's distress, the man touched his chest with his palm and inclined his head slightly forward and said, 'I am truly sorry madam, and I wish I could help, but it is a matter for the police.'

'Can I see a copy of the visitor's book to see if his name is there, just something to confirm that he arrived here at least?'

The man leaned forward and sighed, 'those are confidential records I'm afraid.' He paused, looked around him to see if there was anyone else waiting, then took a bound volume off the shelf behind and placed it on the desk in front of him, 'November you say?' Then muttering to himself, 'enregistré en Angleterre, laissez-moi voir... 14/1923, that is a very old vessel!' then he tapped the register with his forefinger, 'yes, it is here madam.' The man turned the ledger around so that Fran could see it.

About midway down the page, her heart skipped a beat. Cal's familiar scrawl jumped off the page. Fran gasped and said, 'please, sir, please can I just touch it for a moment?'

The man's face softened and, keeping hold of the heavy volume, he pushed it into the trough where documents could be passed back and forth securely, like a bank teller's counter. Fran's hand trembled slightly as she inserted her hand. With her forefinger, she traced the indentation that Cal had made on the page with the pen he had used, around the "Tremayne" and allowed it to rest for a moment on the "Callum." Then she said, 'Thank you.'

With Fran's finger still resting on the page, the man gently removed the ledger from the access tray and replaced it on the shelf. Then, touching his heart again, he said, 'I am sorry that I cannot do more to help. Please accept my deepest sympathies. If you wish to go to the police office, I can ask the concierge to guide you there.'

'Thank you, but that will not be necessary. I have the information I need. You have been very helpful... and kind.'

Slightly unsteady on her feet, Fran walked back outside where she stood for a while taking in the information. Cal had been in Morocco and he had left to carry on with his journey. Almost a year after his disappearance, this was the first tangible proof he had made the journey at all. Before she had seen his name in the harbour master's records, part of her hoped he had, for some unfathomable reason, faked the whole thing, she had read that it been done before by others. She knew it wasn't rational, but she would accept anything if she could just see him again.

A pungent smell of animal dung, organic decomposition laced with the unmistakable feral stench of animal carcasses and the rancid ordure of fish wafted from a large outdoor souk. Thankful that Ben and Teddy were responsible for buying fresh meat and fish, Fran detoured around the wet market and headed towards the rows of traders selling fruit and vegetables.

Sweltering in the early afternoon heat, Fran dragged the heavy cart, now laden with a variety of fresh produce, around the back of the souk and into shade cast by the roofs of some permanent stalls. Looking for something to eat and drink, she was drawn towards a kindly, older woman who was selling little glasses of hot, sweet, mint tea from the back of a wooden barrow, whilst two young girls wearing brightly-coloured kaftans, her grandchildren perhaps, fried strips of dough in an old oil drum, which had been ingeniously welded to a charcoal stove.

Both girls smiled as Fran approached and then sat at one of the little round tables they had set in the shade. The older girl came over and Fran pointed at the tea, held up her forefinger and said 'un tasse' and then nodded towards the younger girl at the stove and held up another finger, 'un pain, s'il vous plait.'

The girls got to work and after a couple of minutes, the older girl placed a glass of tea on the table and said, 'ton machrebi', and then a plate with four doughnuts, 'vos sfenji. Quatorze dirham s'il vous plait madam.'

Fran paid the girl then gave her a few extra coins as a tip. The girls were charming and at ease with adults, quite unlike most children she had met who were the same age back home. She thought about what it might be like to have children and thought, *if they're like this, bring them on!*

Then something caught her attention, a tall western man in a white shirt, loose white flannel trousers and wearing a fedora on his head crossed the opposite corner of the souk from where Fran was sitting and turned down an alleyway towards the covered stalls behind; it was Cal, she was sure of it. Feeling quite faint for a moment, she collected her thoughts and said to the girls, 'je retourne' and ran off in pursuit.

Above the heads of the crowd, for the man was tall like Cal, Fran could see the white fedora bobbing up and down ahead of her. After a few turns, the man made to cross a small square. Thinking that she would be able to catch up to him in the clearer space, Fran began to run, but almost immediately, she tripped over a couple of huge baskets of oranges, which sent her flying. By the time she had picked herself up and disentangled herself from the crowd, the man had disappeared.

Frantic now to find him again, Fran ran across the square. As she did so, she caught sight of him heading into a large covered market, full of brightly coloured baskets. Entering from the bright sun, Fran was momentarily unable to see. She tore off her sunglasses and cast around for the bobbing white fedora, there it was!

Pushing now, to make way against the crowds of mostly western tourists, Fran rounded a corner by a carpet seller and found the man stooping over a large Persian rug. She ran up and almost stumbled into him. Catching her by the arm to prevent her from falling over, Fran looked up at the man and said, 'Cal, Cal, how...?'

Almost as soon as she had spoken to him, the man's face seemed to reform itself in front of her eyes. In place of Cal's features were those of a stranger. The man was much older than her brother, there was a moustache and his chin was longer, more protruding. The realisation caused Fran to collapse out of the man's grasp and onto the floor of the shop.

Thinking that she had fainted, the man loosened the collar of Fran's blouse and the carpet seller brought her some tea. The two men set her down and propped her up against a stack of rolled carpets. Fran looked up at the men's concerned faces and the man with the fedora crouched beside her and said, 'je suis désolé madame, vous allez bien? Vous avez l'air malade, avez-vous besoin d'un médecin?'

Hearing the word médecin, Fran said, 'no, no I'm fine, really, I don't need a doctor, I just thought... you were my brother.' Tears filled her eyes and she said, 'I want to find him, he's lost, I lost him...'

For a moment, while onlookers stared at her dishevelled appearance, Fran felt like she could no longer trust her senses. For the first time since she joined the crew of the Nostromo, she doubted whether she could carry it through. *There were thousands of miles to go, what,* she thought, *were the chances of finding Cal, even if she got to Australia?* Up until this point, she had been certain that she would be able to trace him, but was it all just an illusion, or an hallucination like the one she had just had, brought on by grief at the thought she might never see her brother again?

CHAPTER 16: Stilled life

NOSTROMO WALLOWED, TRAPPED in slack winds somewhere off the coast of Northwest Africa. Hoping they would carry them out of range of African pirate vessels, the prevailing Canary currents had weakened as they sailed a southwesterly course towards South America. First the currents, then the wind had failed and they were now at a total standstill. The doldrums, an almost mythical place where old sailors used to talk of being becalmed for weeks on end had ensnared the boat in a sauna-like combination of heat and humidity. Fran never thought she would struggle to find sleep in quiet seas, but she found herself missing the constant jolt and sway of the boat under a head of wind. To make matters worse, after the dogwatch change-over, she now had the morning watch and for the last two nights she had struggled to sleep.

With a third restless night stretching ahead, the torpor and unbearable heat finally got the better of her and she gave it up. Fran quietly dropped down from her bunk with the idea of making herself a cup of tea in the galley before heading up on deck to chat to whoever was now on watch. In the unaccustomed stillness, she could hear the anxious murmur of hundreds of square feet of canvas as the Nostromo craved a motive force to bring her to life.

Up on deck, a moonless sky and the haze, familiar now as it seemed to accompany the intolerable stillness, gave a close, matt quality to the total darkness that felt claustrophobic, moulding itself around Fran's face as though it might suffocate her. Settling herself on a life raft locker that doubled as a bench seat, Fran was about to take a sip of her tea, when her ears literally pricked up. There was a keening sound, rising to a crescendo then briefly falling silent then rising again; it was almost imperceptible, buffeted by the gentle breeze and murmur of the sails as it drifted back from the foredecks. At first ignoring a sound so inconsequentially small in the bigness of the surrounds, the inexplicability of it finally drove her to investigate. Thinking it might be a seabird trapped somewhere, Fran cautiously made her way towards the sound. Rounding the foredeck sail store, she saw two figures. Assuming they were the watch, she started walking towards them with an idea of offering them tea. As she got closer, she could see the two figures were absorbed in performing some kind of task. Thinking she might be able to help, Fran moved swiftly forward, and then froze mid-step. From where she stood, light from an open hatch below them illuminated the figure furthest from her; it was Mora. Shorts pushed down to her ankles, her face contorted in what looked like pain, the keening sound Fran had heard fell from Mora's slack lips as she supported herself on the bow rails. Still in darkness, Fran could see that the second figure was crouched behind Mora. Although clearly visible to them, so intent on what they were doing, they failed to see Fran who was standing just a few yards away. Then as she tried to leave without them noticing her, Fran accidentally struck her teacup on the rails and they both looked up; it was then she could see that the second figure was Ben and he was naked from the waist down. It was obvious they had been having sex. Seeing that Fran was making to leave, Ben quickly pulled up his shorts and came after her whilst Mora quickly disappeared below.

'Get a good look did ya? You like what you saw then? Snoop'n around, what the hell are you doing?'

Incensed, Fran hissed, 'keep your voice down for Christ's sake Ben, what the hell are *you* doing is more to the point?'

'Surely you saw what I was doing, giving Mora a bloody good seeing to, and why not? She's not get'n anything from the old man and she's been coming on to me these last few days, it was inevitable what was going to happen.'

Seeing that he was getting angry and might do something even more stupid, Fran's said, 'calm down, get a grip!'

'I suppose you're gonna dob us in, yeah?'

'Don't you think everyone already suspects? How long do you think Jack's going to turn a blind eye.'

'It's that bloody bitch Jen tell'n everybody, she's got her nose into everyone's business.'

Taken aback by the vulgarity of the language coming from a person who had, up until now been quiet and rather shy, Fran appealed for reason and said, 'Ben, this is a boat for God's sake! We're in each other's pockets night and day there are no secrets. Sooner or later Jack'll catch you two at it, then he won't be able to ignore it.'

'You gonna tell him then? You two are pretty close, y'know Mora thinks you're fuck'n him.'

'Hah, that's a laugh. If you want to know, I've been keeping as far away from Jack as possible, I know what Mora's like, she's a powder keg ready to explode.'

'That's not how she tells it, she reckons you're all over him,'

'Stop making this about me, it's you I caught with your pants down!'

'If you want to know, we're in love, she's been wanting to leave him for ages, and now she's going to after this trip. We've been seeing each other for a while. That's the plan anyway.'

'Christ, Ben, is there any way you guys can keep a lid on this 'til we get to port? We've got one hell of a lot of sailing to do and we all need to stay focussed.'

'Are you my mum or something!'

Fran put her hand on Cribbs' arm like she was trying to hold him back, then she said, 'please Ben, for all of us. Jack doesn't deserve to have his nose rubbed in it like this, and on his own boat.'

Cribbs was quiet for a moment, then his shoulders slumped, like his rage was subsiding and he said, 'okay Fran... look, I'm sorry. You're a mate I know you are. You've been kind to me and I'm just being a twat. I'm sorry; I'll talk to Mora, calm her down, try and make her see sense.'

Fran nodded, 'right then, I'll see you bright and early in the morning when I come up on watch!'

CHAPTER 17: Purest space

PHILOSOPHERS, POETS, HEDONISTS and sailors have used many words to describe the raw beauty of the sea. There is no beguile, neither is there deceit, nor a hidden purpose, all is uncompromisingly clear and unfettered by curtaining foliage, rearing mountains or deep ravines. Redemption or damnation approaches out of purest space.

Sunrise on the tenth day of flat calm and the morning after her unwelcome discovery, Fran relieved Cribbs and rang the ship's bell for the start of the morning watch. When he realised Jen was Fran's watch-mate, Cribbs shot her a nervous glance and Fran whispered, 'take it easy Ben. If I were going to say anything I would've done it by now, Jen and me share a cabin remember? Like I said it's in nobody's interests that your extramural activities become common knowledge.' A suitably chastened Ben Cribbs headed below to his bunk.

There was no sign of Mora O'Hare, though Fran was pretty sure she would come to see her at some point to, as she liked to put it, 'have a word' at a moment of the young Irish woman's choosing, when she would attempt to regain what she saw as the upper hand. All Fran wanted to do was keep the peace and hold it together until they got safely to Western Australia and the safe haven of Fremantle docks.

As first light broke, neither swell, nor wave crests disturbed the flimsy tendrils of light that crept over the eastern horizon. In the uncertain light that always came before the sun's corona finally burst from the ocean depths, Jen shouted, 'I see a mast, it's another boat!'

Fran took the proffered binoculars from her friend and focussed on an area of sea off the port side. A two-masted yacht, most likely a ketch, sitting perfectly still on the surface of the water, looked like a model in a bathtub. Bow on and lacking sails hoisted on the masts, it was almost impossible to see in the vastness of their surrounds. Fran said, 'you've got good eyesight!'

Jen indicated she wanted the binoculars, then said, 'not really, I was kind of expecting to see it. Gimme a minute and I'll check the flags she's flying; yep, thought so, it's Norwegian. I wondered if we'd bump into him. Skip mentioned that there was a guy called Jensen, I think, doing a solo round the world trip trying to break their national record.'

Jen's nonchalance made it sound humdrum, like single-handed around the world sailing was another-day-at-the-office boring. Like bagging the world's seven highest mountains, or diving to the bottom of the Mariana Trench. Fran pondered whether, because so many had done it before, the incredible feat of single-handed sailing had lost its cache value. And yet, the summit of Everest was littered with the corpses of the hubristic dead who, perhaps believing in their own invincibility, made the surprise discovery, all too late, that they were neither invincible nor infallible. Likewise, the sea was a vast unmarked grave for hundreds, or possibly thousands of crews and individuals from ships and boats who had believed the same thing, as if sailing around the world were routine. Maybe, she thought, that's what happened to Cal, he got lulled into a false sense of security and had made the mistake of believing his own rhetoric.

Just as the two women were checking the decks to see if they could see Jensen and possibly signal to him, McGivern appeared at the top of the companionway. Seeing that Jen was looking through binoculars he said, 'so, have you guys spotted him?'

Jen said, 'yep, skip, he's about two hundred and fifty yards away according to the rangefinder.'

As McGivern approached, Fran watched the skip's face intently to see if there was any suggestion that he might suspect something about what happened the previous night, but his face was impassive, neither sullen nor wearing his usual lopsided grin. If he knew something was amiss, he was giving nothing away.

Just as McGivern was about to say something else, Jen shouted, 'he must've started his engines, the boat's coming over to us.' Then, to Fran, she said, 'at least it proves there must be someone onboard.'

The ketch hove to about fifty yards away from the Nostromo and a man, presumably Jensen, appeared on deck and slowly heaved a sea anchor over the side to ensure he didn't drift any closer. His movements were laboured and ponderous, and not what you might expect from a fit, strong, round the world yachtsman. Having accomplished his task, Jensen steadied himself on the main mast and, using a little megaphone, he shouted over to them, 'ahoy the boat. Are you the Nostromo?'

McGivern shouted, 'yes! Are you Kit Jensen? D'ya need anything?'

Jensen managed a smile and said, 'yes, so you've heard about me?'

Seeing that the Norwegian was suffering some kind of physical distress and wanted to say something more, McGivern simply nodded, accentuating his movements so Jensen could see what he meant and waited for Jensen to continue.

Apparently mustering his strength, Jensen said, 'I could do with some teabags and sugar, supplies are low.'

McGivern nodded again, not a problem, we'll get that over to you.'

Jen said, 'skip, I can take the stuff he needs over in a dry bag, it'd be nice to do some free swimming off the boat, it's always been one of my little fantasies.'

The Skipper briefly checked the conditions and said, 'looks okay, but you'll need a buddy.'

Fran said, 'I'll go with her, it'd be nice to stretch some different muscles.'

Remerging from below in their bathing costumes with Flip in tow, Jen and Fran both shouldered the dry bags they had filled with some teabags and a few choice morsels from the galley they thought a solo yachtsman might be missing after a month at sea.

Jen shouted, 'ahoy the boat. We're gonna come over!'

Seated on the deck, Jensen waved in acknowledgement and then went below.

As they lowered the stern platform and used the stepladder to get down to it, the silence and calm was almost surreal, like deafness, yet tiny sounds were audible. Sensitive to the slightest disturbance, Fran noticed the squeak of her wet feet on the steel rungs of the ladder, the thud of their dry bags as they dropped onto the dive platform and her pounding heartbeat. Standing on the platform, like the blue screen used in movies to enact scenes with special effects, the sky appeared to meld into the ocean's limitless horizon. Diving into the sea's warm embrace, Fan could see that, whilst all was clear immediately around her, a few yards away she noticed a huge mass of protruding fronds that looked like a tangled mat of seaweed. McGivern shouted down, 'Fran, Jen, watch out for that bank of Sargassum weed, the jellyfish love to hide under it, just be careful to keep yerselfs away from it.'

As she swam behind Jen, Fran anxiously scanned the surface. As a girl, she had been stung by a Portuguese man of war, lion's mane they called them in Cornwall; the pain was excruciating and she had no wish to repeat the experience. As usual, Jen seemed to be oblivious to danger, *oh for the invincibility of youth*, Fran thought.

After climbing the stern steps that Jensen had lowered for them, they found the amidships companionway and descended below. In the shuttered gloom, they passed an open door that led into Jensen's sleeping quarters and saw that he was sitting on his cot. The sailor's tanned face accentuating his bleach blond hair and eyebrows, Jensen's features were chiselled, handsome even, but his face was wracked with pain, which made him look older than he was. Seeing that the man was in distress, Fran said, Mr Jensen, are you alright?'

Jensen said, 'Kit, please, there is no formality out here. I am very grateful that you have come over in person, I have suffered a little with loneliness since the accident.'

Fran, whose attention had been fixed on Jensen's pained features, glanced down to his body and she saw that his arms and legs were wrapped around with bandages. With concern in her voice, she said, 'you're hurt, you should have said something, we could've brought over some medical supplies.'

Jensen sighed, like he had been dreading the moment when he would have to explain what happened and said, 'I had a fire in the galley. It was a stupid mistake, I was tired and I did not realise the gas had not lit on the stove. Then I struck a match to light a gas lamp and boom! My clothing caught fire. I was confused, there was a fire in the galley and a fire on me.'

Always practical Jen said, 'I'll make some tea.'

Jensen said, 'the galley is a mess, please be careful.'

Taking a seat on the cot, Fran said, 'I've had some first aid training, I can take a look at those wounds.'

At first, Jensen seemed reluctant to let Fran remove one of the bandages on his arm, but checking her patient's reaction more closely, she concluded that this might be more due to embarrassment than pain; then she noticed the bottle of morphine tablets on the bedside table.

Nodding at the dusky brown bottle, she said, 'have you been taking morphine?'

Jensen nodded, 'yes, the pain is unbearable without it.'

Fran's face filled with concern, 'we must get you over to the Nostromo. I can clean and rebind these wounds properly there...' Fran paused, the burns on Jensen's forearm, whilst not very deep, were an angry red colour and very swollen. Looking into her patient's face she said, 'these are badly infected.'

I know; I have been very much neglecting them. Perhaps not wanting to know how bad they are.' His features wrestled with a mixture of emotions, fear, but also determination, then he said, 'I am not leaving the boat, she is all I have and I will not abandon her.' It was like he was talking about a person.

'Kit... these wounds are infected... they need medical treatment.'

Jensen nodded, 'I have antibiotics in the medical cabinet in the galley; I'll take some of those. I am not leaving the boat!'

Just then, Jen brought in three mugs of tea and gave one to Jensen. Fran stood up and said, 'I'll get those antibiotics', then indicated to Jen that she wanted her to follow. Once they were in the ruined and blackened galley, fearing that Jensen might overhear, Fran whispered in Jen's ear, 'his burns are bad and they're infected.'

Jen said, 'what should we do? We can't leave him.'

'Agreed. I think we should ask skip if we can tow him nearer to shore somewhere so he can get some medical help.'

Back on deck, the women found that the two boats had drifted further apart and that McGivern and the rest of the crew were now watching from the Nostromo's stern rails. Fran held up and pointed to one of the two-way radios they had brought with them. Getting the message, McGivern nodded and held his up. Pressing the transmit button, Fran said, 'there's been a fire and Kit's badly burned. I've patched him up, but we can't leave him.'

McGivern's voice cracked over the radio, 'will he come with us? Join the crew? There's not many places we can let him off, we're in the middle of the South Atlantic.'

Fran said, 'he won't leave the boat.'

There was a pause after she released the transmit button, then there was more crackling and she could hear snatches of a conversation between McGivern and O'Hare, then McGivern said, 'well, there isn't much we can do for him.'

There were more muffled sounds on the radio then O'Hare's voice, 'and where are we going to find help out here, tell me that!'

Fran said, 'we could at least tow him over towards land so he has a chance of a safe landing.'

Just as McGivern was about to say something, O'Hare shouted, 'and risk get'n it from the pirates around the African coast, not a chance!'

Fran immediately pressed the transmit button hard, cutting her off and then said, 'we can't leave an injured sailor. It could be one of us asking for help. It's an unwritten law of the sea; at the very least it's bad manners to just leave someone who has serious injuries!'

Whilst a back and forth argument took place about what to do, the slight wind, which had continued to rise through the morning, began to gust more strongly. Over on the Nostromo, O'Hare turned to Ben and Marty, 'you two, get them sails up, we're leav'n. If they're not come'n over, then they can stay where they are!'

McGivern took the radio from O'Hare, and, with a note of desperation in his voice, he said, 'c'mon on Fran, Jen, c'mon, just come back over, he's got supplies, we can't tow him any closer to land, it's too dangerous.'

Whilst the Skip used all the charm he could muster, Fran could hear O'Hare's voice in the background shouting, 'I said get them sails up, we've got to catch this wind or we'll never leave here.'

Flip, who had become more and more anxious as events unfolded, saw that Marty and Ben were about to obey orders. Before either of them could use it, he rushed forward, unlatched the mainsail winch handle and said, 'don't anybody touch those sails. That's my girlfriend and my friend over there. We're not going anywhere until they're back on this boat!'

O'Hare smirked and said, 'oh, the boy finally speaks. You've found yer tongue there big man!'

Flip shifted position so he was between the rest of the crew and the halliard winches and said, 'I mean it, Ben, Marty, Teddy, don't you do it or, God help me, I'll smash your heads in. Maybe you'll get me but one of you'll have a serious head wound, and we're thousands of miles from help, so go figure what would happen.'

On the other boat, seeing what was happening, Jen grabbed Fran's arm, 'I'm scared for Flip. I'm afraid they might do something to him, maybe hurt him.'

Fran's shoulders slumped like she was momentarily beaten, 'I never thought it would come to this. Jesus!' then she hit the transmit button and shouted into the radio, 'At least send more medical supplies over on a line, we can't leave Kit here without more fresh dressings for his burns. C'mon, have some common decency at least.'

Without saying anything more, McGivern secured and then threw a line with a float tied to the end towards Jensen's boat. Seeing it, Jen dived in, retrieved the line, secured it to a deck cleat and gave a thumbs up sign to signify they were ready. McGivern hoisted a bag and sent the supplies over to the other boat on the line. Sullen now, he turned to O'Hare and said, 'we're go'n to motor over to them, the sea's get'n up now.'

Then McGivern disappeared back towards the helm and the rest of the crew stood in silence. Whilst the two women made their farewells to Jensen and swam back over to the Nostromo, Flip kept hold of the winch handle just in case somebody tried to change the skip's mind. Back on board, Fran and Jen walked past the rest of the crew while they were setting the sails, none of the men met their gaze and none of them spoke. Fran assumed they were either embarrassed or ashamed, she thought to herself they should be both. Voicing her thoughts, Fran said, 'call yourselves sailors, you should be ashamed of yourselves!' Ben, Marty and Teddy looked away whilst Jen and Fran went below. Before he followed them, Flip tossed the winch handle over to Marty so he could use it to raise the mainsail.

Back in their cabin, as the women began stripping off their wet costumes, Flip said to Jen, 'I hope to God *we* never have to rely on Ms O'Hare's tender mercies on this voyage!'

Jen reached out a hand and tenderly pushed her fingers through Flip's tousled hair and said, 'you were stunning out there darling.' Then, gently pulling him towards her, she kissed him and said, 'what would you have done if we'd stayed and they'd raised the sails?'

Flip's face flushed red and his eyes narrowed, 'the way I was feeling, I'd have smashed in someone's skull if they'd so much as touched the halliards!'

At the start of the middle watch, with gusting winds in her sails, the Nostromo rapidly pulled away from the stricken Norwegian and his boat. Still shocked by what had happened, although it was not their turn on watch, Fran and Jen along with Flip, who didn't want to let Jen out of his sight, went back up on deck. Pointedly ignoring Marty and Ben who were setting the sails to make more speed in the rising wind, Jen stared through night sight binoculars to see if she could pick out the Norwegian's mast beacon, but it was nowhere to be seen. Before it had got dark, Jen had been heartened to see that Jensen had raised the mainsail and jib so he could get underway and might even be following in their wake.

As they stood huddled together by the midship's rails, Fran shouted, 'look! It's a maroon it must be Kit! He's signalling he's in trouble.'

Pointing upward, Flip followed the line of a bright light with a long fiery tail behind it as it made an ark in the night sky. As they watched, the ball of light appeared to be coming towards them like a missile. Astonishment in his voice, Flip shouted, 'it's not a flair, it's a meteorite and it's coming straight at us!'

As the meteorite dropped from the sky, reacting instinctively, Flip pulled the two women down onto the deck with him. Just as it seemed like it might hit, there was an explosive sound like a depth charge; the meteorite missed the Nostromo by just a few feet.

When they got to their feet, Fran stared at the spot where the cosmic visitor had landed in the sea and said, 'it's like the fates have spoken, made it known there'll be a price to pay for leaving Kit like that.' After a pause, she said, 'what drives someone to willingly set out across the sea alone in such a way? It makes no rational sense to me.'

Jen said, 'you mean Jensen?'

Fran nodded, 'and my brother... I sometimes think that almost anything can happen out here. The ocean is another world, it makes its own rules and so do the people that sail on it.'

Flip nodded, 'yeah, and we better be watching our backs from now on.'

CHAPTER 18: Storm force

SINCE THE INCIDENT on Jensen's boat, Fran noticed that two factions had emerged within the crew. In one camp was Teddy Styles the Bosun and Marty Childs the Bosun's Mate, who clearly felt loyalty to McGivern and had almost certainly been chosen as crew by the Captain and his Mate, O'Hare. They had shown themselves to be weak and unable to stand up to O'Hare and make up their own minds on what to do when the chips were down. Chosen by O'Hare personally, Ben Cribbs formed a subset of one within the McGivern/O'Hare camp as it was now clear he had been having a clandestine affair with O'Hare for some time. The other camp was more straightforward and consisted of Fran with Flip and Jen, with whom she had formed a strong bond of friendship.

Probably due to male pride at being faced down by a younger man, both Styles and Childs now demonstrated a streak of vindictiveness towards Flip, which manifested itself in a myriad of small ways, including allocation of all the menial tasks, from replacing the bilge filters to unblocking the wastewater pipes in the crew toilets. Although the sting associated with this was countered by the help Fran and Jen gave to Flip with his chores, the malice behind it was a concern and only resulted in reinforcing the factions. As turning the Cape of Africa quite literally loomed large on the horizon, Fran worried that lack of cohesion in the crew could only lead to trouble. As if to confirm her fears, over the week following the incident, they had drifted badly off course towards the Brazilian coast. It was a circumstance she felt was as much due to lax management of the crew by Styles as the adverse winds and ocean currents. In the end, the day they rounded the Cape of Good Hope turned out to be rather an anti-climax with light winds and anticyclonic conditions that persisted for several days afterwards. With the Cape behind them, the Nostromo entered a natural wind tunnel known as the Roaring Forties, the strong and sometimes gale force winds from the west much favoured by sailing boat captains and their crews heading for the antipodes. As a result, whilst still more than five thousand miles distant, the prospect of landing in Australia now seemed to be within their grasp.

Factionalised along the same lines as the crew, watches were now rather unfairly allocated between the two rather unequal-sized groups, which meant that Fran, Jen and Flip were always on watch together and missed out on changeovers. Back on mornings, Jen and Fran had to fit preparation and clearing up after the crew's evening meal in between sleep and going on watch at four a.m. Alas, the calm weather could not last. On the third evening after rounding the Cape, the roaring forties, the southern hemisphere's strong westerly winds, with their well-earned reputation for mayhem and destruction, finally made their presence known. Having been lulled into a false sense of security by a stretch of calm weather, Fran cursed as a pan of water hurtled off the stove and narrowly missed scalding Jen in the process. Alarmed at what could have caused a serious burn, Fan said, 'God! I'm sorry, what with all this fair weather sailing we've been having, I seem to have totally forgotten how to balance the gimbal stove!'

Jen said, 'no harm done, my years on school and university tennis courts have made me pretty agile in an emergency!'

Fran bent down to dry the floor and said, 'I've got a feeling we're going to get back into practice over the next few hours, there's definitely some weather coming in. I'd better head up top and check how bad it's likely to get.'

Although still only early evening, grey clouds scudded like express trains across a darkening sky. Looking for the glow of light that should still be visible in the west where she had enjoyed the aching beauty of South Atlantic sunsets in recent days, a vast cloud bank with an inky black, almost purple centre brooded menacingly just above the horizon. As she watched, the huge squall cloud touched down onto the ocean surface. Appearing to draw strength from contact with open water, the storm gathered pace and ferocity as it moved up behind them blowing the first sheets of curtaining rain ahead of it. In the growing darkness, as Fran held onto the cockpit rails before she went back down below, the deck began to lurch violently and she could see wave crests gleaming white and growing in size like the gnashing teeth of some grotesque sea creature bent on their destruction.

Unknown to Fran, also on deck in the gathering tempest that would soon engulf them, ensconced in the place they liked to meet behind the sail store, O'Hare and Cribbs stood together in the wash as the first huge waves began to crash over the bow. Bracing themselves, Ben shouted, 'at least in this, there won't be anyone snooping around!'

O'Hare laughed, 'Y mean Fran Tremayne? Don't you worry about her, or Jack, for that matter. Look, Ben, I'm a partner in the charter business, if me and Jack part ways, I'm get'n half of it, and he'll not be wanting to do that. We can have our bit of fun now, and if it gets to be more than that, then I'll find a way for us to be together; after all, I can do whatever I damn well like. Me and Jack started out as business partners, and that's the way it's go'n to stay as far as I'm concerned from now on.'

Registering the rather noncommittal way that O'Hare referred to what he saw as their love affair, Cribbs cupped O'Hare's face between the palms of his hands and a mixture of concern and lust danced across his features in equal measure. Lust for all the nights before the voyage when they'd spent hours rolling under the sheets together whilst McGivern was away on business and concern that they might soon come to an end. He had been with this raw Irish beauty long enough to know she was not a keeper and had no doubts that he was just another in a long line of her lovers. Desperate to show his love for her before she went below to McGivern, Cribbs kissed O'Hare long and deep and wished it would never end. At that same moment, looking to see who was on watch and wondering why they weren't reefing the sails, the Skipper came round the corner and stopped in front of them. The passion of their embrace and the utter disregard for the wildness of the approaching storm caused something to snap in McGivern. Pushing Cribbs away from his girlfriend, the Skipper grabbed O'Hare by the wrist and said, 'come here ya bitch, I want a word with you!'

Caught off guard by the Skipper's sudden appearance, Cribbs shouted, 'you can't treat 'er like that McGivern!'

'Oh yeah? Just watch me! But don't you worry ya little shit, I'll be have'n words with you later!'

Leaving Cribbs sprawling on the deck, McGivern dragged O'Hare down the companionway steps and into their cabin, where he threw her on the bed and slammed the door. Scarcely able to control his rage, McGivern bent down and shouted in her face, 'you slut, I suspected someth'n was going on between you and that little shite! I know he's been sniff'n around you for a while. I thought you were foc'n someone while I was away in Dublin, I know that self-satisfied look you get on yer face like you think yer get'n away with somethin'. That I don't mind so much, that I can live with, but since when did you start do'n this in front of my face? You're take'n the piss now!'

'Oh, and this is from a man who can't get it up no more. A man who left his wife for a younger woman because she was frigid, your words Jacky!'

'Ya can't treat me and our clients like traveller's skivvies!'

'Ooh yeah, the high and mighty Jack McGivern look'n down on me an' mine, com'n from a family of sheep shaggers, that's all you are Jacky!

'This boat and the crew are our clients and this is our business! Can't you see you're not just hurting me, you're hurting yourself. This is our company that we built together.'

'What are you talking about! The charter business is our business, sales is our business, all this cruise'n around the world is just so as you can play the big man, the, master of his boat, how foc'n pathetic! I'm bored Jacky, I just needed a foc, an' you're not man enough to give it to me, is that so hard to understand?'

Not waiting for McGivern to say anything more, O'Hare pushed passed him, tore open the cabin door and started climbing the companionway back up to the decks. Enraged even more by the young woman's hard words, which she had heard her use to others, but never to him, McGivern stumbled after her and caught her by the wrist again.

Pulling her into his body, he held her to him like a disobedient child. He loved her and part of him wished he could calm her rage, make her see sense, but, like a belligerent child, she fought hard, punching and kicking, stoking his rage even further until he shouted in her face again, 'you're not listening to me you bitch!'

Just then, a huge wave broke over the side of the boat and the wash momentarily knocked McGivern from his feet and O'Hare wrenched herself free. In desperation, he reached out to catch hold of her ankle. At that moment, for McGivern, it seemed like time began to run in slow motion. As he lunged forward and caught hold of O'Hare's ankle, she fell backwards and struck her head on the deck rails; it was a heavy blow and a trickle of blood appeared on her cheek. McGivern felt a pang of concern and pity in his heart, that their love, that wild thing that had grown between them, had come to this. Regret filled the captain's being and, in that moment, all he wished for was to hold her in his arms again and tell her how much he loved her. It was then that their eyes met for a split second, but it seemed like much longer for the Skipper who saw that she had a startled look of terror on her face as she realised what was about to happen. Just then another wave washed over the deck and she disappeared from view as she tumbled over the side into the raging sea below and was gone.

McGivern lunged towards the rails and almost followed his girlfriend into the raging sea as he shouted himself horse into the dark, his words flung back at him by the wind, 'Mora, Mora, Mora, my love, Mora!'

Hearing the Skipper's shouts, Cribbs ran forward, spun him round and said, 'where is she? What have you done, you bastard!'

'She's gone, gone over the side. I couldn't stop her. She pulled away from me in the cabin. I tried to stop her!'

Cribbs grabbed McGivern's shoulders and might have hurled him over the side, but others appeared beside them at the rails, it was Styles who shouted, 'for God's sake get yourselves clipped into the safety line or get off the deck!' then he grabbed Childs by the shoulder and shouted, 'ring the alarm, get everyone up on deck, do it now!'

Still clinging to the rails, McGivern wailed, 'we need to turn the boat around', then he disappeared into the dark.

Seeing that Childs was about to go after him, Styles said, 'stay here, help me get these sails reefed properly.' Just then the boat veered to port. In the raging sea and high winds, the vessel heeled over almost to the rails. There was a screeching, grinding sound and the two men watched as the mizzenmast crashed down onto the cockpit roof. The immediate effect of the mizzen sail entering the water was to drag the Nostromo over even further, causing both men to stumble. Childs was swept over the side and into the sea before his fall was broken by his harness. Just then, having heard the alarm bell, and seeing what had happened to Childs, Fran dragged herself along the deck on her hands and knees using the safety line, so she could help the Bosun to get him back onto the deck, then she said, 'we need to cut the halliards or the mizzen will sink the boat, it's dragging her over. I'm going to get the cutters.'

Jen and Flip passed Fran on her way back to the cockpit and she said, 'Teddy and Marty are reefing the mainsail. It's a complete mess. I think the Skip is trying to turn the boat for some reason. I'm getting the cutters, I need help cut the mast free!'

As Flip and Jen got to work on freeing the sail, Fran went back to the helm and found McGivern wrestling with the wheel. She said, 'skip, stop that now, it's taking her over. The mizzen's already gone. You've got to stop!'

Almost incoherently, McGivern shouted, 'she's gone over the side!'

'Who's gone?'

'Mora, she's gone. We need to go back for her.'

As McGivern girded himself for one more huge effort to turn the helm wheel, Fran threw herself forward, directing all her weight at his centre mass. The Skipper fell backwards landing heavily on his back, smashing his head on the deck. After securing the helm, Fran checked on her captain. McGivern was stunned, but breathing steadily, so she clipped his harness into the safety line and went aft to help Jen and Flip cut the mast free. Heaving with all their strength, the three friends finally managed to leaver the mizzen over the side along with the remainder of the sail and rigging wires.

With the sails now reefed and the mizzen rigging cut free, the Nostromo righted herself. With the storm at its back the boat rode the winds as if it were part of the elemental forces driving it. Struggling to maintain her balance as the deck reared up and down beneath her, Fran set the helm on an easterly heading locked it in place and then turned her attention to McGivern. If the Nostromo appeared to be in control of the forces driving her, its master lay in a crumpled and dejected heap on its deck. Crouching down, Fran grasped the Skipper by the loose folds of his oilskin, but he was a dead weight and it seemed hopeless. Having finished the task of reefing the sails, Flip and Jen came aft to check on the Skipper and to help Fran drag the unconscious man over the threshold of the companionway doors and down the steps; it was a task that required a supreme effort. Halfway down, framed in the light from the cabin below, Cribbs appeared at the top of the companionway. His jaw was set and rage flared in his eyes, he said, 'give that bastard to me and I'll make sure he goes where he deserves to go, down there with Mora. God help me, I'll take him with me.'

Flip shouted, 'don't be a fool! We've already had one person over the side, we don't need another. Can't you see the Skip needs help!'

But Cribbs wouldn't be put off. Seemingly deranged, with a maniacal look on his face he said, 'he's pushed her over the side, it was him, he did it on purpose, he's killed her so I couldn't have her!'

As he was speaking, Cribbs slowly came down the steps towards them, but, encumbered by the awkward angle of the Skipper's prone body, when he grabbed at his collar, he was unable to do anything to shift him. For several moments Cribbs put all his strength into dragging McGivern back up the steps, but in the end, he was forced to admit defeat and collapsed on the steps. It was then that he broke down. Huge sobs shook Cribbs' body and all he was able to do was to repeat over and over, 'why! Why... why... why', until he became silent and gave himself up entirely to his grief.

CHAPTER 19: Adrift

DAWN, AND ALONG with it came a break in the storm. Exhausted, the crew sat, or simply lay on the decks like the fish, some large with shimmering iridescent blue scales, that had been abandoned there by the sea. Whilst the crew had avoided the agonising death of drowning in water, the fish had drowned in an excess of air. Having gasped their last, their eyes, filmed over in death, stared upwards, as shafts of light shone under the receding clouds and bathed the deck in a golden orange light; like a benediction. But, like the fish, not all had been saved. A crew member had been lost; two men mourned her passing, but one of those men struggled to accept it. Jack McGivern turned his back on the destruction wrought by the flailing rigging and stared out to sea. Amongst the breakers created by the incessant wind and heavy swell, McGivern could see the shape of a small boat. Fixing his eyes upon it, he reached into his pocket and drew out a slim, solid silver whisky flask, unscrewed the cap and took a long swig from it, then another and another. Replacing the cap, he turned it over in his hand to look at the inscription he knew was there on the bottom, "*My love always*." The flask, a gift from Mora to celebrate five years together, was a palpable reminder, if one were needed, that she was gone. Feeling a stab to his heart, he refocused his attention on the boat he could see floating in the wash. His rational conscious mind knew it to be a mirage, a hallucination created by his irrational mind, his heart, to keep alive a hope that it might still be possible to find Mora. Feeling the pain of loss in his chest, McGivern took another swig from his flask, this time he drained its contents. After glancing once more at the inscription, the Skipper threw it over the side where it dropped into the sea, making an inconsequential splash in the vastness of the ocean, just as Mora's body had done. Keeping his eyes on the mirage, he spoke to himself, and to her, 'rest in peace my love: ar dheis Dé go raibh a hanam[18].' Then, after a moment more, the mirage disappeared from his sight and McGivern turned his back on the sea, went below to his now empty cabin and empty life, closed the door and locked it.

Fran knew the Skipper would be in his cabin and she knew that the crew now had mixed feelings and loyalties towards him, but she remembered him as a fair and kindly man who had given her a chance. He was also a man that stood high in Jimmy Belts' estimations, and that was no small thing since there were few men and even fewer women who had passed the Belts test, as she called it. If you did pass the Belts test, you knew your stuff; you were solid and you were a good crew mate, which was a high bar in her old friend's estimation. But, like all of us, McGivern had his Achilles heel, and his was the drink. Where her father had no redeeming features when he was drunk, or sober for that matter, Fran knew she could still talk to McGivern, still reason with him. So, with some trepidation, she tapped on the Skipper's door and said, 'Jack, it's Fran. I want to check that you're okay. Can I get you something?'

Behind the door, she heard scuffling sounds, then a delay before the key turned in the lock on other side of the door. Finally, McGivern cracked the door ajar. Although mostly hidden, Fran couldn't believe the transformation in the Skipper's features. He was haggard and appeared to have aged ten years in the space of twenty-four hours, but what a twenty-four-hours it had been. McGivern said, 'thank you, I've everything I need'; he nodded towards the open drinks' cabinet sitting next to his writing desk. A heavy reek of alcohol wafted out of the cabin as if to emphasise the point.

Fran suddenly felt a wave of emotion and struggled to say anything for a few moments then said, 'Jack, I think we need to find somewhere to lay the boat up and do some repairs. I've found an island up ahead, it's not much, but if we could find an anchorage and shallow water

---

18 An Irish blessing on the death of a loved one translates as, "May her soul be on God's right hand."

out of the forties[19], we can get ourselves sorted.' Seeing there was no answer, Fran continued, 'I'll understand if you might not want to join us, but... we're going to say a few words for Mora up on deck.'

After a pause, McGivern said, 'I've already said my goodbye.' His words were slurred and almost incomprehensible. After another few moments he said, 'do what you think needs to be done; y' can leave me out of it.' Then he slowly closed the door and Fran could hear the key being turned in the lock.

Back on deck, Fran found Flip and Jen standing a few yards away from the other members of the crew, who were deep in conversation. Jen said, 'what did he say?'

Fran dejectedly shook her head, 'he's packed it in. I'm afraid he's retreated into the bottle and it's a big bottle.'

Jen raised her eyebrows and said, 'what of?'

'Jameson's Irish whiskey, he's got a drinks' cabinet full of the stuff in his cabin and he's locked himself in there.'

Flip blew out a long sigh and said, 'well, that's great! I had a look at the boat just now. The helm hood's smashed and the wheel's badly damaged, but functional. There's something wrong with the rudder mechanism though 'cos it's very stiff. The GPS navigation equipment's totally gone, so we've basically gone back to the early days of sailing ships. The rest of the rigging looks okay, so that's something positive.'

Fran gave a grim smile and said, 'let's go and see what Teddy and Marty are doing. I set a course that'll take us north of the fortieth parallel for a bit, so we get out of the slipstream of the prevailing westerlies. It'll give us a breather. I also found an atoll on the map. It looks like it could be a good place to anchor. The Skip's fine with us stopping there. To be honest, I don't think he cares either way.'

Approaching the amidships rails where the rest of the crew had formed a huddle, Fran said, 'I think we should say a few words before we do anything else, to pay our respects to Mora. Skip says he's staying in his cabin.'

---

19 Shortening of the Roaring Forties, a weather pattern of severe winds that sits between 40 and 45 degrees south of the equator.

Styles nodded, 'I'm not sure I'd know the right words...' The Bosun's voice trailed off and both Childs and Cribbs remained grimly silent.

Fran said, 'unfortunately, I've attended quite a few services for lost fishermen, so I do have some words I want to say.' Moving to the rails, Fran turned her back on the others and looked out at the vast limitless horizon and composed herself for a few moments before she said, 'Dear God. Your ocean is so big and we who sail on her are so small. Please receive unto your safekeeping the soul of our dear shipmate, Mora Jay O'Hare. Grant unto her, we beseech Thee oh Lord, fair winds and following seas... Amen.'

Fran then bowed her head; made the sign of the cross and turned back to face the rest of the crew who, reflecting on her words, remained bowed for a few moments longer.

Into the silence, Fran cleared her throat and, struggling with her emotions, she said, 'so... what's the plan?'

Assuming that Fran's question had been directed at him, Styles spoke up like he was voicing his current thoughts. Starting mid-sentence he said, 'loss of the mizzen we can live with, 'cos the other masts look okay; it'll just slow us down. The helm's going to be a problem though; it's partially jammed, which probably means the gear'n gone again. It'll work, but we need to take a look at it.'

Jen said, 'we can go down with the scuba gear and check to see if the mast damaged the rudder after we got it over the side.'

Styles shook his head, 'no one's go'n over the side just now, the sea's run'n fast and God knows what's down there, probably sharks most likely. No, it's out of the question 'till we find somewhere to land.'

Childs said, 'yeah, and the navigation equipment's gone too; smashed to pieces I can't see it's gonna be working any time soon.'

Fran said, 'there's loads of water got down below. We didn't latch the storm hatches closed properly. I just checked and most of the dry goods cabinets are full of water. I think we've lost a lot of our supplies.' Then she paused and said, 'and it looks like the drinking water tanks might be leaking seawater.'

Styles nodded, 'okay, let's hope it's just some sea water get'n into the system somewhere; I'll check it out.'

Having said what he was going to do, Styles headed back to the helm and Fran followed him. After checking to see whether there was anyone around that might overhear them, she said, 'if the GPS is gone, are either you or Marty okay with using dead-reckoning and standard navigation?'

'I did a bit of that a while back', then Styles' face grew angry and he said, 'are you doubting I'm up to the job then?'

Fran refused to back down and said, 'show me, plot a course for today's sailing taking into account the winds, currents and the position of the sun at noon using the sextant.'

Styles grimaced like she had punched him in the gut, then Fran said, 'I thought so; you don't have a clue, do you? I also know that Marty hasn't a clue either, so that means there's nobody else on the crew leadership other than the Skip who knows old-school navigation and he's out of it!'

'He'll be right soon enough, he just needs a bit of time t'get his head together, I mean, he's just lost his girlfriend and we've lost a member of the crew.'

'Time is what we don't have. If we're gonna need to land somewhere, out here, even something as big as the Isle of Wight, we could miss it by miles if our navigation's out; we wouldn't even know until we'd sailed by it. But something the size of a small atoll, no chance!'

'So, you've got an idea where we could land then?'

Fran grabbed a chart role and unfurled it on the table, perused the squiggles and lines and arrows and finally tapped her finger on the map, 'there, it's a biggish island, and...' here she took a magnifying glass, peered intently at the place she had pointed out and then said, 'yep, I'd say it might have a decent natural harbour on its leeward slide. If we're lucky, we might be able to lay the boat up and do some running repairs.'

'So how big's your island?'

'About eight miles long and two miles wide.'

'Sounds doable, I mean navigation-wise.'

'Yeah, right, but the problem is that we'll be approaching it end-on, from its narrowest side. Out here, that's a pretty small target to hit, it'll need some accurate navigation.'

'And so you're some hot shit navigator then?'

The Bosun's profanity and his tone of voice made Fran's ears prick up. The man obviously assumed she was challenging his authority, so she said, 'actually, I am pretty good at this if truth be told. I've had loads of formal training at the Yacht School in Falmouth and I've done quite a bit of navigation for our boat crews when I've been out with them fishing.' Then something happened, Fran felt a strength enter her body, a confidence in herself that she hadn't noticed before and she knew then she was not going to take any pushback from the Bosun, especially one that was unable read a chart properly. She thought, *maybe O'Hare was right, maybe Styles is incompetent and she only just noticed it*. To the Bosun she said, 'not that I'm blowing my own trumpet or anything, but I've totally got this, and if that's a problem for you or Marty, that's tough shit! Personally, since I'm the one in charge of the navigation, I'm the one in charge of the boat!'

Hearing Fran's raised voice, and thinking that she might need some help, Jen and Flip appeared around the door of the cockpit and Flip said, 'are you having a problem?'

Styles glared at the younger man and said, 'oh, here's the boy wonder himself!'

Fran glared back, 'enough! I've heard enough!' Then to Jen she said, 'please could you ask the others to come back here, we're going to have a straw poll on who's gonna be running the boat from now on.' The younger woman said nothing, just smiled and headed up on deck.

A few moments later, Jen returned with Cribbs and Marty. Both men were clearly displeased to be summoned in such a way, but Fran was not going to back down and she said, 'right, this is going to be as straight forward as I can make it. The Skip, how should I put it, is not well and it turns out that he's the only one that can navigate without the GPS, except me that is. So, I'm asking for your support. The way I see it, in these circumstances, the person doing the navigation is the person in charge of the boat, so is there anyone who's got a problem with that?

Taking their cue, Flip and Jen said, 'not us.'

Looking pointedly at the Bosun and the Bosun's Mate, Fran said, 'are you guys okay with that?'

Styles said, 'I think I might have a problem with that.'

Childs nodded, 'and me too, actually.'

Everyone then looked over at Cribbs who was brooding and sullen. He had been watching from the sidelines and not saying much. Fran thought, to give him his due, after all that had happened and the shock he must be going through at what happened to O'Hare, he was still in control of himself, so she said, 'it looks like you've got the casting vote Ben.'

Cribbs said, 'I'm with you Fran, all the way, it's not a problem for me.'

Fran nodded, 'okay that's five against two; I already checked with the Skip and he's fine with me taking on the navigation, that's a majority for the Tremayne camp. So, if that's settled, then let's crack on. Up ahead, there's a small atoll called Nendar Island about five hundred nautical miles away. I suggest we land on it so we can get ourselves together and do some repairs to the rigging. At the moment there's a decent wind, so, if we keep a tight heading, I think we should arrive there the day after tomorrow.'

Into the uneasy silence Fran said, 'right, that's settled, I'll set the course. It's east by southeast on a heading of one hundred and twenty-two degrees. We've got a wind abaft, but we'll need to trim the sails to account for the loss of the mizzen.' Flip and Jen, with Cribbs ambling behind them, set off in the direction of the mainsail halliards but Childs pointedly stuck his hands in his pockets and Styles said, 'I'm going to take care of the Skip. If you've written him off, I think it's unfair after all he's done for you.'

Fran softened her tone and said, 'I haven't forgotten, but Jack was a different person six months ago. A lot has happened since then and somebody needs to take control of this boat if we are to finish what we started. My dad was an alcoholic I know the signs. I'm sorry for what's happened, it's a tragedy we'll all have to deal with it at some point, but for now, we need to ensure that the vessel and the crew stays safe so we don't have any more accidents.'

CHAPTER 20: Paradise

WITHOUT HELP FROM the Bosun or his Mate, who both stolidly refused to do anything on-board and took their meals together in the galley alone, or the Skipper who stayed locked in his cabin, the following two days were hard work for the four remaining hands. Cribbs found the constant work and round-the-clock watches were a way of warding off painful memories around O'Hare's death. At the end of eight hours on deck, with only two hours sleep before he was on watch again, he slept the slumber of the dead. With Cribbs' help on some of the technical matters around handling the rigging, Fran, Jen and Flip continued to forge a strong and very effective team. Fran's confidence in handling the Nostromo grew steadily and she found herself wondering why it had all seemed so difficult with a full complement of eight crew. Sure, there was no proper break from being on watch, but she was acquiring the knack of power-napping and a nuanced feel for when the boat was riding true to course or when she needed to have the sails trimmed a little.

At noon on the second day after she effectively took command, using the sextant, Fran measured the height of the sun above the horizon. Combined with sightings she took the previous night on the Southern Cross and the lunar distance between it and the moon, a slight anxiety began to grow in her that she might be out in her calculations. Placing the sextant down, Fran used a pair of powerful binoculars to scan the horizon. At the limits of the instrument's magnification, she saw a shadowy object amongst groups of towering cumulous clouds sitting along the gentle arc of the earth's circumference, like beads on a string. As she focussed in and out trying to confirm a sighting, somebody behind her cleared his or her throat.

Looking round, she found Jen holding a thermos flask and a dilly bag full of sandwiches, 'I thought you would need something to keep you going.'

Fran smiled, 'thanks, you must've read my mind.'

Reading the look of concern on her friend's face, Jen said, 'are you getting worried about hitting Nendar?'

'Yeah, you could say that. I mean, if I miss the island, I'll lose the crew's confidence, then what?'

Standing beside her at the foredeck rails, Jen said, 'gimme a look through the binoculars. Like you said, I've got good eyesight, better than 20/20 actually.'

Fran watched as Jen crouched down, balanced her elbows on the rails and adjusted the differential magnification on the right eyepiece before peering through the instrument, carefully moving the focus wheel. She seemed so composed and assured, confident that she would find what she was looking for, like it was preordained and all she needed was confirmation. Fran couldn't remember anyone having so much confidence in her before, not even Jimmy. Both her mother and father had said many times to her face that she was good for nothing, *well*, she thought, *here is a person who believes in me for once.* Despite her friend's confidence, Fran anxiously bit her lip while Jen methodically scanned the horizon.

'Bingo! I can see something. At that distance, it can't be a ship, it's too big, so it's got to be land; take a look.'

Fran took the binoculars, knelt down, then, crouching behind her, Jen held out her arm in front of her and said, 'see my twelve o'clock? The sighting's at five past, just south of east on our current heading.'

'Hah, I've got it! Yes, it's land, got to be. If we're about fifteen feet above sea level, then that's about six or seven miles away.'

Over the next hour, all doubt about the sighting of land dissipated and the crew gathered on deck to watch the island grow from a black outline to a large rocky outcrop, which then acquired a green covering and finally a spectacular fringing reef. Seabirds appeared and then a pair of doves, tempted away from the island, they swooped around the masts eyeing them up for their potential as a new home.

Walking back to take the helm, Fran asked Ben to keep an eye on the depth finder readings, as the charts indicated shallows quite far out on the westerly side of the island. From her position at the wheel,

Fran watched the distant shore to port as she took the Nostromo along the coast towards the eastern shore and around the tip of the atoll where she expected to see a natural harbour on its northern flank.

Birds wheeled around the steep, rocky outcrop they had seen when they first spotted the island. Below the black, volcanic rock of the crag, a tangle of trees and lush jungle plants gave way to palm trees, fringing a long uninterrupted crescent of white sandy beach that ended in a protruding reef and the natural harbour she was looking for. As everything fell into place, just as she expected, the tension dropped away from Fran's shoulders. All the studying she had done at sailing school had paid off. But, she thought, she wouldn't be telling her instructor, mealy-mouthed Meadows; she wouldn't give him the satisfaction. Then her gut tightened in revulsion as she wondered how many more unfortunate female students he had managed to seduce since she last saw him.

Sailing into the wind shadow of the island, Fran fired up the engines and motored towards a curving band of rock, which formed a small rocky bay and the natural harbour she was looking for. Ben called out, 'eighteen feet, twelve feet.' Having checked the tide height on the chart, Fran decided to drop anchor and investigate a safe channel to the harbour rather than risk going further in. Then she noticed boats, two large motor yachts tied up to a concrete extension of the natural harbour. Part of her was relieved the island was inhabited, but part of her wished that it might have been a pristine, unspoiled piece of paradise yet to be sullied by the presence of humanity. Dream on, she thought, this is the twenty first century, not the nineteenth.

Dropping the anchor, Fran felt the hook set, she then motored up wind and had Flip drop the second anchor. She smiled to herself, shut down the engine and settled back on the polished wooden helm seat for a moment's reflection. Watching the sway of palms in the tropical breeze whilst she munched on one of Jen's sandwiches, Fran spotted someone wearing a white tee shirt and shorts approaching along the shore. When he was close enough the man shouted through a megaphone, 'ahoy! What boat?'

Finding the ship's hailer, Fran shouted, 'The Nostromo out of Dublin.'

The man waved and replied, 'you're very welcome. What's your draft?'

'Eighteen feet.'

'Then you'll be fine to come into the harbour if you want, but you'll be fine there too. If you don't mind, before you land, me and my associate will want to come aboard and have a chat.'

With that, the man began walking back along the beach to the harbour. Even from the distance they were from the shore, Fran could see he was tall, had a long unhurried gait and, from the few words he had spoken, he had an Australian accent. Fran was wondering when she would hear the Aussie drawl, but never expected it would be so soon.

Not wasting any time, the man on the beach arrived alongside the Nostromo in a large inflatable outboard motorboat, accompanied by a shorter and more powerfully built man. Together, they seemed to make up a pair. Although they were physically dissimilar, both men were assured, similarly attired and climbed up the aft ladder and over the stern rails with an almost balletic economy of movement, as though their entrance onto the deck had been carefully choreographed in advance. Fran noticed that the shorter man hung back from his taller partner, keeping to his blind side. Both men's eyes continually assessed their surroundings and the people around them in three-dimensional space, the deck, the rigging and below, noticing entrances and exits. Recognising Fran, who had now been joined by Flip and Jen, the taller man walked towards her and said, 'Peter Burgess, nice to meet you.' Then, nodding to the man standing behind him he said, 'this is my associate, Simon Tideswell. I hope you don't mind us coming aboard so soon after your arrival, but, as I said, there's certain checks we need to make before we can let you come ashore.'

Fran shook Burgess' hand but noticed that Tideswell continued to stay slightly behind and to the left of his partner and did not attempt to shake her hand or make any kind of greeting or eye contact. A chill of concern began to inch its way up her spine as she wondered what they had let themselves in for.

As Tideswell's eyes continued to move around the decks, Burgess said, 'am I speaking to the Skipper?'

Fran said, 'no, he's below and I'm thinking he might not be available to meet with you just now.'

Burgess nodded and Tideswell seemed to tense slightly, like he was preparing himself in some way. After moment, he said, 'no worries if your skipper is indisposed, but we'll need to talk with him at some point, it's just a formality. So, if skip's not available, can we have a chat somewhere out of the heat maybe?'

Fran nodded, 'I'm so sorry Mr Burgess, please come over to the cockpit, I can show you the charts, our course and our registration documents.'

Burgess nodded and he and Tideswell followed Fran forward towards the helm and the cockpit area. Passing Jen on the way, she spoke quietly so the two men might not hear, 'go and see if Jack's around or whether Marty or Teddy'll come up and talk to these guys.'

Looking slightly alarmed, Jen nodded and trotted off towards the companionway and disappeared below; Tideswell kept his eyes on her as she disappeared down the steps.

Moving forward, alongside his partner, Tideswell passed the helm but didn't join Burgess and Fran in the cockpit preferring instead to continue towards the bow and out of sight. Meanwhile, Burgess seated himself by the chart table, waited for Fran to join him, then, appearing to relax he said, 'sorry if this seems rather cloak and dagger, but you need to know this is a privately owned island in international waters, so there's actually no national jurisdiction. Basically, we're it here on Nendar; it's just me and my associate, Tidy, we call him.' Chuckling to himself, Burgess said, 'actually he's anything but. His kit was always a bloody mess, every time I inspected it at any rate!'

Then Fran twigged and thought to herself, *they're ex-soldiers, of course!* Then she said, 'so you and Mr... you and Tidy, served together?'

'Yeah, for our sins, we were in Australian Special Forces together, SASR Boats. For a while we were seconded to the Special Boat Service of the Royal Navy no less. All white gloves stuff, purely advisory, but we spent some time in the UK and thereabouts before we left the Service. So, we're that obvious yeah?'

Fran nodded, 'my uncle was in the army for a while; I know the type.'

Considering this for a moment, Burgess said, 'we're kind of the official welcoming committee here. The island's owned by a business syndicate, Terra Tours, that runs the place as a resort, hideaway, whatever you like to call it, but it's not open to the public, so we need to know why you've landed. By the way, what's up with your Skip? We kinda need to talk to him.'

'There's been a tragedy, the Skip, Jack McGivern, his girlfriend was lost over the side in a storm; he's in a bad way mentally. He's not been out of his cabin for days and I've kind of taken over running the boat. He was...' she paused a moment considering, but then concluded it would be better for everyone if she was completely honest with the man sitting opposite her, so she said, 'he was there at the time of the accident, that's all I'm able to say, I think he reckons he was responsible in some way. We're headed to Australia, Fremantle docks hopefully, barring further accidents that is.'

'Understood. Mr McGivern's a bit cagey about it right? From what you've told me, he has a right to be. The Australian authorities are gonna want to have a chat with him when you guys get ashore. They can be pretty thorough about these things, so he needs to prepare himself.' Lowering his voice he said, you don't think he did her in do you? It wouldn't be the first time. We had a client here I'm sure she did in her husband. There was nothing to prove it either way, but you get a sense for these things. '

Taken aback by Burgess's candour, Fran said, 'no, no, nothing like that, they argued and had a difficult relationship sometimes, but...' Fran bit her lip and didn't want to say any more. She was beginning to realise that O'Hare's affair with Cribbs would be incriminating to both men.

Noticing Fran's discomfort and reluctance to say anything more about the accident, Burgess changed the subject and said, 'I see you've got some damage to the rigging.'

'The mizzen mast went in a storm, it almost took the boat down with it.'

'And you sorted it, yeah?' Fran nodded, 'that must've taken some guts.'

'I had help from the crew, but for a while it was touch and go.'

'I bet. I've been in an open boat in mucky conditions a few times; I know how things can go south pretty rapidly. But you're in luck, Tidy's a dab hand with fix'n boats, he'll have y' right no worries. I reckon he could fix you a new mast and sail, he's got all the gear he'd need in his workshop. Just let your Skip know and he can have it sorted in a jiffy. Look, if you're gonna be here for a few days, why don't you let us show you around, and the rest of the crew if they like. We've got a fully equipped dive school and no one to teach at the moment; we're always looking for training dummies to practice on.' Here Burgess winked to let her know he was joking.

The following day, after their arrival, Fran, Jen and Flip took Burgess up on his offer. Not taking no for an answer, Buddy decided he would come along. After O'Hare's death, since the dynamics of the crew had shifted, Styles, who had really taken to Buddy, increasingly ignored the little dog, possibly because his mistress was one of the 'mutineers' as he saw it.

All three were excited at the prospect of a dive, especially Jen who was living the dream as far as she was concerned. Leaving Tideswell to talk to McGivern and Styles about the repairs, they shouldered what gear they had and headed over on the launch to the makeshift pier to meet Burgess, who they could see was already standing waiting for them. Spotting him, Jen said, 'he's keen. You said he was the one who suggested you come on a dive. Are you sure he really meant it when he said bring the rest of the crew?'

Fran said, 'Jen, you really are an incurable romantic! He said bring the rest of the crew if they wanted. We're going to be "test training dummies for them", unquote. They only get guests every now and again, so maybe they're bored.'

Flip hugged Jen and Fran close as they sat on either side of him, 'this has always been a dream for me, learning to dive. I can't believe I'm gonna do a training dive without even having to pay anything!'

'So, ladies and gent, this is the Nendar dive school.' Burgess motioned behind him with his thumb at a large, whitewashed building constructed in a vast rocky crevice under a steep cliff that hung over a huge, deep rock pool that had been fitted out with steps down to a sleek-looking speed boat.

Flip whispered, 'this looks like something out of a James Bond movie. I didn't think these sorts of places existed!'

Overhearing him, Burgess said, 'you might not be thinking that after you've been here for a while mate. There's definitely nobody wearing a tux and there's no dry Martini.' Then, after they had gathered on the expansive stern deck of the dive boat, he said, 'I thought I'd take us out to a wreck about six miles out. It's an old steel-hulled merchant ship that foundered on the reef in the 1900's, likely blown there by the hurricanes that sometimes hit this area. It's a simple dive where we like to take novices, but it's exciting enough to make it interesting. We're going do some snorkelling and breath exercises first, then try out the aqualung and do a test dive. It's what we do with the paying clients. I like to give novices a proper feel of a dive on their first day, that way if any of them are skittish I get to know it right away and not when they're forty feet down where they panic and start trying to get to the surface without following proper decompression procedures.'

On their way out to the reef, Fran chatted to Burgess while Jen and Flip canoodled at the back of the boat. Burgess said, 'they're newly-weds, right?'

Fran said, 'no, actually, they've been going out for ten years; they're a young, old married couple. Their words, not mine.'

Burgess laughed; it was genuine, his face brightened and he glanced over at Fran as he did so and said, 'yeah, I kind'a get that. I had a girl back in Aus when I joined up. We kept it going for a while, but when I did the selection for Special Forces, she saw the writing on the wall and gave it up.' Seeming to prefer to change the subject when things might get too personal, Burgess said, 'you said your family are Cornish fishermen? So, you must know your way around a boat.'

'I've known my way around a boat since I was a girl, but I've been afraid of going out on them up until I did the training to crew on a yacht. This trip has totally changed my relationship with the sea. I feel like I've got the hang of it; not mastered it you understand but developed an understanding of it – I feel comfortable being out on it in a way I never thought I would.'

'Right, yeah, totally, the sea's like this big thing that can swat you like a fly, but if you know how to ride the wave, it's fine. Tidy and me, we served in Afghanistan – five tours, that's enough for anyone. Roadside bombs, you name it we saw it, but you want know what the worst of it was? The child soldiers, some of them only thirteen or fourteen, it destroyed my faith in humanity. This place has cured that, helped me move on.'

Fran stayed silent and nodded, it sounded like a confessional, and so she let Burgess speak his truth. Then he said, 'Tidy and me are sort of captives here. Neither of us can go back to what we did before, so we live here for four months on and two months off, but after those two months are up, we can't wait to get back here. Anything more complicated and we start to think too much about what we've done and what we should never have agreed to do. So here we stay, babysitting the filthy rich, but it's something we know about and can do well.'

'You've certainly found yourself a piece of paradise here.'

'Paradise? Or a gilded cage.'

Fran was surprised by Burgess's almost poetic turn of phrase, which set her thinking that the man she was speaking to was more than what people might assume to be just a ruthless soldier. It was clear he had a conscience, but was unsure whether that made his admission about what he used to do for a living better or worse. A killer with a conscience seemed almost worse than a killer without one, like he knew what he was ordered to do was questionable but went ahead and did it anyway.

A dive beneath the ocean is to enter another world. A world as expansive as the one on the surface, but constrained by the clarity of the water, however, sinking down into the crystal depths around Nendar was like being suspended in air as a surreal aquascape stretched out for what seemed like miles in all directions. Crowds of colourful fish, some large, shouldered past the divers like they were on their way to an important appointment somewhere and had forgotten their manners, or perhaps they didn't see humans as a threat since they had possibly never seen one. Below, through the hazy mist created by its depth, Fran could see the shape of a huge ship resting on the floor of the ocean. On seeing it, Fran thought immediately of the sailors who had sailed within it and who had lost their lives in the sudden cataclysm that led to its destruction. She felt a powerful sense of a loss that could not be shared by anyone other than someone who had been raised in a fishing community.

Like he did on the way out, after the dive, Burgess again ensured that Fran was close by as he piloted the launch back to the dive school. Shouting over the roar of the powerful engines he said, 'you must think we're full-on loners, me and Tidy, live'n out out here on this rock, thousands of miles from anywhere, but you'd be wrong. Him and me like company as much as the next man, but it's got to be the right company; and I'm very selective. You did well, taking on a boat that size with just a few of the crew working with ya. Y'know two of your guys, Styles and Childs; it's like a double act, right? Well, they've already asked me if they can stay until our relief flight comes, so it looks like you've got two of your crew jump'n ship.'

'I'm actually glad they're going, it's been tough carrying them, worse than if they were grudgingly helping. They didn't like it when I took on running the boat.'

'Yeah, but from what you're say'n they don't know anything much about navigation. I can't believe a bosun and his mate are clueless about reading charts.'

'I think the crew was the Skipper's girlfriend's choice, she liked to have control of things.'

'Right, I get it; she hired a couple of lump nuts so she could be the top dog. I've seen the same thing in the army, but when the shite hits the fan, it all goes to pieces; people get killed that way.'

Burgess's simple and incisive analysis seemed to perfectly sum up the situation on the Nostromo. Until that point, Fran hadn't seen it, but the tension, the lack of cohesion, it was all down to how the crew had been chosen, not on the basis of the right mix of skills and experience, but on whether one person could exercise control over them. All along, it had been an accident waiting to happen; how had she not seen it after the incident with Styles and the storm with the rudder being damaged during the shakedown?

CHAPTER 21: Paradise lost

STANDING OVER A large steaming grill pan of snapper she was cooking for the crew's evening meal, Fran envied Jen and Flip, who had gone ashore on the pretext of taking Buddy for a walk. The little dog had been unsure about whether he wanted to leave the security of the mother ship and had offered a few barks in protest, but he had gone anyway. Jen had become his new best friend since she had taken over Style's job of feeding him the odd treat. Fran also felt a little jealous; after all, the couple's walks were just that, a pretext, for what they actually would be doing on a secluded beach somewhere on the other side of the island.

On the upside, Childs, Styles and Cribbs had taken themselves off to oversee repairs Tideswell was doing on the broken mizzen. The old soldier was making a new mast by repurposing a spare one-hundred-and-twenty-foot aluminium equivalent that he just happened to have lying around. Fran knew from the tales her uncle used to tell of his time in the British Army, that sappers liked to have a spare part for everything they had in the field. If they didn't have something, they could make it; he used to refer to them as "geniuses". Perhaps Tideswell started out as a sapper before he became a special marine.

That just left the Skip, nursing his latest open bottle of Jamesons whilst he brooded in his cabin. McGivern had briefly emerged to talk with Tideswell and discuss the repairs he could do and the price, but that had been several days ago, so it was a surprise when Fran heard a footfall at the galley door and saw the man himself standing there. The Skipper was in a pitiful state. His hair was dishevelled, he had grown a straggling beard and his eyes had the ineffably haunted look of a condemned man. Deeply moved by what she saw Fran said, 'Jack, you look all-in, come and sit down here with me while I cook.'

McGivern managed a weak smile and said, 'it was the smell of food that brought me down to the galley', then he sighed and said, 'Ben's going to the police when we get into Fremantle. He's going to make it his mission to get me thrown in jail. As if it wasn't bad enough Mora's gone, I'm now go'n to be accused of kill'n her. Then there's Teddy and Marty say'n they're jump'n ship and stay'n on the island. It's a bloody mess.' McGivern's shoulders sagged and he lent forward to cradle his head in his hands like somebody who was in abject misery.

Fran took the cooked fish out of the oven, wiped her hands, sat down next to the stricken captain and said, 'Come on Jack. Jen, Flip and me, we'll see that we get the Nostromo to a safe port. We'll be there for you too, if the police want to ask their questions. We're right behind you. We know what happened, it was a tragedy, a terrible tragedy, I've seen it with fishermen at Polldon, the skipper blaming himself for the loss of one of the crew, always asking if he could have done something different that could have prevented it.'

'But I *was* there Fran, don't you see, I *was* there, I could've stopped her. I'll never forget the look on her face when she realised she was go'n over the side; it'll haunt me 'til I die, God help me! I don't know whether I'm go'n to be much use to ya; I'm not much use to m'self.'

Fran patted McGivern's arm and said, 'Jimmy had faith in you and I have faith in you. You'll get through this. It'll be tough sailing with four, but we can do it.'

While she was talking to McGivern, Fran noticed something moving past the galley porthole. It was fast and sped past her field of vision in an instant, but it made her stop mid-sentence, then she said, 'Jack, I just saw something coming into the bay. I'm gonna check it out.'

Up on deck, in the distance, Fran saw two jet boats skimming towards where the Nostromo was anchored. As she watched, the boats split up, one heading for the harbour and the other coming towards them. Her stomach lurched. Fran had always wondered about the possibility of an attack since O'Hare mentioned it when they had suggested towing Jenson closer to the African coast. The boats were fast and their crews looked like they meant business. Making sure she stayed low and out of view, she ran below and shouted, 'Jack, there's a bunch of guys in a launch coming straight for us!'

The Skipper's eyes went wide and he leapt to his feet, 'Foc! They'll be foc'n boatjackers, Jesus! C'mon, into my cabin now!'

Once in McGivern's cabin, Fran fought her way to the porthole through the debris lying on the floor. The men were just half a mile away now. Going a full speed, Fran could see the launch coming towards them was bouncing crazily on the light swell leaving a long, white wake behind it like the contrail of a jet plane, 'Jack they're coming, they're gonna be here in a few minutes!'

Jack tugged Fran's shoulder and spun her round, 'here, take this, it was my daddy's.' Seeing Fran recoil when she saw a pistol in his hands, he said, 'don't be so surprised, the McGivern's were Irish Republicans. He gave me this when he got carted off to jail by the British, it's kind of a family heirloom, but it works.' McGivern released the magazine of the Colt 1911 and showed Fran it was loaded. 'D'ya know how to use a gun?'

Fran nodded, 'my uncle, he showed me. He said a lot of the deep-sea skippers carry a pistol for protection.'

McGivern nodded, 'very wise, especially out here. Look, it's simple to use, there's a grip-safety.' Handing the gun to Fran he said, 'that's it, chamber a round, now it's cocked an locked, just depress the grip-safety and it's ready to fire.'

'What are you going to do?'

'I want you to stay down here out of sight. I'm going up there to talk to them. Try and get away, don't worry about me. I'll try and keep them busy, distract them. Just get away, keep go'n and don't look back.'

With a grim look on his face, McGivern left the cabin. Moments later, Fran heard heavy boots on the decks above. Checking the pistol, she pushed it into the back of her jeans and carefully made her way into the corridor, which ran the length of the boat and connected with a large aft storeroom, or lazarette. The store was full of equipment, tools and other maintenance supplies, including engine spares and the deep freezers. Unusually, the Nostromo's lazarette was the only below-decks storeroom that had a hatch connecting it with the outside, in this case, the aft platform. On board old sailing boats like the Nostromo, Fran remembered that the lazarette was also used to store the bodies of crew who had died at sea; she had Jimmy Belts to thank for this happy piece of information. When it was down, the aft platform could be used to move heavy pieces of machinery, equipment and bodies, to and from a boat moored alongside.

With the lazarette's aft sea hatch at her back, Fran took up position behind a large stack of cases, holding tinned food that was strapped securely to a supporting bulkhead, and thought about her options for escape. Every muscle in her body was ready to make a move. Straining to hear what was going on up on deck, Fran could hear stealthy movements coming from the companionway steps. Should she escape now? Perhaps use scuba gear to swim under the boat and wait her chance. Then she remembered that all the aqualung equipment was stored in one of the forward lockers. She knew McGivern was taking a risk for her, shielding her and trying to give her time to escape, but what if she turned the tables around? She touched the hard butt of the Colt then unlatched the hatch cover and climbed out onto the aft platform, which had been lowered by Jen for her daily swimming sessions.

Slowly, Fran climbed the aft stepladder and raised her head, so her eyes were level with the deck. Her view was obscured by the aft compartment store, but she could hear two voices, McGivern's giving short terse replies and another man, shouting commands and threats, spoke with a South African accent. Fran had heard a second man below, so maybe, she thought, there were only two men on-board; the rest having continued to the inner harbour. Fran thought of Jen and Flip and hoped they had managed to stay out of the boatjacker's way.

Fran crouched down and inched forward so she could peer around the corner of the store. The helm was unmanned, so she moved forward to get a clear view of the amidships. Standing near the entrance to the companionway was McGivern. In front of him at a slight distance, was a man wearing a white flannel short-sleeved suit; he was holding a machine pistol, pointing it at the Skipper's gut. Fran was just twenty feet away from the two men. The realisation that she had a clear shot gave her a "call of the void" feeling, like she got when looking over the edge of a sea cliff, like she might jump, but this time she did. Exploding out of cover, and firing the pistol as she did so, Fran ran towards McGivern's assailant. While the Skipper had thrown himself on the deck after the first shot, the man had swung the machine gun towards Fran, but he was too late, the second shot ripped into his stomach and the third entered his chest. Firing until the magazine was empty, Fran watched the man drop down onto the deck like a stone and fall forward onto his face. Not wasting any time, McGivern snatched up the boatjacker's machine pistol and fired at the second man as soon as he emerged from behind the cockpit. The expended power of the bullets hitting his body wrenched the man backwards off his feet and down the companionway steps; he was dead before he hit the lower deck.

'Holy Jesus, you got 'im, Christ, I can't believe it!'

Unable to find anything to say in reply, Fran ran forward and looked anxiously over towards the harbour buildings. Expecting to see the other boat coming back towards them, instead they heard semiautomatic fire in three-round bursts, the trademark sound of professional solders engaging the enemy on two sides. McGivern said grimly, 'Burgess and Tideswell taking out trash by the sound of it.'

Fran was startled, 'or the other way round!'

McGivern turned and looked her straight in the eye and said, 'I've heard professional soldiers at work before when I was a kid in Belfast. The boatjackers chose the wrong island and the wrong men to tangle with.' Then, he stepped towards Fran and took the empty pistol from her and said, 'and the wrong woman.'

Taking one of the Nostromo's outboard motorboats, Fran and McGivern hurried over to the island to see what had happened. As they entered the harbour, they saw a jet launch drifting away from sandy shore where the boatjackers had beached it. Fran could see that one of the men was slumped at the wheel of the drifting launch while another two lay face down on the sand, they hadn't even got as far as the harbour buildings before the two soldiers had picked them off. While Tideswell continued to scan the horizon and the entrance to the bay, Burgess hurried towards them, 'are you guys aright, we heard shots.'

Fran said, 'we're fine, only two of them got on the boat.'

Burgess nodded, 'what's their status?'

McGivern said, 'dead, both of them.' Nodding towards Fran he said, 'she got one, and I got the other.'

Burgess smiled at Fran, 'so the pistol shots were you? Christ you've got some guts; I've said it before, but I'll say it again, you are full of surprises Ms Tremayne!'

Fran's face flushed red like she had won unexpected praise from someone she admired, then said, 'I don't know what came over me, it just seemed like it could be done, should be done. I saw a chance and took it; a moment of pure madness maybe.'

Burgess said, 'or pure guts.'

Fran said, 'do you know if there'll be others?'

'You mean on the pirate's boat? Yeah, probably, so we need to be watch'n out for them. Most likely, they'll run for it now they know their mates have copped it. We saw them coming on our radar. You can't be too careful out here. We have a coastguard's scanner. All bona fide skippers or boats scheduled to come here have a beacon, like you did. We can usually check the identity of boats coming here before they land. That's unless they're bad guys, then they don't have a beacon and they don't answer our radio call to them, or they try to block our radio scanners. So when they arrived, we were ready; it was game over for them before they started.'

CHAPTER 22: Roaring forties

'WE'RE GET'N OFF here in six weeks' time. Why don't you look me up when you're in Aus?' Burgess pressed a tattered business card into Fran's hand, then said, 'that's my address, I live in Perth, City Beach, just a few miles from Freo.' Burgess laughed, and said, 'so you see, you'd have no excuses for not com'n to see me.'

'Is there... a Mrs Burgess?'

'Nope, as I said, it's just me at the moment and nobody on the horizon either.'

'Peter, you know I can't think straight until I've found out what's happened to Cal. My head's just not in the right place just now.'

'Totally understood. But if that was to change, or if you find him and it all works out, look me up. I'm a great cook and I've even got a little fishing boat; you'd feel right at home!'

Fran leant forward and kissed Burgess on the cheek and said, 'I promise. If anything changes, I'll come and see you.'

Fran had replayed her last words to Burgess over and over in her head since they left. Part of her basked in the respect bestowed on her by a man that probably rarely gave it out, but she felt no warmth, just a cold, hard appraisal that could just as easily be negative as positive, like the binary logic of a computer. She had spent her life growing up around such men, her father and uncle included, and knew she could never live with such a man or give him her heart, since he would be unlikely to recognise love or know how to reciprocate. So, as they passed the island on their starboard and headed away from the lonely spec in the most desolate ocean in the world, Fran bid a silent farewell to Peter Burgess and his taciturn associate, Simon Tideswell.

As they tacked down towards the 40th parallel, Nostromo re-entered the maelstrom of winds known as the Roaring Forties, that they had briefly escaped when they sampled paradise on Nendar Island. As they did so, all thoughts of sand, long beaches and warm sun were replaced by chill blasts from the Antarctic ice sheets and a seemingly endless procession of low-pressure systems. With swells of up to forty feet, wind speeds reaching seventy miles per hour drove the boat along at up to thirty knots. Their now diminished number, quite literally a skeleton crew, had little time for sleep in between watches, as they were buffeted by gales lasting three to four days at a time.

One positive aspect of their brush with death at the hands of the boatjackers was McGivern had left his cabin and re-joined the crew. With little energy left to vent his resentment on the Skipper, Cribbs also now saw that their very lives depended on working together. At the mercy of the elements, which could at any moment sweep them away without a trace, the crew worked at the relentless task of trimming what little sail they dared raise, ensuring they kept to their course and the wind abaft. But the fury of the wind was not the only element they had to battle, freak rollers that could spin the boat around and sideways on to the path of the waves could strike at any time to push the boat over so the masts were just a few feet from the sea's surface.

On the twelfth of fourteen nights the crew endured during their passage to Australia, sleeping in her oilskins, Fran had managed to snatch an hour in her bunk during a lull in the wind, but it had now returned with a vengeance. Resting behind the security of the lee cloth of her bunk to prevent her being flung onto the floor in the more violent gusts, she heard the bell for all hands-on deck and immediately dived over the top. Just as she was tossed onto the floor after leaving the security of her bunk, Flip staggered through the door of her cabin and said, 'you won't believe what's coming our way.'

'Try me!'

'It looks like a tidal wave! Skip says we've got to turn into it otherwise we'll be swamped or capsized!'

Following Flip up on deck, Fran stooped to clip into the jack-line and glanced to port, it was then that she saw it. A giant wave crest gathered a luminescence imbuing it with a bilious green glow that radiated out from its base, making it stand out against the swell in the inky blackness. As the wave grew nearer, its size and extent became clear. As the crew struggled to keep their footing on the bucking deck, it was as though a giant hand had grasped the edge of some vast carpet and was pulling it up towards the sky where it must inevitably break over their heads.

Gathering at the helm to help McGivern with the wheel, as the base of the wave drew close to the Nostromo, the Skipper shouted to his crew, 'now!' Heeling over to starboard, the bow struck the wave square on, penetrating and briefly disappearing into it as it broke over the deck and washed the crew into the sea.

As Fran felt herself tumbling over the side and into the broiling water, her safety line tugged hard, forcing the breath from her body as though a giant fist had struck her midriff. Flailing with her arms and legs to right herself, Fran swam towards what she thought might be the surface. As she did so, a profound sense of calmness entered her limbs, like the depths were calling to her. *Was this*, she thought, *the siren song from Davey Jones's locker*? Remembering Jimmy's warning about how easy it was to obey his summons to rest in the deep, Fran kicked with her legs until her lungs might burst. Breaking the surface, she was almost immediately struck by the vast, black bulk of the Nostromo as it spun out of control. Rendered senseless in the water and unable to climb up the steep sides of the boat, she felt a tug on her safety line; somebody was hauling her upwards. Buffeted from below by the swell, like the fish that sometimes became stranded there, Fran was forced upwards and onto the deck.

McGivern, for it was he who had hauled her back on deck, shouted, 'we turned over, everyone's back on board, it's a miracle! We did it, we came through it, I would never have believed it, but she went right over!'

The morning of the thirteenth night after leaving Nendar Island dawned fine and shafts of sunlight played on the surface of the limitless eastern horizon. It was like nature had resumed its course and the previous night's fight for survival had been nothing more than a nightmare. In the relatively easy swell, Fran cleared away the chaos caused by the storm and brought a flask of tea up from the galley for McGivern, who had taken the helm for a few hours to allow the crew some rest. The masts had survived the battering and the crew was safe, despite the damage caused by the storm above and below decks, he felt buoyed up. He smiled as Fran struck eight bells and joined him under the helm canopy to sip their tea and eat a few chocolate biscuits. Smiling back at her captain she said, 'it's good to have you back.'

'It's good to be back. I feel like a weight's been lifted off. Mora's gone and I accept that she's gone. There's a hole there where she was in my life, but it doesn't yet seem real. Maybe it won't hit me until I get back home.' Then, pausing a beat, he said, 'what'll you do when you get to Freo?'

'Continue my search for Cal. I know he's still alive, I can feel his presence sometimes, just when I'm waking, it's like he's there beside me; either that, or I'm hallucinating from lack of sleep.'

'No, I don't think so. After the accident, when I still felt Mora was there, I couldn't rest. I could see her everywhere I looked. Then one day, it was like she left me and I knew she was gone and would never be coming back. You need to find the truth about your brother. Once you have, either way, you'll be able to rest easier for the knowing.'

CHAPTER 23: Freo

FREMANTLE HARBOUR ON a sunny morning at the beginning of the antipodean summer positively hummed, chugged and whirred with activity. Throngs of people strolled, laughed and drank in the bars and restaurants along the broad quayside; it was overwhelming. After reporting into the harbour authorities and immigration, Fran knew how Buddy must feel when he left the boat. The ground swayed under her, her legs needing to feel the movement of the decks to be comfortable. It was land sickness, but it was more than that, it was the sensory overload. Unable to enter Australia, Buddy was effectively quarantined on the Nostromo for the foreseeable future. The little dog's internment on the boat meant she would need to find a job nearby so she could check on him during the day, while she made enquiries about Cal.

Walking along the boardwalk from the deep-water berths, Fran took in the vast array of yachts in the Fremantle marina; it seemed like the whole world had arrived in Perth to party. Looking closer at one particularly battered ketch, Fran was startled when a man wearing a Fremantle Dockers baseball cap, bobbed his head out from under the helm's bimini hood, 'g'day, you're not think'n of buy'n her are you, cos she's not for sale. Ha ha, just kidding ya! Are you off the big boat that's just arrived?'

Fran nodded, 'yes, but it's not mine, I'm just crewing.'

'That's good, 'cos there were a couple coppers sniff'n round her earlier this morning.'

Remembering what Burgess had said about the police, she guessed that Cribbs had already been to see them; now it starts, she thought, but to the man she said, 'what do you think they're looking for?'

'They were border police; so I'm guess'n they just want to check with your skip that the papers for the crew are all in order. So, where ya from? You sound like a Pom by your accent.'

Wondering whether all Australians were so direct, she said, 'yeah, Cornwall actually.'

The man gave a broad smile, 'a few years back, me 'n my wife chartered a boat and sailed around England. Cornwall's where they do the fishing, right?'

It was Fran's turn to smile, 'I'm a Tremayne, we're fishermen through and through.'

The man winked and said, 'well bugger me! Look, why don't you come aboard, I've got a fresh pot of coffee on the go and the wife's just out grocery shop'n, she'd love to have a chat with ya.'

Fran yielded to the man's insistence and joined him under the helm hood where he held out his hand, 'Mike Kerns, good to meet ya.' Then he nodded over towards the Nostromo, 'the coppers are back and it looks like they're take'n a couple of your crew mates with them.'

Fran's heart sank; she hadn't expected things to happen so fast, then she said, 'I'm going to have to see what's happening, sorry, I've got to go.'

'No worries, we'll be have'n a few beers over at Cherubs later on if you want to join us? It's the big brewery place at the far end of the marina.'

Climbing quickly back onto the marina boardwalk, Fran hurried back to the Nostromo's berth and caught up with the group of police and what she could now see was McGivern and Cribbs being taken away to a waiting police car. Fran rushed up to the Skipper and said, 'what's happening?'

McGivern shook his head and, since the police were not going to allow him to stop, he continued walking. Thinking he wasn't going to say anything, Fran was about to speak again when he said, 'it's about Mora's accident, they...'

Before he could finish, Cribbs shouted, 'accident? Accident? It wasn't any accident, you bastard! You're not get'n out of it that easy.'

One of the police officers, scowled and said, 'sir, we can do this in cuffs if you like. If you come nice and easy, it'll be better for everyone concerned.'

As they continued walking, a policewoman stepped out from the group, addressing Fran, she said, 'we'll need to speak to members of the crew as well, do you know where they are?'

'The others, a couple, they went shopping early this morning at the E-Sheds? Is that right?'

The policewoman nodded, 'yeah, they're just at the back of the port area. If you don't mind, we'd like to speak with you now. It's just a few questions, a formality really.'

It sounded easy and straightforward, but Fran knew it would be anything but. The policewoman's question was clearly a veiled demand, not an invitation, so she nodded and said, 'yes, I'll come now.'

In the back of a separate police car from the one McGivern and Cribbs were riding in, Fran's journey to Cannington police station took in a scenic route over the Canning River Bridge and through the western suburbs of Perth City.

Arriving at the station, the policewoman that had rode with her guided Fran through signing in with the desk sergeant, after which she was shown into an interview room and left to wait there. Fran had watched enough police dramas on TV to know this was part of the "softening-up" process before the interview started. The room was stuffy, overly warm and had the musty aroma of sweat and bad-tempered defeat.

Eventually the same policewoman returned to the interview room and sat opposite Fran at the table, the only piece of furniture in the room besides the two plastic chairs they were sitting in.

The policewoman said, 'I'm going to need to record our interview.' Placing a recording device between them on the table, she clicked it on and said, 'PC Anne Cousins interviewing, please state your name for the record...'

Here Cousins nodded at Fran who said, Francesca Eloise Tremayne.

'Ms Tremayne, is this your first time in Perth?'

Fran thought, *first the easy questions*; then she said, 'it's my first time anywhere outside the UK actually.'

'The crew, it's just the five of you? That's not many people to handle such a large boat; it must be, what? More than a hundred and fifty feet?'

'It's a hundred and eighty feet and yes, there are two members of the crew who are no longer with us.'

'They've disappeared?'

'There was a disagreement about what happened with... Mr McGivern's girlfriend.'

'Where are they now?'

'After the storm, we put in at Nendar Island; it's a tiny coral atoll about three thousand nautical miles from Western Australia. It's a private inhabited island; they stayed there after we finished repairs to the mizzenmast. Mr McGivern became unwell and was unable to continue as skipper after Mora, Ms O'Hare, was lost. I took over running the boat because I have experience with navigating without GPS, which was smashed in the storm.'

'We'll need to speak with your other crew mates, what are their names?'

'Martin Childs and Edward Styles.'

'Do you know who owns Nendar?'

'It's a company called Terra Tours.'

After noting this information down, Cousins changed tack and said, 'so you've sailed all the way from England? How long did that take?'

'About three months.'

'In all that time, did your skipper, Mr McGivern, ever speak to you about his relationship with his girlfriend, Ms Mora O'Hare?'

'The Skip, Mr McGivern, and I didn't know each other before I crewed for him, I was recommended by a mutual friend.'

'Did Mr McGivern ever show any interest in you, romantically, during all the time you were on-board?'

Fran knew where this was going, so she said, 'no, our relationship was strictly professional. We became friends, but never anything more than that.'

'Were you aware of a relationship between your fellow crew mate, Benjamin Cribbs, and Ms O'Hare during the voyage?'

'Not at all, it was a complete surprise...' Fran stopped herself mid-sentence.

Seeing now where she needed to go with the interview, Cousins said, 'go on.'

'What I mean to say was... was... that I saw Ben, Mr Cribbs, with Ms O'Hare.'

'When you say with, do you mean in a romantic or sexual way?'

An image of Cribbs thrusting into O'Hare from behind flashed before her mind's eye and she said, 'yes, I saw them together one night.'

'When you say together, what do you mean?'

'They were... making love.'

'Do you think Mr McGivern was aware of the affair; it was after all on a boat, it would be difficult for them to have an affair without his knowledge, surely?'

'I think he ignored it, accepted it.'

'That's a little hard to believe, why do you think that?'

'He said it to me once; the age difference, I think he was realistic about her seeing other men.'

'That's quite an assumption, you said you weren't close or friends with Mr McGivern before you were taken on as crew.'

'It's what I thought.'

Cousins nodded and said, 'at the time of Ms O'Hare's disappearance, where were you?'

'It was at night and I was on early morning watch. I was below, sleeping in my bunk, when I heard the alarm bell sounding for all hands on-deck. There was a storm.'

'What happened when you got up on-deck?'

'All hell had broken loose. The sails needed to be reefed immediately. We could barely stand on-deck.'

'I know enough about sailing to know that the sails should've been reefed as soon as the storm started to get up.'

'What can I say? I was below, I came up on-deck and did what needed to be done.'

'While you were on-deck, did you see Mr McGivern or Mr Cribbs?'

'We were all wearing oilskins with hoods up, it's difficult to know who's, who.'

'A perfect situation for someone to do something without you seeing who it was?'

'It wasn't intentional, it's just the way it is during a squall.'

'Do you think Mr McGivern or Mr Cribbs might have caused Ms O'Hare to fall over the side during the storm?'

Without warning, Fran was caught unawares by her emotions and tears welled up in her eyes. Cousins said, 'take your time to answer; there's no rush.'

Fran shook her head emphatically, 'I didn't see anything. The first I knew something had happened was when the Skip ordered us to go-about and tried to turn her with the helm wheel. I had to stop him. It caused a huge strain on the masts and the mizzen broke off. I then had to help cut the rigging free, or the boat would've gone down.'

'What mental state was Mr McGivern in at this time?'

'He was mad with grief and shock. He said Mora, Ms O'Hare, had fallen overboard and we needed to go-about.'

'So, he tried to go back for her?'

'Yes, but it was impossible. If we had tried to come about in the storm, we'd have foundered for sure.'

'So, you effectively stopped him?'

'For the safety of the crew, yes.'

Cousins seemed satisfied and she eased herself back into her chair and said, 'you showed courage Ms Tremayne, it sounded like a terrible ordeal. That's all my questions for now, but please could you remain in the Fremantle marina area for the time being or leave a message with me if you travel elsewhere; I'm guessing you're living on-board the vessel, the Nostromo?'

'Yes, I'll be there for a while anyway. I lost my brother almost a year ago. He was sailing single-handed to Australia. He would've landed in Fremantle. I'm hoping I can find out what happened to him.'

Cousins leant forward again and said, 'sincerely, I wish you luck Ms Tremayne, but the chances of finding him aren't good.'

With that, Cousins turned off the recording machine and said, 'you're free to go. I'll take you up to the front desk so you can sign out with the sergeant.'

After negotiating the buses from Cannington, Fran was in serious need of a drink when she arrived back into Fremantle. The summer had started with a vengeance and the tall, concrete buildings in the city concentrated the heat and air pollution into a stythe that made her skin prickle with sweat. As suggested by the driver, Fran stepped off the bus at the Fremantle markets and immediately enjoyed the Freemantle 'Doctor', a cool breeze coming in off the sea, as she walked back to the marina. As she passed the ketch where she met Mike Kerns earlier in the day, she heard him shout to her, 'hi, hi! Fran!' Fran retraced her steps and, as she got closer, Mike said, 'yer two mates, they've already gone to Cherubs. Me and my missus are heading over there now if you want to come with.'

Fran gave a grim smile, 'yeah, that'd be great, I could do with a drink.'

'That bad, eh? Y'mates mentioned about the accident with your Skipper's girlfriend.'

Thinking Mike Kerns must know everything there was to know about what happened at the marina, Fran said, 'yeah, but we can't say much more 'cos the police are investigating.'

'I know the drill; one of my mates lost his wife overboard on a trip to Bali. He was cut up bad, but the police had him in jail for a while. It was terrible. Your Skipper will likely get the same treatment, the police are hard-arses here in Australia.'

At that moment, a pretty, middle-aged woman about the same age as Kerns emerged from below and tapped her husband on the shoulder. Kerns said, 'oh, here's my princess.'

The woman said, 'don't you be giving me any of that princess nonsense.' Then, addressing Fran, she said, 'Frieda Kerns, nice to meet you. I'm so sorry about what's happened with your crew mate, it must be such a shock.'

Aware that women's chatter might eat into his drinking time, Kerns said, 'right, let's head over, y'mates'll be there already.'

Already becoming accustomed to Kerns's almost oracle-like knowledge of everything and everyone in Fremantle, Fran wasn't surprised when they found Jen and Flip sitting under an awning outside Cherubs Brasserie, sipping a couple of ice-cold beers. As soon as she saw Fran, Jen rushed over, gave her a hug and said, 'God, it was bad, wasn't it? Having to go through it all again. It's like they were trying to make you say something that might incriminate you.'

Fran said, 'that's not the half of it though. I mentioned about finding Ben and Mora together that night.'

'Christ! That's pretty incriminating for Jack. We didn't mention anything about it.'

Aware that Kerns and his wife were listening in, and not wanting to have McGivern's police investigation at the top of his next edition of the Fremantle news, Fran said, 'it's okay, don't worry. When I said I was looking for Cal, the policewoman was very sympathetic, but said it was a pretty slim chance I'd find him after all this time.'

While they were talking, out of the corner of her eye, Fran saw a light bulb expression come over Kerns' features and he said, 'Cal, Cal... Cal who?'

Spinning round in surprise, Fran said, 'Cal, my brother, Cal Tremayne.'

Kerns considered for moment then said, 'Cal Tremayne from Cornwall. When you said you were from Cornwall, at first I didn't put two and two together, but now I remember. It was about this time last year that a friend of ours said they'd met a guy that'd sailed single-handed from England. My mate was real impressed and said he was very friendly, but seemed lost, so they took him under their wing for a while, showed him around. They'd definitely know where he's gone if he's not still around here.'

The effect of Kerns words were immediate, Fran slowly descended into a chair in a mixture of shock, pure joy and relief. For moment, she couldn't speak, and for the second time during the day, tears stung her eyes. Jen came over and knelt in front of her, gently held her shoulders and said, 'it's him isn't it. It's your brother, you've found him.' Then she began to cry too.

CHAPTER 24: Big Jim

A FEW DAYS after being questioned by the police, Flip, Jen and Fran were told they were no longer part of the investigation for the time being. Relieved that she wouldn't need to make any more journeys over to the Cannington Police Station, Fran was anxious to continue her search for Cal, but Kerns confirmed the friends of his who had met her brother were away on a cruise for a couple of weeks and could not be contacted.

The possibility that she was so close to finding Cal was deeply frustrating, almost to the point of causing Fran physical pain. If her brother had been in Perth for months, what had prevented him from making contact? The only explanation she could think of was that Cal had wanted to disappear. Yet this made no sense to her and was, on reflection, deeply hurtful. It meant that Cal had deceived her, effectively putting her through months of anguish unnecessarily. This was not the big brother that she knew and loved. As Fran's mind searched for answers, Ben Gate's disturbing revelations about Cal's time at boarding school and evidence from her brother's own diary that he was struggling with his sexuality provided the only inkling of a clue. Perhaps Cal wanted to break free from his past, and that included his own sister? These thoughts swirled around in Fran's head occupying her waking hours and long, sleepless nights.

Meanwhile, Jen and Flip had been able to find work at one of the bustling Fremantle fish markets, starting at the end of the month. While they waited for their temporary work visas to be approved they started planning a trip up to Coral Bay, a wild and unspoilt surfer's paradise located in Western Australia's remote north. The big question was how would they get up there? So, when Flip, ostensibly on a shopping trip, called Jen to say he had a surprise for her and that he would meet her for a coffee later that morning, Fran tagged along with her friend to see what he was up to. Breakfast having finished;

the heat of the day was just beginning to make it uncomfortable to sit outside when a huge, and very battered Holden station waggon pulled up opposite where they were sitting outside Cherubs. Fran and Jen stared aghast when Flip's face appeared at the car's open driver's side window. Beaming with the sort of pride that an owner of his first car might have, Flip said, 'so, what do you think?'

Still in a state of surprise, the women slowly rose from their seats; it was then that they noticed the huge effigy painted in black on the car's bonnet. Trying to make out who or what it was, Flip, who had by this time struggled out of the flaccid old driver's seat said, 'it's Jim Morrison, you know, the lead singer of the Doors.'

Jen said, 'oh my God, it is! It's like the album cover; I can't remember which one, but it's actually quite good.'

Fran said, 'it's pretty striking, it'll definitely get the attention of passers-by, I'll say that.'

Always practical, Jen said, 'how much was it?'

Flip polished his fingernails on his chest and said, 'three hundred dollars'; I beat them down from six hundred. They even threw in some fishing and camping gear.'

Jen laughed, 'they must've seen you coming my love!'

Slightly crestfallen, Flip said, 'we could sleep in it, the seats fold down; it's what the guys who had it did on their trip over from Broom.'

Jen's eyebrows went up, 'blimey, it's been right across Australia then! By the way, who are they?'

'A couple of French guys I bumped into at the backpackers. I said we were looking for a car to go up north and they said they were selling cos they were going home.'

Peering into the driver's side window, Jen said, 'its got two hundred and eighty thousand miles on the clock.'

Flip's face fell, 'they said it was in kilometres.'

Jen said, 'that's probably what they were told by the backpackers that sold it to them. Two hundred and eighty thousand miles, that's more than ten times around the world.'

Flip said, 'well, it's been properly tested then. They've put on a new set of tires, well, not new, but they're not as worn out as the ones that were on, they said.'

Fran was beginning to feel sorry for Flip, so she said, 'I think you've done well to find something at such short notice.'

Jen pursed her lips and then said, 'that still just leaves us with six hundred dollars for our little road trip that'll have to cover food, petrol and keep us going when we come back. This thing's likely to be a gas-guzzler.'

Fran said, 'but you could save on motel bills by sleeping in it at the side of the road.'

Breaking into Fran's positive train of thought, Flip said, 'or in the tent that comes with it.'

Jen still looked unconvinced, so Fran said, 'look, I'll lend you guys the money, you can pay me back once you start work at the fish market.'

Jen's face lit up and she said, 'or, you could come with us; it'd split the cost of everything.'

Fran glanced over at Flip and saw that his features were wrestling with mixed emotions. There was relief he had Fran's support about the car and that she might contribute to the cost of the trip, but there was also disappointment that he might not have his girl to himself. All those moments of passion in the outdoors might be interrupted, or not happen in the first place. Pondering Flip's conflicted expression for a moment, Fran said, 'wouldn't I be a bit of a gooseberry if I came along with you?'

Jen said, 'not at all, you're literally part of the family, I'd miss you if you didn't come along.' Flip suddenly looked excited by the prospect of being in the company of two woman, let alone the kudos value and said, 'mmm, a ménage a trois, brilliant!'

Jen scowled at him and said, 'oh shut up. Men, it's all they think about!'

Fran was conflicted. She had not been looking forward to being left in Fremantle on her own with just Buddy for company, whilst she waited for the Kerns' friends to return from their sailing trip. It would give her too much time to brood over Cal's disappearance. But she didn't want to intrude on Jen and Flip's time together. In the end, her need for company and a distraction overruled what her common sense was telling her, so she made arrangements to leave Buddy with the Kerns' and packed her bags for a road trip; after all, there was a tent to sleep in and some camping gear.

With almost seven hundred miles of hard driving ahead of them, the trip up to Coral Bay was going to take at least two days. With Perth far behind them and Big Jim, as they had decided to christen the car, going well, it looked like the road part of the trip was going to be a breeze. Being a more experienced driver, Fran had taken the wheel for the first part of the journey out of Perth and up to the seaside town of Geraldton.

Having discovered that Big Jim's ancient radio and CD player both worked passably well, Jen had bought a pile of old Doors and Neil Young CDs she found in a second-hand music store. Quickly deciding to change over to Neil Young after finding the Doors to be too depressing, Fran was cruising at a steady fifty miles per hour when she heard a pipping sound behind her like an impatient driver, signalling they were trying to pass. Since they were on a dual carriageway, this made no sense, so Fran stuck her arm out of the driver's window and waved them through. Instead of the expected irate motorist, the white and blue-spangled bulk of a Western Australian Police Department road traffic vehicle pulled round them with blue lights flashing on the cruiser's light bar. Checking their speed, Fran slowed the car and pulled off the road behind the police cruiser.

Fran said, 'I'm not sure what's wrong, I was only doing fifty.'

Jen, who was sitting next to her said, 'maybe something's fallen off?'

Flip, who was asleep on the back seat said nothing and kept on snoring.

While the two women were considering options, a police officer appeared at both the passenger and driver's side of the car. The one on the driver's side tapped on the window with his knuckle; Fran buzzed it down and said, 'what's the problem officer? I don't think I was speeding. We're from England.'

A flicker of a smile played across the police officer's stern face, before he said, 'I'm going to need to see your driving licence, insurance documentation and road tax certificate.'

With these documents in hand, the police officer that had spoken to Fran returned to the cruiser while his mate stayed where he was. After a few moments, the first police officer returned and said, 'do you realise that this car is still registered to a Mr Steven Waring of Shenton Park, Perth?'

Having now woken from his slumber, the women turned to Flip and Jen said, 'darling, there's a problem with the owner's documents, something about a Mr Waring.'

Flip yawned and said, 'that's not the name of the guys I bought it off, they were French, I think the guy's name was Eunice, I can check.'

Having overheard the conversation, the police officer nodded, 'I think the last owner hasn't properly changed the documents to their name. I suggest you do that straight away in the next town and even then, you're liable to have some problems. Mr Waring is a well-known drug dealer; he's currently serving time in Perth Penitentiary. The picture of Jim Morrison was his calling card if you like, so as buyers knew what he was selling. I'll try and let my colleagues know, but you're likely to get stopped again by other officers. My advice is to paint over old Jimmy there as soon as.'

Not able to find the heart to paint over Big Jim's namesake, the trio of travellers decided on a compromise. Flip sorted out the car's ownership papers but left the bonnet the way it was and took the hit; they were stopped three more times before they finally arrived at Geraldton that evening.

Flip, who was driving when they were stopped for the fourth time said, 'look, they're getting friendlier every time they stop us, I think it's a joke with them now; y'know, let's see how many times we can stop them before they get to Coral Bay.'

Both women laughed and Jen said, 'I think you might be right. Looking at the map, there are far fewer towns up ahead, so we might not get stopped so often after Geraldton.'

Stopping the night at a dusty lay-by at the side of the road, they decided to try out their sleeping arrangements. Whilst Flip and Jen snuggled together in the back of Big Jim, Fran erected the tent, which, surprisingly, had all the poles and enough pegs. Halfway through the night, Fran knew she had drawn the short straw when she heard snuffling outside and a large lump appeared under the groundsheet. Screaming loudly, Fran unzipped the tent, opened the car door and jumped into the passenger seat.

Hearing the commotion, Jen's face appeared from the back of the car, 'what is it?'

'There's a rat under the tent!'

'Do they have rats in Australia? Aren't they all just cuddly marsupials? C'mon, let's have a look.'

Flashlight in hand, the two women crept up to the tent and examined the offending lump. Jen, who was used to dealing with rats from her days working in horse-riding stables, carefully lifted the groundsheet. Dazzled by the beam, a pair of startled eyes stared out from under the tent. The creature had dewy bulbous black eyes and a rash of spiny prickles all over it.

Jen said, 'I think it's an Echidna, basically a marsupial hedgehog. He looks very friendly, but we should move him out from under the groundsheet in case you squish him during the night.'

CHAPTER 25: Grey clouds over blue water

JANES BAY, NINGALOO Point, typified the understated vastness of the coastline around Coral Bay in the northern region of Western Australia. There, above the twenty eighth parallel, while the southern part of the state baked in thirty-eight degree heat, the surfing cognoscenti of Perth came north to cooler temperatures and to challenge the wild surf during a year, when fickle La Nina heat and rain would swell the breakers and intensify the surge of the incoming tide. The rollers, the intense azure of the Indian Ocean and the languid acceptance of the groups of surfers made it seem like anything could happen, anything was possible; here, you had permission to be whoever you wanted to be. Fran felt unfettered by convention, it had slipped away as they left Perth and the police patrols behind. The acrid fragrance of marijuana floating in the air provided a cloak of infinite possibilities.

Eager to explore away from the campsite, Jen tugged at Fran's hand, 'c'mon, let's get us some body boards from the surf shop and have a go at some 'Pommy' surfing!'

Jen's youthful energy was overwhelming sometimes. Up until she had joined them on their road trip, Fran hadn't considered how much older she was compared to Flip and Jen. She had started to feel out of place; did people think she was Jen's mum, surely not, but there was a significant age difference that put them at different places in their life journey. Then there was something else. She had pushed it away from her thoughts a few times, but she couldn't help noticing how different she felt around Jen when they were alone together. There was the connection of friendship of course, but there was something more, a frisson of something forbidden, which had seemed out of reach on the Nostromo. Now she realised it was a longing that only needed a sign from Jen and she felt that it might ignite into something more. This place, where they were, was the perfect setting for such a metamorphosis, but what about Flip? Where did he fit in this transformation?

Flip had been feeling increasingly left out on a road trip that was supposed to be the trip of a lifetime for them. Originally, he had the intention of proposing to Jen on some romantic beach as the sun when down, but now a friendly interloper had tarnished that vision for him. He liked Fran, but he often felt she was cold towards him, yet he had given her no cause to be. For this, he felt aggrieved. He was not a molester or predatory male that she so despised. He felt rejected by Fran and he saw that Jen was becoming increasingly close with her.

Brooding alone at their campsite, the sight of couples and families enjoying the sun and each other's company somehow brought Flip's feelings of isolation into sharper focus. Consequently, the appearance of both perpetrators of his current malaise from behind a large dune did nothing to jolt Flip out of his morose thoughts. Noticing her boyfriend's dejected appearance, Jen scowled and said, 'don't you want to do some Pommy surfing, we're gonna get some body boards.'

Dismissively batting his hand in their direction, Flip said, 'nah, you go, I'm gonna catch some rays, maybe take a swim in the lagoon.' With that, Flip made to head back towards Big Jim who was already attracting his first admirers of the day.

Jen shouted after him, 'suit yourself mopey boots!' Then to Fran, she said, 'c'mon, lets leave him to it.'

Following behind Jen, who had already started walking briskly back towards the beach, Fran said, 'is he okay? He seems miserable; it's not like him.'

'Oh, I don't know, sometimes Flip can be a glass half empty sort of a guy. We had to start using condoms 'cos I missed my pill. He took it as a rejection, now he's giving me the cold shoulder. The last thing I want to do is get pregnant; we're just not ready, actually, to be honest, he's not ready. Let him stew for a while, he'll snap out of it once I start giving him what he wants.'

Jen's turn of phrase sounded transactional, and Fran was surprised by it. She had seen other friends, couples, who did the same thing, you do this, or I won't do that; it all seemed like such hard work. Flip and Jen had always seemed so carefree.

Rounding a small point, the two women strode purposefully towards the breakers through groups of young surfers wearing colourful boardies. Their laughter and exuberance was infectious and Jen snaked an arm around Fran's waist, pulled her into her body and said, 'I'm totally lov'n this, there's such a vibe here. I was expecting palm-fringed beaches and tropical vegetation, like on Nendar, but this is somehow better; it's the people, they're so alive!'

Standing in the marbled spume created by the crashing waves, Fran held up the string that was attached to her body board and said, 'what are these for?'

Jen examined her's and said, 'it's got a loop with it, what do you suppose we do with it?'

Just then, a group of women appeared beside them with longboards tucked under their arms; one of them said, 'look darlin' that's the leash. It goes round your arm above your elbow. If y' don't put it on, the board'll get washed away and you'll need to go all the way back to the beach to get it every time y'take a spill.' Motioning that she wanted Jen's board, she bent down and pushed the plug at one end of the leash through a hole in the top corner of her board. Then, holding the leash, she said to Jen, 'now give me your right arm.' As the woman slid the strap into position she said, 'there, see?'

Jen said, 'thanks! We're so useless at this!'

The woman smiled a huge, generous, happy smile and said, 'from England, yeah? You guys have a great day. Just keep clear of that dump'n surf over there and keep between the red flags, the riptides can be lethal.'

Encumbered by the boards now attached to their arms, Jen and Fran waded into the surf and launched themselves into crystal clear blue water. Tucking the boards under their bodies, the two women paddled with their arms out to there the waves were building before they broke onto the beach. Thrust into the air by the incoming waves, they both turned in unison and Jen shouted, 'paddle as hard as you can!'

Thrashing her arms furiously, Fran stayed close to Jen and tried to follow what she was doing, but she was slower and Jen caught a huge wave and managed to crest it on her board. Missing the wave Jen was on, the one following it crashed onto Fran's back and washed her off the board. The force of it delivered her unceremoniously back onto the beach on top of Jen who shouted, 'wipeout! Strike one for the Indian Ocean!'

Finding themselves laying entangled in the surf together, Jen made to help Fran get to her feet, but instead it morphed into an embrace. The closeness and vitality of the younger woman's body flipped a switch in Fran's head putting her subconscious in the driving seat for a moment. Grasping the back of Jen's head, Fran drew her close and kissed her on the mouth. Jen immediately opened her lips and they were lost in the ecstasy and excitement of the moment. It was done, something had been unleashed and they wanted more.

Struggling to their feet, Fran and Jen almost bumped into the same woman who had helped them earlier, she was smiling, then she waved the sign of peace in their direction and said, 'you guys were awesome, but you've gotta avoid getting too close out there, that is, until you get back on the beach,' then she laughed and trotted off to catch up with her friends.

Watching their guardian angel trotting off down the beach to catch up with the group of other women, Jen said, 'c'mon, I wanna find somewhere.'

Fran looped an arm around her friend's shoulder, she felt drunk on an emotion she didn't recognise, then she said, 'to do what?'

'You know... I don't want to stop what we were doing.'

Not caring anymore who saw them, the two women held hands as they walked over to a dense patch of dunes. They saw footprints of others who no doubt had the same idea. Jen threw her towel down and followed it onto the ground. Fran felt a tug of an invisible cord that now joined them and she lay next to her, cupping Jen's body with her own. Almost immediately, they resumed their embrace. Fran felt Jen's fingers unfastening her swimsuit, exploring her body and she said, 'I don't know how this goes.'

'Neither do I, but let's go with the flow.'

Much later, returning to the campsite, Fran and Jen found groups of exited families and couples rushing about taking down tents and packing things into their vans. Wondering what was amiss, the two women hurried over to their tent and found Flip surrounded by an anxious group of fellow campers. Jen said, 'what's happened?'

Flip looking visibly shaken he said, 'I was attacked by a crocodile.'

Someone standing behind them said, 'yeah, it was a saltie, a big'n. He was out in the lagoon. We were wondering if was safe to swim there, and now we know. You were bloody lucky he didn't get ya mate!'

After the crowd had departed back to their tents, Flip said, 'I had just started swimming, when something moved in front of me in the water. I stumbled backwards, but it rushed at me. It came straight out of the water, I thought it wouldn't stop, but it eventually did.'

Jen stifled a smile, 'you've never been good at running darling, but you outran a croc; he's got much shorter legs, so no contest!'

His anger starting to flair, Flip said, 'I could've been killed. A couple of the guys had to chase it with sticks to make it go back into the water. Everyone's packing up and moving to another camp and we should do the same.'

Apparently unmoved by Flip's distress, Jen said, 'oh, don't be so melodramatic, it's probably swum off and is halfway out to sea by now.'

'Melodrama, that's what you think it is? Anyway, where have you been all this time?'

Jen's smile was replaced by a scowl and she said, 'oh, so that's what this is all about. You could've come with us, but you chose to sulk instead.'

Flip looked up and saw Fran give Jen a sideways glance, he caught the look, his face froze and he said, 'you two have been up to something haven't you?'

Jen sighed, 'and what do you mean by that?'

'Just what I said, I've seen you two whispering together. Now you're giving me the cold shoulder. This was supposed to be our time together, now all you're doing is spending it with Fran of all people!'

Jen looked over at Fran and said, 'we're friends, we've spent months together on a boat if you haven't noticed.'

Flip shouted, 'I've been noticing all right! I've been noticing you two spending more and more time together. I'm not stupid you know I've got eyes. The last few days, you've been all over each other.'

Flip saw a guilty look pass over Fran's face, then he knew, like it had been obvious all the while, but he had refused to believe it. After a few moments of dawning realisation, he said quietly, 'I can't believe it. Cheating with a woman, not even another guy, but with a so-called friend.' Flip fell silent for a long moment then he covered face and sobs came hard and long; it stung Fran's heart and, unable to bear it, she looked away.

Her face now ashen, Jen whispered to Fran, 'you'd better go, just for a bit while I talk to him.'

The next morning, Fran took an offer from a couple of surfers of a lift to Coral Bay to catch a bus back to Perth. Unable to part from Fran, Jen went with her in the surfer's car. Sitting in the back seat together, Jen said, 'it'll be okay. What we did, I don't regret anything. I love you, but I love Flip too. I need to sort myself out.'

When they arrived at the Ningaloo Bay Backpackers, to give them some privacy, the two surfers, stepped into a kiosk. Alone for a moment, the two women kissed long and hard, but Fran eventually pulled gently away and said, 'it's for the best just now. Flip's a lovely man. You two have something special. I never wanted to come between you. I just feel so damaged. I don't want to hurt either of you. Love, friendship, it sometimes gets mixed up and I don't know where to draw the line between the two.'

Jen cupped Fran's face with the palms of her hands and said, 'if it makes you feel any better, I've had flings with women before. I've never thought it was, like cheating, 'cos it wasn't with a man; but now it does... God! I'm rambling. What I'm trying to say is, you're the first woman I've fallen in love with. It's the same kind of love I feel for Flip, but more intense somehow, like it's new, like Flip and me years ago when we first got together.' Then, grasping Fran's hand, she said, 'please let me know how you get on and if you find Cal. I want to see you again, please, please don't let us part like this.'

It was all so hard and wretched when they said goodbye that Fran thought her heart might break. With nothing more to say, Jen got back in the surfer's car and the old Holden pickup drove off back towards Janes Bay. The truck kicked up a trail of red dust, which could be seen for what might have been five miles until the vehicle disappeared around a bend in the road and was gone. Distances were truly epic in Australia, which made partings more protracted, and more finite.

Fran wondered if she would ever see Jen and Flip again and concluded that she probably never would. After more than eleven thousand miles and over three months at sea, that included storms, near death, loss of a crew member, mayhem and a brush with the police, the closest thing she had known to a loving relationship had ended and it was all her fault. She had experienced a moment of madness, where she had risked a cherished friendship for what, an urge, a fleeting gratification of a passion she didn't even understand? Flip didn't deserve that. If meeting the young couple had taught her anything, it was that not all men were selfish and self-centred like those she had met in the past.

Feeling numb, Fran found a poolside table at the Backpackers where she could wait for the overnight bus from Broome to come and take her on to Perth. When it finally arrived, during a brief exchange of drivers, Fran boarded the bus and found a window seat about midway down the coach. Leaving the bright morning light and twenty-eight-degree heat, Fran was plunged into a dimly lit, cool, almost cold environment. It was like entering a space capsule designed to shut out all trace of the exterior environment. Sharing the next twenty-four hours of her life was a group of Aboriginal people; men, women and a few children, who were huddled under blankets at the back of the bus. Fran nodded in their direction as she took her seat.

As Fran settled herself in her seat, the new bus driver, a profusely sweating man wearing a damp white shirt with button holes stretched to breaking point over his paunch, noticed his new passenger, made his way down the aisle, bent low so that his head was close to Fran's and said, 'now if those Abos give you any trouble, any trouble at all mind, you just let me know, okay?'

Fran nodded and glanced over to where her forlorn and dejected-looking fellow passengers were sitting and said, 'there's no problem, we're getting along fine.'

Unconvinced, the driver said, 'just keep ya valuable stuff nearby when you use the bathroom, y' can never be too careful.'

Since the driver made no real attempt to ensure the Aborigines didn't hear what he was saying, Fran was sure they had overheard him. After he had returned to the front of the bus, Fran looked apologetically in their direction, but they all turned their heads away, the driver's message had been received and understood.

As the engine started up and a blue cloud of fumes briefly enveloped the bus, Fran pondered the three weeks she had so far spent in Western Australia. She concluded, that for all its primal beauty and its natural wonders, Australia was totally enthral to a Western-style culture that appeared to have no place for an ancient people who had endured and thrived in a country where thousands of white settlers had perished as they tamed its harsh, uncompromising environment. What had supplanted the original inhabitant's reverence for wild nature was a beer-swilling culture prone to a loutishness that wouldn't have been out of place in London. Too much money, the mines and carefree consumption had left little intrinsic wonder, but nothing could expunge the raw beauty of the place, and its danger.

CHAPTER 26: Terra incognita

ARRIVING BACK AT Fremantle marina the following morning, it was like Fran had never left, but the 'ghosts' of old crew mates lingered and she expected to see Flip or Jen amongst the groups of purposeful-looking nautical types wandering along the quay. As she headed out along the boardwalk towards the dark, three-masted bulk of the Nostromo, Fran heard a familiar voice, 'if ya look'n for yer skipper, he got carted off by the police again. The word is, he's been remanded in custody.'

Following Kerns' example, Fran dispensed with a greeting and asked, 'when was this?'

'Day before yesterday. It was quite a to-do, with a police van and everything. The Skipper's Mate's been banged up since you left. The boat's been a crime scene, so y' likely not be able to get aboard her. The good news is they don't seem to be look'n for you or yer mates. Oh, and Tina and Lenny are back off their cruise; I'll introduce you to them now if y' like. They're moored up a few boats down. They got hit by a tropical storm and took on some water, they're busy on their boat.'

Kerns' never-ending stream of information was interrupted by a bark and, after a familiar scrabbling sound of feet, Buddy appeared on-deck. 'He's a right character is Buddy; he's been great company for the missus whilst I've been away fish'n. C'mon, I'll do the introductions.'

As Fran and Kerns approached a modern-looking sloop-rigged yacht, Fran could see that the boat's clean and shiny lines had been somewhat tarnished by the ravages of the storm and they could hear voices and the sloshing of water below. Never daunted, Kerns shouted, 'ahoy the boat.'

In response, a woman about the same age as Fran popped her head out from the top of the companionway and waved. Her colourful headscarf held a luxuriant and unruly head of curls off her face, which Fran could see was lean and sinuous with prominent cheekbones and a dazzling smile. The woman looked fit and full of life and seemed unperturbed by the damage done to the boat.

Stepping aboard, Kerns said, 'Tina, this is Fran, the woman I told you about whose look'n for her brother.'

After giving Kerns a welcoming peck on the cheek, Tina said, 'c'mon, have a seat under the bimini while I fetch us some drinks; it's just cokes I'm afraid, the galley's a mess!'

After a moment, Tina returned accompanied by a taller, older man with a balding head and greying whiskers, who hovered on the margins of the group and gave the air of a man who had been disturbed from an important task. While her partner opted to remain silent, Tina served out the drinks then sat on the helm seat and said, 'I'm sure you're wanting to know about your brother. You have no idea how glad I am to be bringing you some good news after what must've been a terrible ordeal!'

Fran, who felt like she had been holding her breath since she stepped onto the couple's boat said, 'thanks so much for seeing me, it's a nightmare, sorting things after a storm; we had a couple of bad squalls on the boat I was crewing', Fran nodded over at the Nostromo and she noticed that Tina gave Kerns a knowing look.

Tina then said, 'First off, Cal, isn't it?' Fran nodded, then Tina said, 'he kept himself to himself for a while after he got in, but he had a problem with some pulled deck cleats, he saw us and we started talking.'

At the mention of Cal's boat, Lenny broke his silence and said, 'it was a very unusual vessel for a round the world solo trip, I mean, all wood, it must've been real old.'

Fran nodded, 'the Nautilus, it's a ketch-rigged boat my brother found in a Falmouth boatyard, it was love at first sight.'

Clearly his favourite topic, Lenny's eyes brightened and he said, 'he'd done an amazing job on refurbishing her, but some of the deck planks looked badly damaged, so I advised him to see one of the local boatwrights. It was then he said he was headed to Papua New Guinea of all places. He seemed to be in quite a hurry.'

Tina said, 'he mentioned he was from Cornwall, that his name was Cal and that he had a sister.' Tina stopped abruptly, reached over, squeezed Fran's hand and said, 'I guess that's you honey.'

Fran nodded, 'it's been such a long time; I'd given up hope... you're the first people I've met who've seen him. It's just hard to believe. I mean, he never contacted me.'

Tina looked like she was searching for something reassuring to say, but all she could come up with was, 'maybe he was distracted. His boat needed a lot of work. He did seem very agitated about getting on with his journey.'

Lenny said, 'when he mentioned he was going to sail over to Papua, he said he was looking for something, a new start he said. It felt like he was trying to tell us something in some kind of roundabout way, but never got around to it before he left.'

Tina said, 'he talked about orphanages and maybe teaching English. He'd made contact with a mission over there, but didn't say which one.'

Fran said, 'when do you reckon he left?'

Lenny said, 'he was gone before Christmas for sure. Y'know, it's like migrating birds, one day y' see 'em, the next they've gone, but y'don't know exactly when.'

In answer, Fran just nodded. Her head was spinning, like she was suffering from information overload. After over a year of not knowing anything about what had happened to Cal, now she was getting more information than she wanted to hear. None of it made any sense. It was like her search was over and now she was going into uncharted waters. Fran again wondered what had happened to Cal to make him sail halfway around the world and then disappear into the interior of a country she'd heard from news reports was like the Wild West, an untamed primeval wilderness with a people who were wary, and even hostile, towards strangers. What, she wondered, had compelled him to go there?

Needing to know what had happened to the Nostromo and her captain, Fran left Kerns talking with Tina. As she was stepping onto the gangway and off the boat, Lenny followed her out onto the boardwalk; it was clear he had something else to say. Turning his back on his wife and Kerns, he bent slightly so as to shield his words from the other's ears and said, 'I didn't want to say this in front of Mike. He's a friend but he can be a terrible busybody. Look, your brother Cal, I said he was in a hurry to leave Freo and didn't say why, but that's not strictly true. You said you came to Aus to find the truth, so I need to tell you that Cal said there were people pursuing him and he asked, pleaded actually, for us not reveal his whereabouts if someone were to come looking for him; that's why I was cagey when Mike said there was a woman looking for her brother, then I put two and two together. Cal was a man I could've been friendly with if we'd had longer to get acquainted. What he didn't know about boats wasn't worth knowing, not the new gear, anyone can read about that in Boat Owner magazine, he knew about real sailing, the skills you need to be a seafarer rather than just a yachtsman.'

Fran recognised the man Lenny was talking about, it was the old Cal, the one she knew before he had changed and become secretive and uncommunicative. The new version of Cal she was searching for had disappeared without a trace and sent a false distress signal. The possibility that people were looking for her brother frightened her, but also explained the subterfuge. To Lenny she said, 'that explains a lot. It really didn't make sense to me that Cal sent a false distress message. Did he say who was looking for him?'

Lenny shook his head, 'no he didn't, but I could tell he needed to confide in someone. I'm not a Christian or anything, but I believe that Cal will find peace in helping others. He spoke quite a bit about wanting to do good in the world and that was why he wanted to work in a mission school.'

'Thank you for letting me know, I really appreciate it.'

'You just take care of yourself. Whoever is looking for your brother might be dangerous, so take care, and good luck.'

Sensing a story might be unfolding without his knowledge, Kerns almost leapfrogged over to the midships rails and would have joined Fran and Lenny on the boardwalk, but Fran had already begun walking briskly towards the Nostromo's mooring. After watching Fran walking away for a moment, Lenny then nodded politely in Kerns' direction before heading back down below to continue pumping the bilges.

After having spent time on a couple of the smaller boats moored at the marina, Fran felt, once again, the huge presence of the Nostromo as she approached her at her mooring. The worn gold lettering on the stern, the replacement aluminium mizzen mast and the patches of worn paint on the midships were war wounds inflicted by her trials and tribulations at sea. Like her crew, Nostromo had suffered. Fran reflected on the fact that many sailors fall in love with their ship as she felt her chest swell with a unique kind of pride that only a crew member can have for their vessel, their refuge and the only place they can call home in the vastness of the ocean. She was going to miss the Nostromo.

Climbing up on the decks that had once bustled with activity, casting off, hauling on the halliards and the countless tasks associated with a large vessel leaving its berth, the sense of silence was almost deafening. Its crew having abandoned her, the Nostromo was now a ghost ship. Not sailing adrift on the ocean like the Marie Celeste, but something worse, without a crew or the elements to propel her, she sat ignored and alone.

Walking towards the companionway, she suddenly had an urge to ring the ship's bell, just one more time; four pairs, eight bells, the end of the watch; it seemed appropriate like the last post to mourn a dead soldier. Heading towards the steps leading below, Fran suddenly noticed McGivern sitting in the shade of the cockpit. Fran thought, *well, well, Mike Kerns doesn't know everything that's going on after all.*

As she approached, the Skipper roused himself from his reverie, gave a tight-lipped smile and said, 'I thought it was you. You've always had a fascination for the old bell.'

Fran picked up her pace and hurried over. As she entered the shade of the cockpit canopy, she could see that McGivern was in despondent mood. His clothes were dishevelled and his chin whiskers were transforming themselves into a thick beard. Even so, if he hadn't looked quite so dejected, she would have thought him quite dashing. Sitting next to him, Fran said, 'what happened? Is it over?'

McGivern nodded slowly, 'the police said there wasn't a case to answer. Mora's loss...' the captain stumbled over his words for a moment and then said, 'her loss, was through misadventure and Ben was an unreliable witness.' Then she saw a bitter anger in his eyes and he said, 'it's not the name I would have for him. The backstabbing fealltoir!' Glancing up to the heavens for a second, he said, 'but there is some justice to come out of it, the police have kept Ben in custody.'

McGivern's use of Gaelic as a voice for his bitterness seemed like he was regressing to his Irish roots in the hills around Kilkenny, where a man's word was his honour and a man's wife or chosen partner was sacrosanct.

Fran said, 'so what'll you do?'

'I'm get'n a crew together here in Freo for a trip back to Ireland. It's hard working the clients on my own, but I've gotta get used to it.' Leaning back in his seat, the skipper appraised Fran for a moment and said, 'the rest of the crew's jumped ship, but my faithful Cornish fisherman stays?'

'No, I'm afraid I'm jumping ship too.'

'I'm think'n the only thing that'd part you from this here ship is news of your broder.'

His use of the Cornish vernacular made Fran smile, 'yes, I know where he's gone, but I've now got to find out why.'

'Mysterious.' Then, noticing that Fran seemed reluctant to say more, he said, 'are you able to tell me where?'

Fran sighed, 'I can't. Not until this is over.'

'Is he in danger? Do y'need my help?'

'He might be, but... I'm afraid if I go in all guns blazing it might make things worse by attracting more attention. I need to do it in my own way. You're not the only one who feels cheated by someone you thought you could trust.'

'Don't be too hard on the man. There'll be a good reason and when y'know it, it'll mend your hurt. As they always say, blood's thicker than water.'

A chill ran down Fran's spine as she entered Cherub's Brasserie. She knew it was a chill of remorse rather than one caused by the hard-pressed air conditioning; this had been Flip and Jen's favourite place. Hastily, she crossed the strangely quiet foyer area where just a few groups of people sat at tables that were usually crowded with holiday makers. Australia was the world's playground it seemed, but not for her, she had business to do.

Arriving at the back of the bar area, she stood in front of a huge floor-to-ceiling cork board festooned with handwritten notes, pages torn from spiral notebooks, business cards and post it notes. Fran scanned the many and varied pleas, requests and the odd amusing anecdote searching for notes left by boat masters looking for crews. If you wanted to sail around the coast of WA or over to Bali, you were in luck, because there were tens of messages requesting yacht crews. Then she saw it. Like the others, it was a piece of lined paper torn from a notebook. Cleverly, the paper had been turned at ninety degrees so that the lines pointed downwards to act as guides to cut the bottom part of the note into strips where, on each strip, the contact mobile number was written. At the top of the page, printed in capital letters across the lines was a simple message, *"Have you ever fancied crewing a sailboat over to Papua? Well folks, here's your chance. We can't pay you, but we promise food, a bed, hard work, sun, sea and an all-you-can-eat meal in Port Moresby's Café Pacific as a reward – and a swim off the stunning coral reefs of course ☺"*

The offer was almost too good to pass up, but examining the fringe at the bottom of the page, she noticed that none of the little strips were missing; nobody was interested it seemed. Or perhaps they knew something Fran didn't. The date for leaving was just a few days away, so after tearing off a strip, she bought an ice-cold steam beer and sat down on one of the comfortable leather seats lining the walls next to the bar.

Sipping her drink, Fran tried to conjure an image of Papua New Guinea, but failed completely; her mind was a blank. Apart from watching a couple of less than encouraging documentaries on BBC TV, as far as she was concerned, Papua New Guinea and the familiar-sounding name of its capital could have been somewhere around the far side of the moon, a place cartographers used to label with warnings for the unwary traveller, "terra incognito, terres inconnues, here there be dragons." Take your pick of language, the meaning was the same.

For Fran, Papua New Guinea was a place on her mind map as empty of detail as regions lying outside the Second Century map of the Ancient Roman Empire drawn by Ptolemy, and just as forbidding.

CHAPTER 27: Ampersands

CAL AND FRAN, Fran and Cal, brother and sister; inseparable. Tom and Jean were the perfect partnership, brother and sister, they were symmetry in motion, like cheese and biscuits, Marmite on toast, like Cal had been for her, the perfect match. During their cruise around the Northern Australian coast, Fran marvelled at how they worked together on the boat. She was where he needed her to be and vice versa. Throughout their two weeks together since they left Fremantle on the coastal cruise and now the passage across to Port Moresby, she had often found herself wishing it could have been her and Cal. If she had felt like an intruder in Flip and Jen's relationship, she had felt superfluous to Tom and Jean's. She found herself wondering whether she would ever be part of a couple, half of an ampersand, and cease being the outsider looking in?

Cal had been the perfect brother who had always been there for her through thick and thin. He had been a shoulder to cry on and protector when she needed him most. Then he had been sent away and her life and their relationship had never been the same. Over the last few days, the filmstrip in Fran's head had again started playing and replaying moments from her life with Cal before he set out on his fateful voyage. Now she knew he had been alive all the time she had thought he had gone forever, he had kept the simple truth of his existence from her... why? Fate had given her a chance to rewrite the arc of their relationship on her terms, but what would that look like?

Fran was almost afraid to find out what he had become. Then there was Ben Gates' disturbing revelations about Cal and their time together at boarding school, were they just the lies of a friend who had become a rival in some way? How could Cal have come to begrudge Fran the miserable life she led after he had been sent away to school? It just didn't make any sense. Had they become too close? Was that, as Ben had said, really why her parents had sent Cal away? And why he had become resentful of her? The thought twisted in her gut like a knife. Tom and Jean were brother and sister, they clearly loved each other, but they were not in love. They had their own families and friends. This was the new arc that Fran wanted for her relationship with Cal, not one of desperate need, but one of mutual trust and affection.

With only three crew on board, watches had fallen rather awkwardly, but the forty-four-foot ketch with its two relatively small masts and sail area was a breeze to handle after the vast acreages that needed to be hoisted aloft or reefed in on the Nostromo. Even though the watches were exhausting, Fran reprised her role as ship's cook and Buddy as the trusty old sea dog. That's not to say the little dog didn't have fierce competition from the incumbent ship's mascot, Bojangles the Persian cat. During the first few days of the voyage, it looked like the arrangement might not work. Buddy's exploratory sniffs and barks had been met with spitting and a hefty cuff or two from Bojangles meaty paws. But the cat's generally high level of indifference to most everything, except for the odd haul of fresh seafood delivered to him by Jean after a spell of fishing, meant that, in calm seas, Buddy had a pretty free rein on the upper decks.

Evenings aboard the Trixie-Belle were times when Tom and Jean liked to catchup and have a meal together at the galley table. Like their vessel's playful name, these occasions were full of humour as brother and sister joked with each other, played cards or one of the vast collection of games they had brought with them. To Fran, these occasions offered a porthole into a world where families were happy and where good humour and love banished the harshness of the outside world, like a protecting veil. Sometimes, for no reason that Fran could understand, the happiness of brother and sister triggered intense memories of her childhood.

The sunny uplands where Tom and Jean had been brought up was the polar opposite to the Tremayne household, where the sudden tumult of violence and brutal language were ever-present possibilities. One of the earliest memories Fran had of her childhood was of an incident when she fell into a stream whilst on a walk near Polldon. Fran's mother had been ferociously angry; perhaps she had received a beating from her husband the night before and needed to vent her rage. Using one of her stock and trade threats she said, 'just wait 'till I get you home and tell your father.'

Even all these years later, Fran could clearly remember the terror she felt as her mother dragged her by the arm along the street. Quickly changing her dress in the kitchen, she had just handed her wet clothes to her mother for washing, when she heard the sound of a key turning in the lock of the front door. The sight of her father returning home, most likely drunk, caused her to immediately wet herself. She could feel the urine leaking from her underclothes, flowing down her leg and onto the tiles of the kitchen floor. Seeing what had happened, her father slapped her face so hard that she soiled herself. Fran's screams of terror ignited a rage in her father that caused him to slap her again and again. Perhaps she had eventually become unconscious because she could remember no more of the incident. Why, she thought, could she only remember the bad times? Was there no compensating happiness? She now knew all too well that the filmstrip of these memories had no off switch, no pause button and there seemed to be a never-ending library of horror stories to choose from.

At the end of her journey to find Cal, her childhood memories had become more intense and real. Was this the moment when the filmstrip would end, or would her brother's truth simply add to her repertoire of stories?

On the last but one evening before they were due to arrive in Port Moresby, Fran was preparing some freshly caught sardines when Jean sniffed the air and said, 'geez! I'm glad we brought you along!'

Fran chuckled and said, 'I'd reserve judgement until after you try it. It's only grilled sardines.'

Craning his neck so he could see into the grill pan, Tom said, 'yeah, but you've got priors on the last couple'a weeks, I'm sure I've put on weight when I'm usually losing it on these little trips.'

'I got the knack of galley cooking on the way down here, you should see the slop I used to serve out to the fishing boat crews when I was aboard!'

Seeing that supper was nearly ready, Jean sat down at the table and said, 'you must be shak'n, you're gonna be see'n your brother day after tomorrow.'

Fran's face assumed the expression of conflicted emotions she had when she considered the possibility of seeing Cal again and said, 'I don't know what to think, it's been so long, I can't even see his face anymore.'

Jean smiled at her brother and said, 'I dunno what I'd be like if I lost this old lump.'

'Hey, less of the old, I've only got one year on you.'

'A year and a half bro!'

Fran said, 'I had a whole speech planned for when I finally catch up with him, but I don't know where to start.'

Taking his customary role of male explainer to the two women onboard, Tom said, 'there'll be a reason why he kept quiet all this time, just let him speak his truth.'

Fran said, 'if there is, I don't know what it could be. We were joined at the hip, he was the love of my life when I was a girl growing up.'

After the tension of sailing through the Torres Strait, a narrow passage harbouring many treacherous shoals and reefs separating the tip of the Cape York Peninsular of Northern Queensland from the southern flank of Papua New Guinea, a vast inlet opened up and a spine of snow-capped volcanos could be seen forming a line, like an army advancing on Port Moresby, which, when it eventually came into view, appeared to crouch defensively in a natural harbour on the western flank of the Papuan Peninsula. To Fran, the distant form of Papua New Guinea shrouded in early-morning haze resembled the shape of a giant dialogue comma, like there was a question to be asked, or answered. Of all the places she had come into harbour since she left home, the outline of the island state seemed to be the most mysterious and enigmatic. As they approached further into the lee of the Papuan Peninsular, the wind was sucked out of the sails and Tom, at the helm, started up the boat's engines.

Chugging into the Port Moresby Yacht Club Marina, they were met by a dazzling array of floating wealth, which seemed contrary to the image of grinding poverty Tom and Jean had painted of the country. Seeming to answer her unasked question, Tom said, 'don't be deceived, most of these boats are owned by tourists and wealthy landowners. If you own land here, you're minted; it's one of the most resource rich countries in the Pacific. But if you're a landless peasant living up country, you'll be suffering grinding poverty. After we left uni, Jean and me joined the Australian Volunteers Programme and were posted here for two years. We were teaching English in Aronda, a village in the uplands near the border with West Papua. There was no electricity and no running water, but it was one of the most enriching experiences of our lives. Port Moresby is another matter, it's best avoided.'

Jean said, 'actually, we're quite worried about your safety. The city's no place for a woman on her own to be honest. Kidnapping and rape of local women is rife, even tourists, so you'll need to be careful. We're gonna be moored here for the rest of the week and you're totally welcome to crash here at night. We'll also take care of Buddy for you, it's no place to have a dog in tow.'

Tom said, 'yeah, totally, we'll help all we can.'

Not for the first time on her journey, Fran felt the warmth and kindness of strangers and she said, 'I can't thank you enough. I wish I could be more certain what's going to happen.'

Tom said, 'I'd start at the Pawan Mission; it's over at the other side of the city, to the east of the airport. The Sisters there were very helpful to us when we first landed here.'

Jean said, 'there was a problem with our visas and the volunteer programme couldn't find us accommodation for the whole time we needed to wait. Our stipends hadn't come through, so we were basically homeless for a while. The Mission took us in, fed us and gave us a bed for the night. Like Tom said, I'd start there. There's a lovely old nun, Sister Angelica, she's Spanish, but her English's good, she's been at the Mission for years and knows the city and it's other missions inside out.'

CHAPTER 28: The Mission bell

TAKING TOM AND Jean's advice, Fran took one of the airport buses that stopped at the marina and from there picked up what they had referred to as the Missions bus, which took a winding route through a rash of squalid dwellings squatting in the shadow of Jacksons International Airport, to stop at the churches and missions in that part of the city.

Getting out at a stop a passenger had told her was near the Pawan Mission, Fran spied the open door of a large high-ceilinged colonial-style café. Hurrying inside, she found a table under a huge ceiling fan. Although working, the languid rotations of its grime-covered rotor blades did nothing to dispel the humid heat, but it was cooler than sitting at the tables on the pavement outside.

Shortly after seating herself, a waiter, a young man wearing a red waistcoat, replete with white gloves and a circular pewter tray, arrived at her table with a smile. The menu, one side in English and the other in Tok Pisin, or Pidgin depending on whom you spoke to, had an array of mostly Western-style food. Fran ordered a fruit-filled pancake and a black coffee, leaned back in her chair and imbibed the old-world colonial atmosphere of the place. If she'd had more time, or the inclination, Fran might have taken this rare opportunity to explore this exotic and faraway place, but her thoughts were focussed only on finding Cal, so when the waiter returned, she asked, 'I am looking for the Pawan Mission, do you know where it is?'

The waiter nodded, 'yes madam, it is close, I will show you.' Fran followed the waiter into the street where he said, 'turn to the left and walk here', pointing to a steep slope, he said, 'around to the right, there is the Mission. It is my own church.'

Returning to her seat and her breakfast plate, Fran realised that she had left all her belongings at her table. She inwardly cursed her carelessness, now was not the time to be robbed of all her money, 'get a grip,' she whispered to herself.

Following the waiter's directions, Fran waited to cross the busy street of noisy, honking and unrelenting traffic. Guided by the principal of safety in numbers, she crossed when her fellow pedestrians crossed assuming that bus and car drivers would avoid hitting a large group of people. This, however, didn't seem to be true, since a truck driver bearing down on them from the hill seemed to speed up when he saw the group of people crossing. Perhaps, Fran thought, not safety in numbers, but a distracting number of targets, like shoals of fish confusing a shark.

In common with many of the older buildings in the city, the Pawan Mission church of St Agnes sat atop a flight of stone steps, which elevated its cavernous entrance out of the billowing exhaust fumes. Inside its darkened portal, it resembled many other Catholic churches. Christ's effigy in stained glass with his Apostles and the Virgin Mary. As she entered, for some reason Fran felt a tug of emotion in her chest, perhaps it was the familiar setting, the lines of pews flanking a wide nave leading to the transept and altar bathed in filtered light from the stained-glass windows. The thick masonry and high arches dispelled the heat and humidity outside, like a kind of terraforming aimed at transforming the vast number of environments in the world where Mother Church found herself into an ecclesiastical standard of heat and humidity.

Fran stopped at a row of pews behind the foremost one in front of the altar, then threaded her way along the benches towards the right-hand aisle and sat down. Mid-morning on a midweek day, the church was apparently empty. Not having any idea how she could find Sister Angelica or get a message to her, Fran felt she had no more answers, just questions. Unable to think of anything more she could do, she placed her forearms on the pew in front of her and lowered her head until it rested on them. It felt to her like she had finally been forced to surrender herself to the apparent utter hopelessness of her quest to find her brother. It was then that she heard footsteps. At first, barely audible, the steps grew louder as he or she approached the transept. As it became clear that they would continue on towards the front of the church, Fran looked up and saw a diminutive form wearing a black habit. The nun continued onward, stopped in front of the altar and crossed herself. She then turned and their eyes met. Slowly, the nun walked back towards Fran's row of pews. Fran rose and crabbed her way back towards the nave; as she did so, the nun waited for her and smiled as she approached.

Seemingly waiting for her to speak, Fran approached the nun and wiped away some moisture on her cheek with her hand, which she realised were tears. When Fran spoke, her words came out in a rush, like she had been saving them up and could no longer hold them back, 'oh sister, I have lost my brother. I have been looking for him so long I've given up hope of finding him.'

When the nun spoke, Fran realised that she was quite old, 'my child, you have come to the right place to find hope. Let it speak to you and bring you the comfort of Christ's mercy.' Here, she crossed herself and her eyes rested on the crucifix at Fran's throat and the little wooden spoon hanging on the same thin leather cord, then she said, 'you are Catholic?'

'Yes, my family is very old; the Tremaynes have been Catholics for generations. But... I don't practice my faith. I have come from England to find my brother who I thought was lost at sea, but now I know he is here in this city working as a teacher in a mission school.'

As Fran spoke, her fingers caressed both the crucifix and the little spoon. The old nun saw her gesture and said, 'you wear a crucifix and a gift?'

'Yes, it was given to me by a friend, a kind man.'

'It is a gift of love, I can feel it. You are betrothed?'

'No sister, I am so confused about men. I have been so hurt by them, abused by them...'

'There is much evil in the world and between men and women here also. Out of all the pain and suffering that men inflict on women, we must learn a new way of love. You have come on a pilgrimage, yes? To find a truth to live by? When the world has no answers, there is only God. You say you do not practice His teachings, but I see a grace in you.'

'I have given such pain to others, Sister, I'm not worthy.'

'It is the pain you have suffered finding its way; I can see that you are filled with it. Do not be a vessel for the evil that has been done to you, it will damage others as well as you. You must let it go, or you will never find peace from it.' The Sister's words were powerful, almost prophetic.

Fran said, 'I have been told to look for Sister Angelica. My friends said that she might help me find the mission school where my brother is working.'

'I am Sister Angelica. There are only a few missions with schools that teach English, but it is unsafe for you to travel in this city alone. Sister Immaculata is a Novice, but her work with the poor means that she knows the streets and the missions where your brother is likely to be, let me ask her to guide you.'

When Sister Immaculata was introduced, Fran could see she was young, perhaps much younger than herself. She had the features of a local woman, but her right cheek and temple had been terribly disfigured by scar tissue from two huge gashes, which must have been deep when they were inflicted.

Sister Angelica said, 'like you, my dear Sister Immaculata has suffered great pain while she was growing into womanhood, but her wounds are visible.'

When Sister Immaculata spoke, her voice was strangled and almost inaudible. Touching her throat, she said, 'my wounds inside have healed, but my physical wounds make it difficult for me to speak. You must be patient with me.'

Sister Angelica said, 'it is best if you go now on your search, before it gets dark.'

Sister Immaculata nodded and said, 'Come, Miss...?'

In answer, Fran said, 'my name is Francesca, but everyone calls me Fran.'

Sister Immaculata said, 'just call me Immi, all the children do – they find it easier.' Then she laughed, but no sound came out of her lips, like the ability to laugh had be stolen from her.

As they walked together, it seemed to Fran that the presence of the nun transformed the streets around them. As they passed through a busy street market, some of the people crossed themselves and offered the palms of their hands in supplication. Sister Immaculata responded by inclining her head, but Fran noticed she winced slightly when she did so.

While they had been walking, buildings of solid masonry had given way to squalid, makeshift dwellings made of wood, cardboard, anything that could be found on the street or the city refuse tip. After a while, Sister Immaculata stopped outside a large old building constructed of red brick, she said, 'this is an orphanage with a school, we must see if your brother is here.' As they entered the building, as though she were responding to a question that Fran was about to ask, Sister Immaculata said, 'I found refuge in the church and I just stayed; there was a place for me. I had been raped and beaten since I was a girl. I mention this because the Holy Mother said that you were also abused as a child.'

Unable to reply for fear of breaking down again, Fran simply nodded. The sight of children, toddlers and small babies in cots, brought back intense memories of the times she stayed with her mother in women's refuges in Falmouth. Finding her voice, she said, 'I have stayed in places like this to escape my father. I used to miss my brother so much, we were close, but now I think he no longer wants to see me.'

Looking up to see why the sister had become quiet, Fran's eyes met those of a tall, slim westerner, a man, in his thirties with a beard and head of sand-coloured hair; it was Cal. Realising who she was, he made to turn and might have taken flight towards the door, but Fran shouted, 'Cal, Cal, no wait, stop, please. I'm here alone it's just me. Please stay and talk.'

Cal turned and it was then that he saw Sister Immaculata. He spoke to her and said, 'you knew where I would be. You know that I do not want to see anybody.' Then, looking at Fran in disbelief, he said, 'this is my sister.'

Sister Immaculata said, 'I know Cal, and know that I have brought her to you against your wishes, but now is the time to turn away from what has happened and look to the future. God has guided your sister to you, I am only doing His bidding as His servant.'

Then, taking Fran's hand in hers, Sister Immaculata gently led Fran over to her brother. Taking Cal's hand, she brought the two of them together and placed Fran's hand on top of his. Then she knelt between them on the filthy floor of the orphanage and bowed her head, 'Almighty God, in your presence, I ask you in all humility to heal the hurt that has been brought into the lives of these two people and forgive them their sins.' After crossing herself, she rose to her feet, smiled at Fran and then walked out of the door of the orphanage and was gone.

CHAPTER 29: Tell me the truth

AFTER WAITING IN a street café while Cal finished his work at the mission, they travelled back to the marina where Tom and Jean's boat was moored. Cal said little on their journey across the city, sitting beside her on the bus in morose silence until they got close to the port area.

Exasperated, Fran said, 'at least tell me where you're living.'

Cal pushed his fingers through the tight curls on his head, then said, 'I'm still on the Nautilus, there didn't seem to be a better place to stay. I have a room at the mission staff building, but it's pretty grim and the food's terrible.'

'What are you living on?'

'I have some money stashed away and I get a small wage from the mission that keeps me in food, but I'm not living like a prince or anything.'

'I can let you have some money. It's a long story, but I found some ambergris on Housel Beach. I sold it to a perfume company and I've used some of it to come here.'

'Did you fly?'

'Another long story, no, I crewed on a boat from Dublin.'

Cal shook his head, 'you could never be accused of being conventional.'

After leaving the bus, Cal walked slightly ahead of Fran as he made his way through the crowds around the port. Thinking that he might try and escape from her, she picked up her pace, caught up with him and said, 'where are we going, this isn't the place where my friends are moored.'

'That's the posh Yacht Club marina; the Nautilus is berthed at the public marina. It's nearby, just twenty minutes' walk.'

Walking along a dusty pavement that skirted around the docks, they arrived at a second, larger marina and stopped at a guard station where the access road entered the complex. After he showed his pass, Cal strode off once again.

Hurrying behind him, Fran was becoming irritated by Cal's indifference and said, 'what's the rush? Why are you treating me like this?' When Cal still didn't reply, she said, 'you owe me an explanation!'

Relenting, Cal slowed his pace and said, 'I'll tell you everything you want to know when we're safely back onboard the boat.'

'Is someone following you? Are you in danger? A man you met in Fremantle thought you might be hiding from people who're looking for you.'

'You found me, didn't you? It can't be that difficult.'

'You've no idea what I've been through to find you!'

Cal stopped abruptly and pointed, 'there she is, the Nautilus.'

Peering through the gathering gloom, Fran could make out the familiar masts and sweep of the hull. Once they were aboard, she noticed the boat had finally lost the strong smell of varnish and lacquer that it had when she helped Cal refurbish the interior panels and cupboards. In every sense, everything looked neat and squared away, the galley was gleaming and the floor appeared to have been recently scrubbed. Remarking on the high level of tidiness, she said, 'have you hired a maid? This place is spotless.'

Cal said, 'it's not beyond me to keep things tidy y'know. It's the only place I have to live, so I have to look after it.'

While her brother fixed a drink, beer for him and fruit drink for her, Fran struggled mentally with what had happened. In just a single day, a search for her brother that she assumed would take days, if not weeks, had already produced results. But something was very wrong. The familiar prickle of doubt she always felt in her gut when something didn't feel right began to make her feel uneasy. After Cal settled himself on a bench seat at the opposite side of the galley to where Fran was sitting, almost the furthest from her he could manage in the confined space, Fran knew there was something wrong. Her eyes fell on the navigation rig and chart table with its ingenious gimbal seat. In her mind's eye, she could imagine Cal sitting at the table sending out his bogus distress message at some random point in the ocean as he approached Australia. Unable to keep up the pretence of waiting for her brother to get around to telling her what she wanted to know, she said, 'what has happened? I know something has. I went to see Ben.'

Cal's face darkened and Fran saw a flicker of anger cross his features, 'oh yeah, so what did he have to say for himself?'

'He talked about his time at school, how you fell out, and what happened to you afterwards. Surely this is not about all that? At school, I was bullied too, and worse when I was at home.'

Cal sneered, 'oh, that's all over-egged, a girl's cry for help.'

'So you knew what happened to me after you left.'

'We were both beaten by the bastard of a father we both had, but the other stuff you've mentioned in the past about Dad's so-called mates that used to stay at North Cliff, that's just a figment of your imagination.'

'Said who exactly?'

'Mother actually.'

'So you don't believe anything I've said in the past about it?' Cal just shrugged. Then it hit her. What if Cal had also been abused by Moggs and his cronies and he was still in denial... or maybe he'd been forced to participate in her abuse. An image that she had always blanked from her mind, assuming it was some kind of childhood aberration drifted into her consciousness. It had the feel of a memory that had been packed up so tight, so hermetically sealed that it was impossible to open, but now she remembered. She remembered seeing Cal's boyish face with Moggs', she remembered...

Seeing the conflicting emotions pass over his sister's face, shock, fear, revulsion and then comprehension, Call let his mask of deceit and denial slip. Standing up, he said, 'it's not what you think... I was forced to do it. It was Moggs' little game he had for us, we were the puppets and he was the puppet master, like it was his own little show.'

Not wanting to know any more, Fran said, 'forget all that, all the sick crap that's happened to us, okay, just forget it and tell me why you're here. You're clearly hiding. Look, I don't care what it is, you can tell me. You're frightened of something aren't you?'

Cal's carefully conceived deception had failed, *women*, he thought, *are so damned perceptive; too perceptive for their own good.* Moving closer to Fran, he said, 'you think you're so damned clever coming here, calling me out like you are now. But you've no idea what shit I'm in.'

It was Fran's turn to lose her temper. She stood up and faced her brother and said, 'tell me the God damned truth! That's all I want. Then I'll leave.'

'I killed someone...'

Call's three words knocked her off her feet; she sat down heavily again and, almost in a whisper, she said, 'you did what?'

Grinding his teeth Call screamed at the top of his voice, 'I killed someone, didn't you hear?' Then he said, 'he was a friend. Then we were lovers. He was rich and smart, good looking; we were good together for a while. We lived the highlife in his flat in Soho with his mates. There were all night parties. We got into... just sex wasn't enough for him; we experimented. Anyway, one night, we went too far and he died. I panicked, hid the body.' Disconcertingly, Cal began to laugh, then he said, 'it was like some Agatha Christie novel. I stuck Pete, the guy, in the boot of my car and took him miles out of London; I'm still not sure where. I buried him and then I left him. But they're onto it.'

Fran's eyes were wide, she was frightened, but she said, 'you mean the police?'

'Yeah, they found him. With all the modern crap, DNA fingerprinting, fibres, hairs, Christ knows what, I knew it was just a matter of time. I'd had some run-ins with the police; drugs, drink driving, so my prints and DNA are on file.'

While Cal was talking, Fran felt herself go into another place, a place far away from what her brother had turned into, a fugitive... a murderer. Unable to handle any more, she got up and said, 'I've heard enough. I can't take any more. I'm leaving.'

'No you're bloody not! After what I've just said? Not a chance.'

Fran's anger rose from inside her, it was visceral and it refused to let her be pushed around. 'I'm leaving and you're not stopping me. I'll keep your secret, but I want the Nautilus. It's something good and clean that you did that I was always so proud of and I want it to remember that you were once my brother.'

Cal suddenly rushed at her, using the weight of his body he pushed her down onto the galley floor. His hands were around her neck, and they were strong; they were squeezing the life out of her. Fran could feel the lights going out. In desperation, as her vision began to cloud, she grasped Cal's powerful forearms and tried to loosen her brother's grip. Then the pressure lessened, at first Fran thought she had got herself free, but she realised that Cal had released her. Regaining her senses, Fran saw that Cal was sitting back on the galley bench. He had his head in his hands.

Still shaken, Fran said, 'I want you to leave. Take the stuff you need to stay at the mission and, just leave. I'll be gone by tomorrow morning, so don't come looking for me.'

'Just like that. You come all the way here, and...'

'I'm not going to go to the police, staying here on your own will be punishment enough. You're still my brother, and as a man I know once said, blood is thicker than water. Now go!'

'Fran, please, let's start again. I'm sorry.'

The sight of her brother's remorse tugged at her conscience, but she hardened herself to it.

Without saying anything more, Cal packed some things in an old ex-army kit bag she recognised. As Cal was heading towards the companionway to go up on deck, he turned to look at his sister one last time. Fran stepped over, hugged him and said, 'goodbye Cal, and good luck.'

With tears in his eyes, Cal whispered, 'goodbye', then he climbed the steps, opened the latch on the door and then closed it. Fran heard his steps on the deck, then silence. Locking the door behind him, Fran sat for a moment staring at her own reflection in the darkened windowpane opposite, then she poured herself a large whisky and drank it down in one. She was completely spent.

CHAPTER 30: The Horn

AFRAID THAT CAL might still prevent her from leaving with the Nautilus and fearing another desperate attempt by him to change her mind that might result in the unthinkable, either her own serious injury or his, Fran hastily but stealthily, made her way back to where her friends Tom and Jean were moored at the Port Moresby Yacht Club. As she approached the Trixie-Belle, with her distinctive, orange-lacquered nameplate, she heard Buddy's distinctive bark. Perhaps sleeping lightly, or still keeping the habit of adhering to watches, a light snapped on in the cockpit.

Fran breathed a sigh of relief and shouted, 'Jean it's me.'

Seeing that she seemed unsteady on her legs, Jean offered her hand to Fran to prevent her from stumbling as she stepped onto the deck. 'We didn't expect to see you so soon, is everything alright.'

Fran sat down heavily and said, 'it's all happened so fast. Your friend, Sister Angelica, I think she knew where Cal was; one of the nuns, Sister Immaculata, took me straight to him. I can never thank them enough; or you and Tom.'

Jean smiled, 'so all's well that ends well, right?'

Fran's shoulders slumped and she said, 'well, actually, they aren't all right. Nothing's all right... I promised Cal I wouldn't say anything, but your friends, Lenny and Tina, were right, Cal is hiding. I really can't say anything more, but... oh, Jean, it really is a terrible situation, the worst I could have imagined. Cal attacked me; he's afraid of running into the police and thinks I might turn him in. We came to an agreement, I'd take his boat back to England, wait 'til things die down a bit and then meet somewhere; but I don't see how we can. God, I'm so confused, I don't know what to do for the best. I'm leaving though, right now. I'm sorry, but I'm going to have to ask you to lend me some supplies. There's supplies on Cal's boat, the water tank's full and there's plenty of gas, but there's not much food.'

Jean, who had been listening open-mouthed whilst Fran had been talking, said, 'nothing's changed, we'll help you any way we can, but surely you don't need to leave right now?'

'I'm worried he'll come back; maybe stop me leaving somehow. I'm so, so sorry, it's got to be now. I'll pay you back, I've got your address.'

Jean held Fran's shoulders, she could see that her friend was shaking, 'come on below, we'll figure something out. Tom's out of it, he's taken some sleeping pills, he reckons he's got a touch of malaria, a parting gift from when we were here as volunteers.'

Opening the largest of the aft store cupboards, Jean started loading tinned goods into plastic boxes, 'there's a fisherman's trolley up on the main deck, unfold it and start loading these boxes onto it.'

'I don't know how to thank you.'

Once the stores were loaded on the trolley, Jean insisted on coming with Fran. Before leaving the boat, she slipped a tin of pepper spray into her jeans pocket, 'you never know who you'll meet at this time of night.'

Fran gave a grim nod and they started off towards the road leading around to the public marina.

When they arrived, the Nautilus was still fully lit up, in the way Fran had left her, and there was no sign of anyone aboard. Relieved, she jumped onto the deck and Jean began passing boxes of supplies to her. Once they were piled on the deck, Fran returned to the quay and stood in front of her friend and held out her arms. While they hugged each other, Fran said, 'please give Tom a big hug from me.' She felt Jean's head nod against her shoulder, but when she didn't say anything, Fran said, 'I'll let you know how I get on. Unlike the Nostromo, at least the nav system's working.'

Finding her voice, Jean said, 'yeah, but your brother's boat is less than half her size and, to be honest, from what I've seen, there's not a single mechanical aid on her, is it all manual handling for the sails?'

Fran nodded.

'Christ, you're gonna have your hands full. You're headed for the Panama Canal, right?'

'The shipping's murder in the Canal, everyone says the bureaucracy's awful and the fees are high, also... well, the Nautilus isn't registered to me, which could complicate things.'

'And reveal Cal's hiding place.'

Fran looked into Jean's face. She could see that she had figured it out, so she said, 'yeah, Cal's in trouble if he goes home and I need to keep things quiet and avoid awkward questions.'

'You know what you're letting yourself in for?' Answering her own question, Jean said, 'the biggest fairground ride you'll ever take. The only thing going for it is the sea temperature's warmer this time of year, and'll probably still be okay when you get there in a month or so's time.'

After Fran cast off, started up the motor and set a course out of the harbour, she stood on the stern deck and waved to Jean's dark figure now receding into the distance. She waved until the quay disappeared behind a large yacht. Keeping her eye on the same spot when it re-emerged, she noticed a flashing light; realising it was Morse code, Fran grabbed a notebook and pen. Jean repeated the message, "God speed" and then, "fair winds" - "fair winds and God speed", it was the farewell used by ships in the British Royal Navy.

At the transition point between two of the world's great oceans, the South Pacific and the South Atlantic, Cape Horn, the rocky promontory at the southern-most tip of Chile's Tierra del Fuego peninsular, had loomed large in Fran's imagination since she set sail from Port Moresby. While she sailed down to forty degrees south to re-join the expressway of the Roaring Forties and their incessant gales and treacherous squalls, Fran had taken some time during calm seas along the eastern coast of Australia take on more supplies and to sample Cal's eclectic choice of books and other reading material in his extensive library.

Knowing little about mountaineering, except that at times it could be considered suicidal, she had been intrigued by her brother's interest in books written by mountaineers. Although she'd found several volumes about singled-handed this or Alpine ascended that, Chris Bonington's book, "Everest the Hard Way" caught her eye. The larger-than-life characters of the mountaineers, their often truculent and obstinate behaviours and Bonington's painfully honest narration made compelling reading. His words resonated with Fran's recent experience on the Nostromo. Reading the book, Nick Estcourt's account of his ascent of a treacherous gully beneath a rocky band that sat just below the summit particularly caught Fran's imagination. Cape Horn and the Drake Passage, an aquatic border separating the Atlantic and Pacific from the Southern Ocean was her crux move on a thirteen-thousand-mile return journey. However, unlike Bonington's expedition, there was no team to support her or others to fall back on to take her place if she were to become exhausted or unable to continue. She would be at the mercy of the sea and the elements at their most savage. There would be little chance of rest during incessant squalls that could last for days at a time.

If Buddy were able to speak he would have told his mistress that over the past three weeks she had become a wrath, the Nautilus' living, breathing spirit, which had come to inhabit the very fabric of the boat itself. Fine-tuned to every motion, gasp, tug and sigh, Fran's mind and body had become intrinsically connected to her vessel. If a yacht could have a soul, Fran would be its living companion, like brother and sister. Sleep was rare. At night, Fran's corporeal being hovered within a twilight world of semi-consciousness and vigorous physical activity. Without the luxury of other crewmembers the watch system had been largely dispensed with and, along with its demise, there was disruption to the timing of meals, downtime and chores. Instead, Fran toiled through one long, never-ending day. Even her digestive system had been disrupted, with the need to defecate sometimes ambushing her at some vital moment, like reefing sails or checking the heading.

On the sixtieth day after leaving Port Moresby, she saw it. Through a veil of continuous slight rain driven by a gusting fifty-knot wind, a trio of rocky bastions, like gatekeepers to another world, took shape and grew more distinct as she approached. The mizzen sail had been stowed some days ago as squalls became more numerous, but now, Fran reefed even the mainmast's storm trysail. Alone now, and tight as a drum, the storm jib glowed in a shaft of orange light that shone through a rent in the dark clouds resting on the ocean surface. Matching the jib's own colour, the filtered light caused it to glow like the carapace of a huge tropical insect. With the wind speed now rising, Fran checked her anemometer, sixty knots with higher gusts. The rain intensified and despite Jean's reassurance of milder weather conditions, sleet stung Fran's cheeks. Down below, Buddy took shelter on his mistress's bunk, the lee cloth preventing the little dog from being hurled onto the floor as the deck bucked increasingly violently.

In a maelstrom of curtaining rain and spume, vaporised by the wind from atop of roiling wave crests, the trio of Cape Horn's rocky bastions Fran had first seen were joined by further, vast companions, until it was clear that the whole coast of Tierra de Fuego had been honed by the elements over countless millennia into a perfect ship-wrecking graveyard for sailors. On and on, faster and faster, the Nautilus heeled over to starboard as far as the gunwale. Seawater rushed along her decks, lapped at Fran's boots and broke over the stern sheets. Navigation became near impossible. With the help of satellites, the course was clear, but an ever-present danger of violent changes in wind speed and direction made holding a course through Drake's Passage between the mainland, Wollaston Islands and their treacherous reefs difficult and there were some anxious moments. At some point, which Fran could not remember, they passed the Falkland Islands to port and entered the South Atlantic. The crux had been negotiated. In her exhausted state, Fran entered a euphoric state, which built from within the pit of her being and found expression as a long high-pitched scream of pure joy that she had never experienced before. Hearing the commotion, Buddy barked from behind the companionway hatch, unlatching it, the little dog dived into Fran's arms and the two of them sat together on the deck. At that moment, Fran knew it was the happiest moment of her life.

CHAPTER 31: Cornish lullabies

NOW IN THE North Atlantic, after a hundred and twenty days of sailing, the cupboards aboard the Nautilus were bare and the last few tins rattled at their doors. The welcome sight of a bag of pasta shells, which brought Fran so much happiness, was a stark reminder of the lamentable state of their supplies. Although there was a lack of food, the past week had been one of ideal sailing, with fresh westerlies carrying them along at almost twenty knots, a speed that would have been envied by masters of the old clipper ships who used to vie with each other to bring tea to the tables of English gentry over a century and half ago.

Fran sat with her back against the cockpit, the bow ahead of her and Buddy in her lap, something that would have been nothing short of suicide just a few days earlier but was now a pleasant possibility in the first warm days of early spring. Happy thoughts were growing like daffodils in Fran's mind, chasing away the melancholy that had often settled on her soul in the past. In a happy turn of events, she would, for the first time in her life, experience two springs and two summers back-to-back, like Ron and Gracie, the wealthy retirees she knew in Polldon, who had a second home in New Zealand. Her double summer had been bought the hard way, which made it all the sweeter. She'd sailed around the world, half of it single-handed, and Fran thought to herself, *Sir Francis Chichester, eat your heart out!*

Recalling her oft-felt childhood envy of the old couple who would pack their bags to leave, as the first November storms made themselves felt, forced Fran to grapple with her emotions about going home. Explanations would need to be dreamt up for the reappearance of the Nautilus. She could almost hear herself explaining how she happened upon Cal's boat in Fremantle harbour and was told it had been found drifting mid-ocean. Oh yes, it had been salvaged, towed into port and refurbished. Such a story would never stack up, people would suspect something. Then there was her old life, the chandlery, North Cliff, trips out on Bran and Breo's fishing boat and visits to Jimmy. The only difference being that beachcombing walks would be accompanied by Buddy. Just as the mere thought of it all threatened to crush the newfound exuberance from Fran's soul, she suddenly knew what she needed to do.

In an almost perfect recapitulation of a day over a year ago, Fran sailed the Nautilus into the mouth of Loch Nevis on a crystal clear afternoon. Then as now, a catamaran launch cut a white crescent in the blue waters, arcing its way around the headland as it headed towards the little huddle of white-painted cottages she now knew to be the village of Inverie. The difference was, she was returning as the master of her own boat and on her own terms. Seeming to recognise where he was, or, more likely, feel the happiness radiating off his mistress, Buddy barked a greeting to the launch as it passed. As it did so, Fran tacked over and caught a steady breeze blowing around the headland and watched the sleek wooden hull of the Nautilus cut though the water like a knife. It was like she was experiencing a dream that she might wake up from, but she knew it to be reality, a new reality she was making for herself.

Danny, who was on the quay helping to unload supplies for the village shop, looked up from his task and saw a two-masted yacht running in towards the harbour. It had appeared suddenly, as though it had coalesced from wave-crests in the sound. Then he noticed a woman with long, raven-black hair standing the deck. She was waving, waving to him, he murmured under his breath, 'Fran.' Unable to stop himself, Danny shouted, 'Fran, Fran!'

During the minutes it took for her to bring the Nautilus into harbour and tie up, the two of them waited in childlike impatience. After she stepped onto the quay, ignoring stares from the locals, Danny ran towards Fran and into her arms. They embraced and this time she kissed him long and hard and never wanted the moment to end.

Unable to contain his joy, Danny quipped, 'The boat's shrunk since the last time I saw you!'

Fran smiled and said, 'yeah, it shrank in the wash, but it fits me better now.'

'What happened to the other one?'

'I've no idea, but it's not the last we've seen of the Nostromo, she's that kind of boat.'

'What about you?'

'I think I'll stick around and help plant some trees for a while.'

-THE END-

About the author

A born traveller and adventurer, the author found excitement and solace in wild places from an early age. Having travelled the world using most forms of transport, some practical, others ridiculous, he is always on the lookout for a good story. A tale well told can be an inspiration to all of us. Falling in love with Norfolk, its wide-open skies and the sea, the author has spent almost twenty years of his life in a small village planted in the wheat fields of the Norfolk-Suffolk border.

Acknowledgements

I would like to thank Victoria Curry for editing the manuscript and providing valuable critique. I would also like to thank Sarah Hurn for offering me much-needed technical advice on sailing and for providing me with creative elements for some of the chapters.